RAVE REVIE... AND *THE WIND CALLER*!

"*The Wind Caller* is a nail-biting read of terror and wonder."
— Douglas Clegg, author of *The Abandoned*

"Deftly paced and handled, complete with touches of Cacek's sly trademark irony. You'll find yourself scared of—and rooting for—the wind!"
— Jack Ketchum, author of *The Girl Next Door*

"Cacek doesn't pull any punches!"
— *The Denver Post*

"Cacek is certainly one of horror's most important up-and-comers."
— Matt Schwartz, Founder of Shocklines

"Cacek has a superbly twisted imagination."
— AtuXVII

"P. D. Cacek is the most lyrical—and the scariest—writer to emerge in the horror field."
— S. P. Somtow, author of *Vampire Junction*

"An enjoyable horror tale [with] mysticism, fear, gore, and the abuse of power."
— Necrofile

LESSONS

"Now what are you doing all the way over there?" Luci said to Allison, grabbing the man's right wrist and hauling him into a semi-slumped upright position. "You plan to mark him by long distance?"

"Me?" Allison said. "You want *me* to bite him?"

Turning the hand palm up, Luci slapped the veins in the wrist to full attention and held it out to Allison.

"It's up to you to make the first bite." She wiggled the limp hand at Allison again. "Of course if you don't *want* the honor I can always get Gina to do it…."

The man smiled up at her, winking drunkenly when Allison took his hand and lifted it slowly to her lips.

"Bite deep," Luci said, leaning forward like a home economics teacher making sure the recipe was being followed to the letter. "Make sure you pierce the vein all the way through…but don't take too much."

Allison moaned as her fangs slipped into him—and the sound echoed back in a low baritone….

Other books by P. D. Cacek:

THE WIND CALLER

NIGHT PRAYERS

P. D. CACEK

LEISURE BOOKS NEW YORK CITY

To Timmy Valentine

A LEISURE BOOK®

December 2005

Published by

Dorchester Publishing Co., Inc.
200 Madison Avenue
New York, NY 10016

ISBN 0-8439-5609-7

The name "Leisure Books" and the stylized "L" with design are trademarks of Dorchester Publishing Co., Inc.

Printed in the United States of America.

Visit us on the web at www.dorchesterpub.com.

NIGHT
PRAYERS

"*For your sake we are being slain
all the day;
we are looked upon as sheep
to be slaughtered.*"

—Romans 9:36

"*You said it would be different!*"

—Allison Garrett

PROLOGUE

"You said it would be different! You lied to me!"

Allison picked up the heavy glass ash-tray and hurled it at him. A wasted effort. She knew it would never touch him.

It didn't.

Seth caught it in mid-air and crushed it to a powder between his fingers. She watched it rain down over the side of the bed and into the motel's green-gold carpet. *Ashes to ashes . . . dust to dust.*

He chuckled, and Allison felt tiny shivers race up her spine.

It was the same honey-dripped baritone she'd heard over the din and "wanna screw" lines at the Country Western bar that'd become her home away from home once she realized being thirty-seven and single really *was* the pits.

1

But he'd noticed her—walked right past the perfect grins and perfect boobs and tight asses and offered to buy her champagne. Because, he said, it went with her sparkling personality.

And she bought it.

Was *still* buying it.

Allison slammed her naked rump into the wall next to the dresser and rode it down to the floor.

"You *did* lie," she mumbled, not ready to lose the fight yet . . . not yet. Not any earlier than she had to.

"Never did, pun'kin," he said softly. Easily. Allison heard the bed springs creak as he stretched. She began to claw furrows in the worn carpet. "Besides, what'd you think would be different?"

chuckle chuckle chuckle

"Everything," she snapped. "I thought *everything* would be different."

The springs accompanied him as he got off the bed. His perfect body glowed pale blue in the darkness, his erect penis still wet from their last bout of lovemaking.

Screwing, Allison corrected. *Him screwER, me screwed.*

Period.

Seth smiled at her, his fangs gleaming, and shrugged.

"Life's what you make of it, darlin'," he said, "so I guess the same thing goes for death."

"Now's a great time to tell me," she whispered. "I just . . . I just thought I'd feel different, that's all."

"How can you feel anything, sweet thing? You're dead."

There were a hell of a lot of things they didn't tell her about this job when she signed on.

"It's not fair."

"Hey, babe, what made you think death would be any fairer than life was? It don't work that way."

Allison looked up and shot him the bird. He acted like it was the funniest thing he'd ever seen.

"What? No one ever tell you to go fuck yourself before?"

Seth walked over and knelt in front of her. Allison felt the velvet soft tip of his cock press against her raised knee—and moved.

"See? You felt that didn't you? Nothin's changed."

"That's right," Allison yelled. "Nothing's changed. NOTH-ING!"

Seth reached out and she slapped him away. His eyes flared red for an instant before cooling back to their pale grey-green.

"Now, don't be like that, sweet thing. More things have changed than you know. F'instance, you ain't gonna get any older . . . an' I thought that was one of the *biggies* on your list."

It was one of the things . . . one of the hundreds of things he'd wheedled out of her that first night in the bar over glasses of sparkling wine. He seemed so interested in her "as a person" that Allison dropped the facade she'd carefully cultivated and started pouring out thirty-seven years of unrequited dreams and never-ending disappointments.

And fears. About growing old. Alone.

About dying.

Alone.

And he held her hand and t'sked and said that he could do something about that. If she wanted.

If she wanted: The perfect hook for a woman who'd begun counting the minutes on her biological clock.

Walking hand in hand back to his motel room, Allison had let herself imagine what it would be like to spend the rest of her life with the pale man with green eyes.

The rest of her life lasted three nights.

Allison felt another tingle crawl down her backbone.

"The word's *dead*," Seth said suddenly. "Well . . . *un*-dead if you want to get technical."

"What are you talking about?"

"You an' me, kid. The undead." He leaned forward quickly and jammed his tongue into her mouth. Allison jerked away and tried to wipe the taste of raw sewage off her tongue.

"Aw, don't be like that, sweet lips. We got it made! Everything that's ever gonna happen to you has already happened, babe. Just remember, real feelin's for the livin'. When I did you I gave you *fer*-ever." He nuzzled her neck, suckled the shrunken puncture wounds above her jugular. "Now get on up here and show me how grateful you are."

Her ass squelched against the wall as Seth pulled her to her feet. He was less gentle than he'd been when she was still—

Allison pressed her lips together as Seth spread her legs apart and began dry-humping her against the cracked plaster. She didn't worry about what the occupants in the next room might think. It wasn't anything they hadn't heard before . . .

Over the last seventy-two hours . . .

Seth's fangs broke new ground as he worked himself in deeper. She'd whimpered the first time—not from the bite or the size of his cock . . . but because it had been so goddamned *cold*.

Like fucking a dead snake.

The *first* time.

Now they were both dead snake cold.

Allison yawned into her cupped hand and waited for him to finish.

"Hmmmm," he whispered less than a moment later, "that was nice."

"Thanks."

He kissed her on the cheek as he pulled out, then sank his teeth into her left breast.

For old time's sake.

"Yessir . . . you were one of the best I ever had."

High praise, no doubt. Allison sneered.

"Well, best be headin' out. Dawn ain't far away and there's still a great big ol' world out there, just full of hot-blooded, lonely women." Seth glanced at the pile of clothes laying at the foot of the rumpled bed and wrinkled his nose. An instant later he was dressed in a dark-colored *Kentucky Headhunters* T-shirt and jeans. Allison blinked and felt the carpeting come up and smack her on the butt.

Hard.

"How'd you . . . ?"

"Well, babe, it's been fun," he said, winking at her. "Don't take no wooden stakes, now, y'hear." His chuckle had lost some of its endearing quality. "Get it . . . wooden *stakes?*"

"Yeah, right—hah, hah. But how did you get dressed like . . ." Allison's brain finally caught up with her mouth. "What do you mean it's been fun? I'm going with you."

"Hell no." Seth sat down on the edge of the bed and began tucking his jeans into the tops of his boots. "We had our fun—now we can go spread it around."

"Spread it around?"

Another series of tingles tip-toed up Allison's spine. This time, they had nothing to do with Seth's clogged-drain chuckling. "But I mean . . ." *What DO I mean?* ". . . I mean—in all the movies, the Head . . . you know . . . Vampire always has this army of the undead around him. You know?"

Seth leaned over his knees and shook his head at her.

"Damn girl, you really didn't have no life, did you? Here's a hint," he said. "Movies *ain't* real."

Like this is, Allison thought as she hugged her knees tightly against her chest. "Are there any . . . others like us out there?"

"Suppose so." Seth smiled at her as he stood up, fangs still fully extended. For effect. "But I wouldn't try to find 'em, if I were you. A group of *anything* makes a better target. If you don't believe me just go ask the Jews or Blacks or American Indians. Hang out with your own kind long enough and, one day, somebody'll notice . . .

and take it into their tiny little minds to do somethin' about it.

"First thing you gotta learn is that there's safety in numbers . . . and that number's *one*."

Seth clapped at his own wit as he took a step toward her.

"Second thing is the *'wither thou goest'* shit just don't work for our kind."

He blew her a kiss and winked. "You were one hell of a fine feed, babe."

His outline slowly began to dissolve, blending with the dark and becoming part of it. When he spoke again his voice was as empty as the wind.

Just stop believin' everything you see in the movies, okay? Be seein' ya.

Then he was gone.

And she was alone.

Again.

Allison relaxed her grip and leaned back against the wall.

Alone.

For all eternity.

Empty.

Shit, I'm hungry.

It was the hunger that drove her back to the *Silver Concho Saloon*.

Back to the old hunting grounds. But tonight *she* was the hunter.

Sitting in one of the bar's secluded booths, Allison

ran a finger down the dripping side of the first of a three-drink minimum and watched the action taking place in front of her. Sometimes subtle—mostly overt: Eyes studied potential bed partners for any outward appearance of disease, lips smiled veiled invitations, perfect breasts spoke of fantasies fulfilled. A woman in tight jeans and off-the-shoulder blouse walked past two men in business suits, tossing her bleached curls and pointedly ignoring them.

It was pitiful.

But it did give the term "meat market" a whole new meaning.

Smiling, Allison lifted her glass and saluted the room indiscriminately.

Someone across the room returned the salute.

And all the bravado she'd worked on since leaving (*forcing* herself to leave) the motel room vanished.

Shit . . . it was real.

Allison picked up her drink and stared at the lime curl floating across the top of the tequila.

The whole purpose of her existence now was to attract men and suck them dry. Pretty much the same goal she'd had since high school.

She smiled and shook her head. Seth was right . . . things *weren't* any different.

"If there's anything *purdier* than a beautiful woman laughin' I don't know what it might be."

Allison could smell the blood flowing in his veins—warm and tantalizing—as she looked up . . . slowly . . . letting her eyes drift past the crisp, indigo jeans, up to the real silver belt buckle and matching beer gut, then following the braided leather bolo tie to the crooked smile, ruddy cheeks and bloodshot eyes.

As a vampire she was supposed to have the seductive powers of a bitch in heat . . . and *this* is what it got her? The Pillsbury Doughboy version of the Marlboro Man?

Her stomach rumbled its approval.

Din-din.

Allison swallowed the saliva filling her mouth and remembered to smile as he slid into the booth next to her.

"Hope y'all don't mind." He was making sure she noticed the *real west* twang in his voice. It was the same thing Seth had done. "But I just couldn't stand seein' such a *purdy* young thing sittin' all by herself. Didn't seem right. Name's Buck."

Buck.

Allison took the pudgy dough-boy hand and squeezed it gently.

"Wooo-WEEE, little lady, you're hand's as cold as ice!" He lifted her hand to his lips and blew warm air across her fingers. "But like they say, cold hands mean a warm heart. Ain't that right?"

She pulled her hand back and brought him along for the ride.

"You wouldn't believe *how* warm . . . Buck."

Just to make sure he wouldn't misunderstand her intentions, Allison ran the tip of her tongue lazily across her top lip. She could hear the front of his brand-new jeans creak under the pressure of his stiffening cock. *That* hadn't changed either.

Her new position on the food chain just made it more interesting.

Somewhat.

Her stomach snarled loud enough for *Buck* to notice.

"Whoa, you sound hungry."

"Starving."

Pressing in close, Allison arched her back so her intended dinner . . . companion . . . could see she wasn't wearing a bra beneath the loose-fitting silk blouse.

"You're fucking gorgeous!"

"Sweet talker," she purred, nuzzling his ear, then licking off the drool she left behind. The scent of blood overpowered the Brut aftershave he'd apparently taken a bath in.

Allison nudged him gently in the ribs and told herself she was only asking the next question because it prolonged the delicious cat-and-mouse game.

"You really think I'm . . . pretty?"

Really miss not being able to see yourself in the old looking-glass, don't you, kid?

"Ma'am . . . you're about the most beautiful woman I've ever seen."

Happy now?

Smiling, Allison tossed her short, layered-cut hair and wished she had let it grow out—one last sweeping mane of auburn before the grey started to come in.

An instant later, heavy curls cascaded down past her shoulders.

"What the *hell?*" Allison gasped.

Allison pulled a handful of hair out in front of her

10

eyes and stared at it, open mouthed. It was the color of autumn leaves at sunset, as thick and long as it'd been her first year in college . . . right before she got sick and tired of fussing with it and had it cut.

All she'd done was think about letting her hair grow and . . .

Another inch sluiced through her fingers.

Shit.

"Oh, yeah. That's better."

Allison forced her mouth closed and blinked *Buck* into view.

"Pardon?"

"I'm real glad you let your hair down," he said. "I just love long hair."

Allison tossed her head again. This time the hair swept her face dramatically. Was that how it worked? You just thought of something?

Smiling, Allison hooked a finger into the front of her blouse and watched melons bloom from nectarines.

Now *this* had possibilities.

Inflating her lungs without needing to breathe took some doing, but the effect was worth it. *Buck* was drooling almost as much as she was.

"Damn."

You're so right.

Looking up at him through her lashes, Allison ran a blood red fingernail along his double-stitched inseam until she came to the hard obstruction between his legs. She could feel him quiver from the inside out.

"You know, I never did introduce myself." She pouted.

11

"That wasn't very nice of me, was it? My name's Allison . . . Buck."

"I—I always loved that name," he said, swallowing hard enough to make the concho-slide jump. "In fact, I knew this girl in high school named Allison. She gave great head."

Allison cupped his erection gently and fought the urge to rip it off and hand it to him—still hard and dripping.

"Well, maybe we should go someplace a little more private and see if *I* measure up." *You disgusting, fat-assed son of a bitch.*

Buck licked his lips while her stomach growled again.

"I'm just *so* hungry," she whispered, sliding a finger down toward his ass. "And I bet you'd be able to fill me up in no time."

"Jesus Ch—"

ONE

"—rist into the desert and tempted Him with the riches of the world if . . . and this is the important part, brothers and sisters . . . if He, the only begotten Son of God, would bow down and pay the devil his due.

"But He didn't do it! He told Satan to get lost. He put the devil behind him and that's what you've all got to do! You've got to throw the devil and his ways out of your hearts and let Jesus in! That's the only way. And that way is *up!* Praise the Lord!"

Panting, Mica Poke clasped the tattered Bible to his chest and felt his heart pump through the well-worn pages. It was a hot night, following hard on the heels of a blistering day, but Mica knew Hell was hotter. Knew it and had to make sure others did as well.

It was his job.

Had been for a long time.

He was MICA . . . Chosen Preacher to the People.

One of whom yawned loudly and scratched himself.

A drop of sweat—25% humidity, 75% divine perspiration—trickled down inside Mica's "I'd rather be Praying" T-shirt as he took a deep breath of exhaust fumes and raised his hands toward the urban-lit night sky.

"Lord . . . it's me again. Mica. Lord, look down on these, the weakest of Your children and give them the strength to push their own devils behind them. Times are hard, Lord, we all know that. Shit, it's hard enough to take the polish off a Saint's halo, but I'm hard, too, Lord . . . as hard as the name you gave me."

Mica looked down at his transient congregation and felt his heart swell. The light from the drugstore behind him illuminated dozens of people. Of course, most of them—being tourists—thought what he was doing was just part of the Hollywood night life. Diagonally across from his corner a man in a long, flowing black gown was captivating *his* audience with the joys of Satanic worship and animal sacrifice.

Leaning back against the warm bricks of the Hollywood landmark, Mica smiled down at a homeless woman wearing too many clothes for so hot an evening. She smiled back, then flipped him off and wandered away, mumbling to herself.

Forgive her, Lord.

Rolling the fatigue out of his shoulders, Mica stood up and began again . . . keeping his voice soft and easy. For a while, at least. He knew he wouldn't be able to hold back the Power for long, but since the cops had already warned him once that night about disturbing the peace, he wanted to give it his best shot.

"Now, when I say Mica, brothers and sisters, I'm not putting myself up there with the Old Testament Prophet *Micah*." He emphasized the name, hoping they'd hear the difference. "No sir, I would never place myself so high as that! I am Mica—the rock . . . hard as flint. The Lord made me hard not because this is a hard world, but because we all have to be hard to fight the temptations of this world."

He was shouting again. *Oh well, Lord, You know best.*

"It's too easy to just lay down and let the world screw you whenever it wants. We have to be hard . . . hard as rock . . . hard as MICA to know that the Lord loves you. And I'll help, because that's my job. I've been tempered by the Lord and I'm hard enough to kick all of your asses through the Pearly Gates if I have to. Because the Lord loves every last one of you. AMEN!"

Collapsing against the building, Mica pushed the sweat-damp hair out of his eyes and nodded. His throat was raw and throbbing, and the pocket Bible felt like a Guttenberg in his hand, but that was all right. And if the cops came back and hauled him away that was all right, too. Because he'd done his nightly duty. He'd spread the Word.

Even if no one listened.

But tonight someone actually clapped. And whistled. And pounded the sidewalk with heavy heels. Mica lifted the Bible to his chest and smiled weakly.

"Thank you, but it's not me you should be praising—it's the Lord you should be . . . *shit!*"

The two skinheads who were leaning against the busted out newspaper stand weren't clapping and whistling for him *or* the Lord. All their adoration was directed at the teenaged street whore swishing her ass across Highland.

"Hey!" Mica yelled at them. "Don't you brain dead fucks know you're Loved?"

Only one of the skinheads turned, the other was darting through the cruising low-riders after the whore.

"Sure we do, man," the skinhead smiled. "My friend's trying to negotiate a deal right now. You want in?"

These you don't have to Forgive, Lord.

Before he climbed down from his portable pulpit, Mica looked across the bumper-to-bumper traffic to the robed Satanist. *He* didn't seem to be doing any better. Tourists, as a general rule, were hard to convert to *anything*.

Tucking the K-Mart step stool under one arm, Mica shoved his way through the meandering crowd like a running back trying to find a hole.

"I am as mica," he reminded himself, ignoring the looks he might be getting. "Hard and layered against the temptations of self-will. I am blessed."

The crowds thinned by the time he crossed Hawthorn. The action was on Hollywood Boulevard . . . no one walked down Highland unless they were heading for *more* action on Sunset.

Mica realized he was still mumbling when he kicked

an empty beer can half-way up the steps of Hollywood High's auditorium. He imagined going to school there would be like trying to learn in a cesspool.

"I'm Mica," he told the silent building.

Actually, his parents had named him Milo—after a distant cousin who made a fortune in the sausage industry—some thirty-two years earlier, but the name just didn't have the same impact as *Mica*.

That—and the fact that his first time preaching as Brother Milo had cost him three fractured ribs and a dislocated jaw. When he woke up, still in a codeine haze, an Angel had appeared and touched his aching head softly with her cool hand.

"Your name's really Milo?" she asked. "Damn . . . it's lucky those punks let you *live!*"

It was one of the *clearer* signs he'd ever received and the next day Milo became Mica.

Forever.

Amen.

Not that *all* the signs were that easy to understand. One of the troubles with doing the Lord's work solo was that there was no training manual.

"Except *this!*" Mica said, tightening his grip on the small Bible. He smiled and felt the scar on his forehead twitch.

But, of course, *some* signs were more obvious than others.

His daddy—a devote Fundamentalist—had presented him the scar on his thirteenth birthday when he asked, innocently, if Jesus really had fucked Mary Magdalene.

Mica, then Milo, had seen pictures of men and women fucking (he'd learned the correct term from his best friend Horace Bonner) in magazines his daddy kept hidden behind the paint cans in the garage, and thought it was cool that Jesus could fuck (he liked the word the moment he'd heard it) and still find time to preach.

Mica spent the rest of the week in his room.

Healing.

That had been the first sign.

The second came that night when, groaning and drifting in and out of consciousness, he woke up to find Jesus sitting in his bean bag chair reading one of his MAD magazines.

They had a nice talk (every time he woke up) and Jesus explained that, although He Loved Mary Magdalene the same way He Loved Mica and the rest of the Apostles, He never fucked her. She was a whore, He reminded Mica, and being God, He knew the kinds of diseases He could catch off her.

Right before He left, Jesus patted the seeping gash between Mica's eyes and winked.

The next morning the angry red scar was in the shape of a cross.

The *third* sign.

With his free hand, Mica traced the smooth skin with his fingers and smiled. After seeing the wound his daddy had never hit him again.

"Aw, does big boy have a boo-boo?"

She came out of the shadows next to the auditorium

so quickly that Mica almost back stepped into a rumbling garbage truck. When his ears adjusted back to the steady hum of the waking city, he heard her giggle . . . and the sound went directly from his ears to his cock.

"Careful honey," the lilting voice whispered, "I don't want you *flat*."

Mica nodded and watched her sashay toward him. It was only after the mini-skirted, halter-topped figure stepped out into the piss-yellow light that Mica noticed *she* needed a shave.

"Aw, shit."

"What's the matter?" Although still vaguely feminine, there was a hard edge to the voice. "Disappointed?"

Mica hugged his Bible tighter to his chest and shook his head. Pimps, he could accept, and hookers . . . and crack heads and bag ladies and gang bangers and even Neo-Nazi-fascist-radical-NRA supporting-assholes like the two he just left.

But not these . . . *creatures of Perdition!*

Hunching his shoulders, Mica tried to walk past without further comment. He just had enough time to get home and change before—

"I *asked* if you were disappointed."

Mica kept his shoulders hunched, like a cat warning off an interloper, as he turned. *Is this some kind of test, Lord?* "No. Excuse me. I'm late."

"*I'm* never late," the man said as he stepped directly in front of Mica—the pink lipstick gleaming beneath the bushy mustache. "I can go thirty days out of the month."

19

When he batted glittered eyelashes, Mica felt something snap deep inside him. Two of his portable stool's legs sank into the fake rubber boobs while the second set trapped the trans-whatever's neck. A gentle, but steady push propelled the man back into the shadows.

Where he belonged.

"Hey . . ." The giggle had a touch of nervousness to it now. Mica kept pushing until he'd backed the man into a blind corner next to the auditorium's exit door.

"Not so rough, sweet-cakes, I'll have to charge double."

Three quick cranial thumps against the stucco facade was more than enough to convince the man this customer wasn't interested

Stepping back, Mica pulled the stool away and watched the man crumple, the mini-skirt riding up to reveal heart-decorated boxer shorts underneath.

"Shit," the man whimpered, wiping running snot off his lipstick. "I didn't do nuthin' to you!"

"You're an abomination in the eyes of the Lord!" Mica hissed with as much conviction as his overworked throat could produce. "And damned in the sight of men. You mock the body God gave you, you fucking *queer!*"

"I'm not a queer!" the man yelled as Mica cut across Highland behind a bus loaded with upwardly mobile business-types. "I'm a woman trapped in a man's body!"

"You're a fucking pervert!" Mica hollered back, ignoring the raw tickle back by his tonsils. "God made you a *man!*"

"Then God made a mistake!"

The accusation echoed out of the shadows at him.

Mica almost darted back across the street to finish the job, but instead pressed the Bible against the scar on his forehead and took a deep breath.

"God doesn't *make* mistakes," he whispered.

TWO

This was a mistake.

A *bad* mistake.

And her aim had been *way* off.

Allison molded her bare ass into a waffle pattern on the cyclone fence and watched Buck hop around the deserted parking lot—jeans down around his ankles, his penis flopping out the front of his briefs, his hand pressed tightly against his lacerated left ear.

Oops.

"You goddamned bitch! You fucking *bit* me!"

Buck's Tex-Mex accent had disappeared, along with his passion . . . and ear lobe. Allison silently damned Seth's already damned soul to the lowest pit of Hell for sucking her dry and not leaving her so much as a training manual.

Producing fangs was no effort—she managed that

23

while Buck was ripping her skirt off up against the back fender of his station wagon (they couldn't use the back-seat because it was filled with kid's toys); and she'd even lulled him into near-orgasmic euphoria by running the tip of her icy tongue up and down the throbbing veins in his neck . . . just like Seth had done to her.

But *then* she lunged.

What would Christopher Lee do at a time like this?

"You fucking cunt," Buck screamed as he waddled up and shoved his dripping hand into her face. "Look at that!"

Allison did. And her mouth watered.

"You shit-brained whore . . . how am I going to explain *this* to my wife? I could . . . kill you!"

"Too late," Allison whispered.

"WHAT?"

"I—I, ah . . . I guess I just got—um—carried away." She tucked her fangs down under her lip and tried to smile. "You're just so . . . uh, sexy."

Without warning, Buck grabbed the front of her blouse with his free hand and tore it down the middle. The anger in his face shifted into something else.

Something Allison had seen before.

In Seth's cold green eyes.

Power.

Allison lowered her chin and trembled, letting him think he'd achieved it.

"Yeah, think you're so fucking funny, don't you?"

Instead of waiting for an answer Buck tried ramming the tip of his deflated cock up inside her. When it flopped off the front of her pelvis, he grabbed it with both hands and began masturbating it back to life.

Talk about beating a dead horse.

"Goddamned bitch—try to tear my ear half off so I'll—umph—get into trouble at home. Well, I'm going to—shit—show you s-something that—oh yeah—*really* funny!"

Finally hard, Buck kicked her legs apart and pushed himself in. Allison arched her back to accept him and moaned loudly. She could taste his blood with *those* lips, too.

Her moan turned into a low growl.

"Yeah, you like it . . . don't you . . . bitch . . . tell me . . . you . . . like—"

This time her aim was dead center.

Her virginal incisors busted their cherries in a streaming gush that poured down her throat like liquid fire.

Allison hadn't realized how cold—how *dead* cold she'd been until the blood began to thaw her out. It felt like someone had turned her internal thermostat back on.

With the warmth came memories. *Buck's* memories. Of sunlight and children laughing and the stupid dog that wouldn't stop humping everything in sight and of one-night stands and backseats and beer and her and running the final touch-down in high school and . . .

Low-throated moans harmonized as each of them pushed deeper into the orifice of their choice.

Anyone spotting them would think they were seeing two half-naked people humping each other's legs off . . .

a generally accepted and much revered ending to a chance encounter in a single's bar.

Meat market, she corrected. *And definitely USDA Prime!*

Allison's tongue flicked against the twin punctures as the rushing stream of blood slowed to an ooze.

Not bad for a girl who used to like her hamburgers burnt to a . . .

Slowed?

Oh FUCK!

Allison strong-armed Buck away from her . . . and literally held him there. The six-foot-one, two-hundred pound Urban Cowboy was sagging worse than an old lady's boobs.

But he looked happy.

Head lolling to one side, eyes rolled up into the back of his skull, big shit-eating grin covering the lower half of his face, Buck suddenly whimpered and dribbled his wad effortlessly down the inside of her right thigh.

"Oh, yeah . . . you're the best . . . Dolores."

Whoever Dolores was, she must have been some lay.

Allison released her grip and watched the man crumple to the asphalt like a used condom.

"Oh, shit."

Collapsing back against the fence, Allison stared down at the dying man and lifted her hand slowly to her mouth. She took three nails down to the nub before noticing.

"Shit!" She said, slamming her fists against her naked thighs. "I'm fucking dead and I still bite my nails? I don't even get a break on getting rid of bad habits? This isn't FAIR!"

The memory of Seth's voice—so cool, so condescending—drifted back to her.

What made you think death would be any fairer than life?

Good ol' Seth.

"I hope he runs into a logging truck," she whispered.

Buck's moan snapped her back. Thanks to her now-perfect night vision, she could see that he was quickly fading to the color of old newsprint. Seth had told her . . .

Allison pressed her lips together, found them splattered with blood and greedily licked them clean.

Seth had told her . . . *something* about not draining a person all at once because . . . because . . .

Because in every Dracula movie the victim had to be bitten three times in order for the vampire to gain control over that person's soul creating another member of the undead.

"Yes!"

Allison looked down at the "club's" newest potential member—and suddenly realized why Seth had taken off. Carrying another person is hard enough, but being stuck with someone who would be constantly under-foot and muscling in on your kills . . .

Now, if he'd been better *looking* . . .

"No. No way, nada, negative!"

"Do . . . me."

Shit, he was already making demands.

27

Squatting, Allison pressed her hand down against the man's chest and felt his heart struggling to keep body and soul together. But it wouldn't last much longer. And when he died he'd transform and she'd be stuck with him.

For all eternity.

A marriage truly made in Hell.

His heart skipped a beat and Allison cringed. When the weak fluttering started again she almost thanked God . . . but figured *that* would have only gotten her into more trouble.

Okay, she thought, how does one kill a vampire? Given her present after-life-style, she hadn't thought it necessary to bring along wooden stakes the way she had always slipped a few condoms into her purse.

Just in case.

Okay, no stakes . . . so what else could she do? Dammit, she really should have spent more time *watching* those movies instead of making out or hiding behind her hands. *Let's see,* Allison thought, *how did Chris Lee bite the big one?* There was fire and drowning and sunlight and . . .

Allison cringed. None of them sounded all that pleasant given *her* present circumstances.

Buck's heart started hiccupping. Okay . . . he was still alive (if only for the moment) and if she killed him *while* he was still alive that meant he wouldn't necessarily turn into a vampire once he *was* dead.

Right?

Closing the man's egg-white (*but alive*) eyes, Allison hooked the tip of her nails into the holes on his neck and ripped his throat out.

Now he looked like he'd been attacked by a werewolf.

"Buck?"

Allison lay her hand back across his chest and felt absolutely nothing. Okay . . . he was dead. Good.

He groaned.

Bad.

Allison tore his head off and tossed it over her shoulder.

Sucking the blood off her fingers, she turned and watched for any sign of *after* life. The head landed upside-down against the fence . . . silent, still, pressed to Abraham's bosom. The ultimate Dead Head.

"Thank God."

She flinched at the sound of her hands hitting her face as they clapped across her mouth. What the hell was she doing thanking God? Shit, talk about courting disaster! She was a frigging vampire! One of the Undead. Forever damned. With knowledge and forethought she'd forfeited her soul and—

Allison let her hands drop into her lap and looked up into the night sky.

—and there was nothing HE could do about it.

Smiling, Allison leaned over the decapitated corpse and began lapping the cooling puddle of blood up off the blacktop.

Not as good as fresh, she decided, but still edible.

"Holy-fucking-*shit!*"

29

Allison's head snapped up and turned back toward the sound. Her ass, raised high and proud, was outlined in a white halo of light. *God?*

Dropping her butt quickly, Allison sat up and squinted past the glare. She could just make out the overall shape and size of an electric golf-cart-turned-security-car . . . and the two wide-eyed Rent-A-Cops inside.

So much for a vampire's heightened sense of hearing.

"Do-you-fucking-see-what-she's-doing?"

The words were spilling out of the man's mouth so fast it was even hard for Allison to keep up. She lifted her hand to her eyes and a small glob of Buck fell, white as a snowflake, back to the ground.

"Oh God Oh God Oh God Oh God Oh God . . ."

And *that* was as good an exit line as she'd ever heard.

Three decades (plus) of human conditioning took over and Allison bolted like a half-naked jack rabbit across the empty parking lot.

With the golf cart's little whirring electric motor right behind.

"Hold it right there, lady! Stop, goddamn it! This is Security!"

Halfway across the lot she had the fleeting image of running shoes and instantly felt the hugging comfort of Nike's encasing her feet.

Satin running shorts followed.

Being a vampire and having been caught in the act of feeding was *nothing* compared to charges of indecent exposure.

30

At least not in California.

Thrilled that she'd finally gotten the basics down, Allison concentrated on becoming a bat.

And found out that only happened in movies.

Goddamn Hollywood anyway!

THREE

Hollywood, California, was the modern world's answer to Sodom and Gomorrah, which was what brought Mica there in the first place.

Actually, it was the round-trip bus ticket the First Congregational Church had awarded him for his essay "Ask Not If God Is Dead, But Rather If YOU Are" that brought him. With it he was to compete against the soulless radical youth from across the nation in an Intra-collegiate debate on whether or not God existed at all, win by proving He did, and come home to Tulsa bathed in glory.

Mica (still Milo, at the time) had no doubts that he'd win hands down. God, after all, was on *his* side.

After a brief stop at the Holiday Inn where the contestants were paired up and given rooms (Mica's "roomie" was a wild-eyed, black-haired youth from

Maine who farted a lot and called it Divine Atomization), they were all piled into a school bus and driven to Paramount Studios where the debate was to be taped for later broadcast.

On obscure public access stations.

Late at night.

But even the thought of appearing on television, just like the late-night preachers, made Mica light-headed with anticipation.

He didn't bother trying to explain the feeling to his black-haired seat partner. It wouldn't have done any good anyway. Two minutes after sliding into the seat, he'd laid his greasy head against the window and fallen asleep.

Mica took the opportunity—and blessing—to find someone with whom he might be able to share an *intelligent* conversation.

He found her sitting near the back of the bus.

Alone. As if she was waiting for him.

Mica took *that* as a sign, too.

Her waist-length hair was the color of autumn leaves and the eyes that met his were soft and gentle and matched her voice. Her name was Piper and, although she looked a lot like Piper Laurie's character in *Carrie*, she told Mica she was an agnostic.

And he forgave her.

More than forgave her.

He kept quiet.

They never made it to the debate and Mica turned in his return bus ticket the next day.

Three weeks later, when he called home to explain, his mama cried and his daddy cursed him. But he was an *adult* and they-couldn't-do-anything-about-it-go-to-hell.

Then Mica started to think about what he'd done.

And left two days later.

Without a word.

But he did leave his Bible along with a note on the cheap motel's stationary that told Piper that he forgave her for leading him astray.

Good-bye.

Shit . . . what dredged up THAT old walnut?

Mica blinked his eyes and watched the strawberry blond continue jogging up the street away from him.

Oh.

Eleven years and he still phased out at the sight of red hair.

Leaning back against the side of an all-night video rental store, Mica took a deep breath and licked the salt off his lips. A few years back he actually tried to find out what happened to Piper. He hoped she'd taken his blessings and Bible and found God . . . or at least her way back home.

Wherever that was.

He'd never asked. And he never heard from or about her again.

But he still checked out every red-head who passed. Just in case.

Mica ran his hand through his lank brown hair and watched another jogger—this one a middle-aged Philippino—dart into traffic between a stretched limo and a Ram Van. And marveled at the miracle. Less than a month earlier, at the world famous intersection of Sunset and Vine, Mica had seen a kid in a Raider's jacket try the same thing and become road pizza.

The kid had probably been a Gang Banger, but Mica prayed for his soul anyway.

Hell, he prayed for them *all*.

Every last one of them.

A girl with a green dragon tattooed across her forehead glared at him. Mica tipped his red satin uniform cap at her and smiled. She flipped him off.

A normal exchange for "The Strip."

Stepping away from the building, and back into the thick of the sidewalk traffic, Mica lifted his arms a la Mary Tyler Moore and smiled.

"I *love* this town!"

"Then go fuck a manhole cover," a man wearing a short-sleeved garbage bag over stained long johns growled at him.

Mica spun on his imitation Hush Puppies, grasped the man's knobby shoulders and pulled him in as close as the stench of cheap wine and well-aged sweat would allow.

"You can feel that Love, too, brother—just open your heart!"

The man shrugged away Mica's hands and quickly brushed off his shoulders with excrement-caked fingers.

"Goddamned *pervert!*"

He knocked past Mica and stumbled away, muttering angrily to himself. Mica watched the man until he was swallowed by the meandering crowd and shook his head. Oh well, the night was still young.

Checking his watch against the large neon-encased clock in the Pawn Shop *(We Accept Used CDs)* Mica quickly readjusted his cap and joined the steady flow pushing eastward. It was 9:48 . . . which just gave him enough time to *almost* make it to work on time.

It still bothered him that he couldn't spread The Word as a full-time occupation. But even a preacher has to eat, and the Lord *had* provided him with gainful employment.

Such as it was.

Sighing, Mica stuffed his hands into the black-and-red satin jacket (that was also part of his uniform and probably the reason the man had misunderstood his pure intentions) and ignored the rhythmic grunting that was coming from a narrow alley between the porno bookshop and Army/Navy Surplus store.

Tried to ignore it.

Halfway across, Mica looked in. In the backwashed glow from the streets, he saw four people exchanging points of view. One man was slamming his rod into the narrow ass of a teenaged boy while a second was doing it doggy-fashion with the kid's girlfriend. Mica knew they were sweethearts by the way they held hands and smiled at each other while their clients humped away.

True love—Hollywood style.

Mica mumbled a quick prayer for their enlightenment and hurried away . . . as much for the fact that Luci could be a real bitch if he wandered in late, as for the uncomfortable tightness in the crotch of his jeans.

He could handle the ignorance and injustices and even the overt hatred . . .

. . . but the constant testing was wearing a little thin.

When Allison realized how long she'd been running it was like hitting a brick wall. She stopped so fast she left skid marks. She'd always thought running was the biggest joke ever played on the populace by the medical profession, and had even gone so far as to explain her theory to her P.E. teachers . . .

. . . none of whom had listened, and made her take extra laps just to prove her wrong.

But *now*.

Allison pressed her hand against her chest and smiled. Her heart wasn't trying to explode out of her ribcage. It wasn't *beating*, either, but it was still an improvement.

"Maybe there's something to this vampire business after all."

Smiling, Allison fluffed out her wind-tangled but still perfectly dry hair and walked to the corner sign post just ahead of her.

Lankershim Boulevard and Hartsook.

Where the hell was that?

Leaning against the thin metal pole, Allison looked back in the direction she'd just run in from as if that would give her some clue. The Silver Concho was near the Lopez Adobe on MacClay and San Fernando Road and good ol' *Buck* had followed the Road north another couple of miles before turning into the deserted *(hah,*

hah) parking lot. Somehow, along the run, she'd turned off San Fernando and onto Lankershim and was in . . .

Allison looked back at the street signs and would have gasped if she'd still been able to.

. . . North Hollywood.

The sign post felt cool as she grabbed it. Even though orientation had never been her strong suit in Girl Scouts, she knew the area well enough to know she was roughly twenty to twenty-five miles away from where she'd left Buck. And the Security Guards.

They wouldn't be looking for her in North Hollywood, considering she'd taken off running and it would have been impossible for a woman to go so far a distance in—

She checked her watch quickly and smiled.

—in twenty minutes.

A mile-plus a minute. YES! Finally . . . something that worked!

Giggling to herself, Allison faced back toward Lankershim and watched the traffic lights shift from green to red. There was no reason to draw attention to herself by breaking a minor law . . . especially when she was drawing enough attention just standing there.

She smiled back at the three black men in the rusted-out Impala next to her.

"You sure do have some kick-ass legs, baby," the man hanging out of the passenger's side window said.

"You really think so?" Allison asked, *innocently* sliding the jogging shorts higher up her hips so they could see she wasn't wearing any underwear.

She could almost hear their cocks begin to harden. She *could* smell the blood racing through their veins.

"Oh, yeah . . . you *know* it, baby."

The driver muttered something as the light turned green and was ignored—by everyone but the irate driver in the VW Bug behind the Chevy. A *beep* from the horn only got the Bug owner angry glares and shouted threats.

Allison waved as the Bug peeled out.

"Some people," she said, shaking her head.

"Yeah. You want a ride?" The man's voice was syrupy sweet. "Ain't safe for a pretty thing like you to be out so late."

Ten o'clock. Yeah . . . *real* late.

"Thank you," she said as the back door popped open and another dark face smiled up at her. The man looked like he ate pit bulls for breakfast. "Gee, this is *awfully* nice of you. I guess I really am a little tired. Hope you don't mind if I accidentally fall asleep."

This time the sound of belt buckles being unfastened and zippers sliding open was unmistakable.

Allison added a graceful "oh, are my feet sore" limp as she hobbled to the car.

"How can I *ever* thank you," she asked.

"We'll think of *something*, baby," the man in back laughed.

Allison joined them.

She always did prefer dark meat at Thanksgiving.

FOUR

The moment the late model pick-up pulled into traffic, Allison maneuvered the Impala into its space and cut the engine. Finding a parking spot on The Strip had been hard enough when she'd been alive. She wasn't going to let the fact that she could easily sprint to any location along Sunset Boulevard in mere seconds deprive her of the pleasure of screwing over some other motorist.

Some things didn't *have* to change.

Leaning across the welded chain steering wheel, Allison looked through the insect-splattered windshield at the pedestrians ambling along the sidewalk.

Hookers propositioned plain clothes vice officers, neo-hippies flashed peace signs, tourists huddled together like frightened quail and pointed at the strutting homeboys, taggers nonchalantly shook aerosol cans, joggers jogged and shop owners kept a watchful eye.

Allison smacked her lips. Welcome to *Tinsel-Town Take Out*.

It was a veritable smorgasbord.

One that she'd fit into perfectly once she slipped into something a little less blood-stained.

It was lucky *(for her)* that the three men had decided to rape her one at a time in some back alley. Not that she'd been worried about not being able to handle them . . . but it made things so much easier.

She chuckled softly, remembering the look on the others' faces when she stepped around to the front of the car, buck-assed naked, and said "Next."

Allison's chuckle eased into a purring hum as an overly developed hunk in a speedo and muscle tee sauntered by—arrogantly ignoring her and all the other drooling females.

And she *was* drooling.

And still hungry.

Dammit.

Sitting up, Allison jabbed a finger into her belly and listened to it gurgle. It sounded like an under-filled water bed.

How much could the average vampire hold before it exploded?

That was just *another minor detail* Seth hadn't bothered mentioning before he split.

Bastard.

Let's see, there was Buck and the three dudes in the alley . . . At six-quarts each, give or take a pint when I tore of their heads, that's . . .

"Shit, that's twenty-four quarts!" Even a *non*-human body couldn't hold that much liquid.

Smoothing down the front of the blood-soaked blouse *(that's another couple of cups right there)*, Allison checked her tummy for any unsightly bulge. And relaxed.

Her stomach, though sloshing slightly, was still as flat as the fifty sit-ups a day had made it.

"Guess they were right about an all liquid protein diet."

Funny, she didn't have to pee.

Patting her tummy, Allison looked up in time to see Mr. Speedo going into a gay bookstore. And it didn't bother her one bit . . . not like it used to.

"Different strokes and all that. Well, time for a quick change and—" She glanced into the car's rearview mirror and saw nothing but the driver's side head rest. "Damn. That's going to be a bitch. Well, at least I can change."

A quick check indicated it was still warm enough for shorts and tee-shirts. So be it.

Mint-green satin joggers and matching French-cut tee.

To go.

Now.

Allison looked down at the gore-splattered blouse and joggers and felt a slight twinge race through her atrophied sphincter.

Okay, she thought, let's try something a little simpler: Cut-offs and tube top.

A muu-muu?

43

Not so much as her shoes transformed.

Fuck fuck fuck fuck fuck fuck . . .

Allison could hear the dead men's blood pounding in her ears as she tried to change something. *Anything*.

Nothing.

"Aw, shit . . . now what?" What *other* minor detail had Seth forgotten to mention in his stampede to get out of her death? "Goddamned bastard!"

"We *all* are."

Despite everything that had happened to her over the previous three days, Allison jumped at the sudden intrusion into her well of self-pity. A skinhead in black leather pants and matching vest was leaning up against the driver's side fender—hunched over, arms folded across his bare chest, looking at her like he was used to seeing women covered in blood.

"Your bastard do that to you?" he asked, nodding to the blouse. "Or you do that to him?"

Allison let her hand outline her breasts while pretending to brush the stain away.

"A little of both, actually," she said.

"Good. I like my women to have a little spirit in 'em." He didn't look half bad when he smiled. "You wanna party?"

Allison's stomach rumbled happily.

"Sure," she said, opening the door. She didn't bother taking out the keys. With any luck somebody would steal it . . . and the three headless horsemen stuffed in the trunk. "Thought you'd never ask."

Her fangs were already digging into her bottom lip

when he slipped a hand into her blouse and began pinching her nipples hard enough to make a living woman whimper. Allison smiled and shoved her hand between his legs and matched pressure.

"Damn! You *do* like it rough, don't you?"

Allison pulled in front of him just enough to slide her ass up against his groin.

"The rougher the better, Mr. Clean," she said patting his stubbled head. "You *up* to it?"

"Well, let's just go find out, shall we, bitch?"

He grabbed her around the neck and dragged her through a narrow passage way between two buildings. It looked like it opened up farther back into an actual weed-choked, beer-can-lined vacant lot. Good. She was getting so tired of alley ways and parking lots.

"Hope you don't scream too loud when I take you apart," he growled as he ripped her blouse off from the back.

Allison turned and smiled—fangs fully extended.

"Same goes for you, pal."

"You wanna scream? You wanna holler?" Mica yelled from his place in front of the club. "Well, this is the place to do it! You just *think* you've seen Hollywood until you see what goes on inside. Hot? Brother, only Hell'd be hotter and not *half* so much fun!"

Ain't that the Truth?

Mica took a quick gulp from the Seven-Eleven tumbler he had stashed behind the full-sized cut-out of Luci in her famous *Foxy-Lady* outfit and nodded to one of the regulars—a granny-glass wearing, mid-forties hippy with thinning shoulder-length hair. "Place jumpin'?" he asked, just like he did every night.

"Like fleas on a dog's ass," Mica answered. Just like every night.

"Oh, man . . . Oh, man!"

Pathetic. Grown men acting like adolescents with bad cases of raging hormones, just because women were prancing around a stage dressed like animals.

Sad.

Mica took another long swallow and gave the cut-out—with its silvery fur that clung to every luscious curve of her body, and full tail pulled suggestively between her long legs and held so that it *almost* covered her rose-pink nipples, and the tufts of snow-white fur curling up toward her pert, raised ears—only the briefest glance before wandering back toward the un-suspecting public.

"Yes sir, boys, if you want to see the native *wild life* of Hollywood, step right in! I can guarantee that you won't be seeing nothing like this on National Geographical!

"So, come on all you Big Game Hunters . . . Grab your barrels and step on into the only *Fur-vert* Club in Holly-wood! The *Animals* are getting restless!"

The Lord provided him with the means to support himself and Mica was grateful . . . but, *shit,* he hated his job.

"You wanna scream? You wanna holler?" He took a deep breath and prepared to begin the speech again when someone tugged his sleeve.

"Excuse me, young man."

Mica relaxed his vocal cords and looked down at two old women dressed in matching capri pants and Hawaiian-print shirts. Thick layers of pearls and multi-colored glass beads encased the turkey-waddled necks and hung off the thin liver-spotted wrists. Each was carrying a straw hand-bag that had *Palm Springs* written across it.

Mica wondered if that was where they were from or if they just thought it made them look *chic*.

"Yes, ma'am," he said, tipping his hat, "and what may I do for you this fine evening?"

"We're here visiting Elenore's grandson and . . ."

Mica nodded and *hmmmed* and smiled and stopped listening. Why was it that old people couldn't just come out and get to the *one* point they were interested in? He remembered his granddaddy doing the same thing—ask him for the time and he'd tell you how to build a watch.

Mica unplugged his ears just long enough to make sure he wasn't missing anything important—". . . in junior college out here and he's just doing so well that we . . ."—and noticed the toes of his shoes were over the yellow line painted on the ground ten feet from the club's entrance.

Oops.

Chuckling along with the woman over something the grandson had done, Mica slid his feet well back into the protection of his "office." City ordinances let the clubs on the strip employ barkers, but the cops kept a close eye on them. Get too close to the walk-bys and the club owner would get a harassment charge up the ass.

Luci told Mica she lost more employees that way. Hence the yellow line.

". . . I asked Elenore and she didn't know either so we just thought we'd ask you . . ."

Mica blinked and straightened his shoulders. "Yes ma'am?"

But instead of asking—maybe she'd busted a vocal cord—the old woman who's name *wasn't* Elenore pointed to the glowing red-on-black fur lined marquee above the fur covered doors.

Mica turned and shrugged. It was pretty self-evident as far as he could see.

LUCI'S FUR PIT
The finest FURVERT entertainment in L.A.

"Yes? Ma'am?"

"Furverts?" Elenore said, finally finding her voice. "I've never heard of that. Is it some kind of animal?"

Animals? Yes. That's exactly what they were. Animals.

"Yes ma'am," Mica said softly, inching closer to the yellow line because there were some things more important than job security. "Animals. Big two-legged animals who get their kicks by watching naked women prance around in furry costumes."

Both ladies gasped—*moved* by the spirit of righteousness.

"Yes'um, I know, but this is a free country and there's

nothing I can do about it." He stepped to one side and nodded greetings as two men in business suits walked into the club. "With free will comes the burden of Choice! I can't make these men choose the Path to Glory over the Path of Sin and Corruption. That's their choice. And they will pay for it when the numbers are finally counted."

Another customer—this one obviously under the legal age but just as obviously carrying a fake I.D.—brushed past Mica and his flock and hurried into the fur-lined darkness.

"Bu-but that *child!*" One of the ladies yelped. Mica didn't catch which one. It didn't matter.

"Has as much right to go in there as you do to stay out. It's his choice. We all have choices . . ."

Mica's hand was automatically reaching for the carry-along Bible he kept in the back pocket of his jeans before he remembered it wasn't there.

Damn.

Luci didn't mind him trying to convert the clientele *after* they left—while visions of fur-covered tits and asses still danced o'er their heads—but she drew the line (like the one defining his "office") at him Bible thumping anywhere near the club. Besides, she once told him, bringing a Bible into a well-established den of iniquity was a little sacrilegious, wasn't it?

Was it?

Mica dropped to his knees, ignoring the pain and the bug-eyed shock on the old women's faces, and clasped his hands in front of him.

"The only thing we can do is pray for these poor men to see the Light. Will you help me, ladies? Will you help me pray their choices back from the fiery pit of eternal damnation?

"*You are the salt of the earth,* Jesus told his Disciples, *but what if the salt goes flat?* Well, we can't let that happen, ladies . . . we gotta get down and dirty and wrestle the taste back into that salt. We gotta—"

Mica watched the old ladies' orthopedic loafers burn rubber as they hurried away.

"Next show's in fifteen minutes," he hollered after them. "Ladies welcome."

"Aw, hell, Preacher-boy, don't tell me you got off on another Holy Roller tear. Shee-IT. And get up off your knees, man . . . people'll think you're doing me right here in front of God n'everybody."

Mica stood up and tried to wipe most of the sidewalk grudge off his knees while the club's head bartender/bouncer shook his shaggy head in the neon glow. It was impossible to tell where the man's facial hair stopped and his shoulder-length hair began.

Two ax-handles high by four ax-handles wide—most of that from the waist up—the man crossed his arms over his pride and joy . . . a "real" *you even think about touching this and I'll rip your arm off* Harley-Davidson black leather vest he got the *hard* way (although Mica had yet to build up the courage to ask what that was) and fiddled with the toothpick that stuck out from beneath the greying walrus mustache.

While he casually looked up and down Sunset.

And ignored Mica.

For the moment.

According to the club's dresser and chief gossip, Miriam, the man had been: an outlaw biker, a roadie, a music promoter, porno-star (until his beer belly overshadowed his *other* qualifications), a full professor of philosophy, an undercover cop in Detroit and one of the biggest collectors of anthropomorphic, graphically enhanced, anatomically correct female animal cartoons this side of Fresno. A *Furvert* of the first order.

And the only *real* friend Mica had made in the last eleven years.

They might be one-hundred-and-eighty degrees opposites in the way they viewed life, but that never stopped Gypsy (at *least* fifteen years Mica's senior and a devout cynic) from inviting Mica to his bi-monthly Beer-Bust/Chili Gas-Off/B.Y.O.C(ondom) Orgy at his place in Echo Park. The same way it didn't stop Mica from trying to show Gypsy the errors in the path he'd chosen.

And bailing him out when he had to.

Which was usually right after the bi-monthlies.

But that's what friends were for.

In Hollywood.

"You land yet, Preacher-boy?" he asked. "Or are you still flying through the ionosphere?"

"I landed, Gypsy."

"Glad to hear it, man." Gypsy stared down two Homeys in Raiders jackets and backwards baseball caps before turning his attention to Mica. "You scare the shit out of me when you start drooling holy water."

"World's a big scary place, Gyp. A man's got to have something to fall back on."

Gypsy slapped the seat of his wear-faded jeans and winked.

"I got *more* than enough right here, pal."

Mica slid his hands into the creamy smooth lining of the jacket pockets and shook his head. Gypsy was one hard-assed mother whose views, or lack of them, proved once again that God had a marvelous sense of humor. Why else would He have let their paths cross?

For all his gruff and bluster, Gypsy was still the only *living* man Mica trusted.

The only one he would kill for.

If it came to that.

He just hoped it never would.

Amen.

Hunching his shoulders, Mica scraped the toes of his shoes all the way back to his place behind the line.

"Guess I'd better get back to prostituting my talents, huh?"

"You mean *proselytizing* your talents, don't you?"

Rolling his eyes in a *what's a mother to do* sweep, Gypsy strong armed Mica around the neck and half-dragged/half-walked him toward the entrance.

"Come on, man . . . I think you need a little break."

"But I just *got* here."

"Yeah, yeah, I know. But it was getting a little too close in there. If you know what I mean."

Mica knew all right. Three or four times a night, more on the nights that Luci introduced a new number,

Gypsy would stagger out of the club and offer to bark while his blood-pressure dropped back to a reasonable level.

Without these little diversions, Mica was sure his friend would spontaneously combust.

"Go on. Grab some coffee or some ass," Gypsy said giving him a final shove. "I'll come get you in a bit."

Mica nodded and made it to the second set of fake fur curtains before the music hit him right in the groin. Whining guitars and driving snares accompanied *Jimi Hendrix* as he sang about his "Foxy Lady."

Luci's theme song.

Mica thought about turning around and beating a hasty retreat out to the relative safety of the streets. Out there he could cower next to his best friend and no one would think any less of him.

But him.

No. There was nothing behind those curtains he hadn't seen before. They were just women . . . beautiful women who could entice the shoes off a saint . . . but just women. And he had the strength of his convictions—Bible or not.

Besides, Gypsy would laugh him three ways to Sunday if he scurried away like a frightened little mouse.

No. He was going to face the music . . . and whatever would be strutting her stuff *to* that music.

Taking a deep breath of air laced heavily with controlled substances, Mica lifted his chin defiantly (*You still with me, aren't you, Lord?*) and pushed through the velvet soft curtain.

53

Luci was curling around one of the metal "dance" posts, her silver pelt almost invisible in the pale blue light.

Almost invisible.

Depending on how she moved.

Right now (and from where Mica was standing transfixed) it looked like she was completely nude except for a rhinestone dog collar and modified fox mask. The lush white-tipped tail sweeping the glittered floor looked like it was coming right out of her ass.

"Jesus," he moaned.

"Man . . . you got *that* right," one of the Furverts gasped next to Mica.

Even with the spots following her every bump and grind, Luci saw him as he slipped in, and waved to him. Blew him a kiss. And every furverted eyed followed it back to him.

God . . . she did that to him every time.

Lowering his head, Mica scooted in behind the bar and took Gypsy's high-rise director's chair. He told Mica he needed something that high to keep an eye on things . . . but what it really did was allow him an uninterrupted view of the stage.

Lord, we gotta talk to this boy a little more seriously.

Hoots and hollers erupted as Luci removed her collar and flung it into the audience . . . followed immediately by a fight to determine who would take possession of it and therefore get to stay after the doors closed for dinner and drinks with the Foxy Lady herself.

Mica knew he ought to go get Gypsy before one of the clawing *'verts* got hurt . . . but Luci was still on stage and it would have been rude to run off before she finished her number.

At least that was the lie he told himself *this* time.

FIVE

The blue spot melted into pale pink as Luci arched her back . . . and became every furvert's image of a silvery vixen stretching to meet the dawn.

And the crowd went wild.

Even the five men beating each other into bloody pulps over the coveted collar stopped—briefly—to salivate.

Mica swallowed an extra mouthful himself and tried to find a more comfortable position in the chair. Which wasn't, he soon realized, going to be possible without grabbing the front of his jeans and moving things around a little.

Or a lot.

When he finally gave up, Mica looked up and saw Luci looking in his direction *(again)* and smiling *(again)*—just like the first time he made a fool of himself.

It was the night he walked out on *(left . . . I left)* Piper. More than half the things in his suitcase still had mama-folds in them. Neither of them had bothered to unpack once they found the tiny one-room apartment. They'd made love for most of their three weeks . . . only bothering to put on clothes when hunger drove them to the Tiny Naylor's drive in.

That had been wrong . . . so wrong . . . he'd almost lost himself in the arms of carnal pleasures.

Well, that wasn't going to happen again. To him or *anyone* else!

It was only chance—or, Mica'd come to believe, divine comedy—that stopped him directly in front of the *Pit*. He'd never seen anything like that in Tulsa. And if it hadn't been in Tulsa then it had no right to be anywhere!

The barker that night had been a tall, skinny kid with long curly hair and a face ravaged by acne scars. Mica felt sorry for him *(I'm sorry, I'm sorry, I'm sorry)* but fed him the suitcase anyway.

Nothing was going to stop him from *(making it up to Piper for walking out)* showing the fools the error of their ways. He got as far as the stage before a massive right arm—Gypsy's he found out later—made itself at home against his Adam's apple.

Luci had been dressed as a snow-leopard that night, wearing a green rhinestone collar that matched the emerald sparkle of her eyes. Before he passed out from lack of oxygen, Mica remembered those eyes staring at the scar on his forehead and smiling.

When he woke the next morning, he had the world's

worst headache and a job. The pizza-faced kid, Luci told him as she gently traced the cross with her finger, had handed in his jacket and quit.

Just like that.

Then she smiled at him again and Mica felt all the blood rush out of his cheeks and into his cock.

Just like now.

Luci did hip grinds as she moved farther down the runway, holding the tail up between her legs and moving it slowly . . . so very slowly back and forth. Up and down. Her fiery green eyes sweeping the crowd but always coming back to him.

To him. Alone.

"God—" Mica started, then felt his jaw click shut.

Luci looked straight at him and mouthed something . . . repeated it so he could be sure.

God helps those who help themselves, Preacher-boy.

"How the hell . . . ?"

But by then her gaze had found another target.

The winner of the coveted collar—shirt half torn off and nose running blood—was waving the mangled remains above his head like a banner. And Luci was staring at him. Smiling at *him!*

Mica slid off the chair and muscled his way into and through the shouting Furverts.

Luci had gotten down on her hands and knees, asshigh, swinging the fox tail like a cat in heat. The man with the collar edged his way closer to the stage and shouted something up to her. It must have been funny because Luci reared back up laughing—her heavy, fur-covered breasts jiggling . . . the rose-pink nipples dancing in the light.

Mica shoved his elbow into the sagging gut of a man who hadn't gotten out of the way fast enough.

She was doing it to torment him . . . he knew that, knew it as if it were gospel . . . but kept right on heading for the stage.

And he might have made it, too, if Gypsy's arm hadn't snaked around his neck (again?) and hauled him backwards toward the exit.

But that's what friends were for.

In Hollywood.

Luci saw him leaving, and waved bye-bye.

She was getting better at her technique.

This one hardly spurted at all.

Dusting her hands off on the seat of her shorts, Allison tossed her blouse into the shallow grave next to the body and wiggled into the skinhead's vest. It barely covered her breasts but she wasn't going to run the risk of shrinking them down to a more manageable size. She couldn't face another disappointment just yet.

Reaching down, Allison pulled the oversized safety pin out of the man's left nipple and used it to fasten the vest a half-inch below the exaggerated swell of her breast.

Nice effect from *her* angle, but without a mirror she couldn't tell if it would even pass Hollywood's lax dress code.

"Of all the things I miss the most," she whispered to the dead man, then stopped before she got any further. No use crying over spilt milk, as her grannie used to say. Standing up, Allison brushed at the dried *Buck* stain on her chest. Maybe that philosophy went for blood as well.

"Okay," she said, glancing around, "now where'd we toss that head of yours?"

Hands on hip, Allison turned slowly on the balls of her feet, seeing into even the darkest shadows as if it were high noon. *Where, o where has his little head gone?* Good question.

The moment they entered the vacant lot, he'd thrown her against the wall and pulled her shorts down to her knees. Same old thing . . . right down to the sweet nothings he was grunting into her ears. She'd managed to keep from yawning while he told her—in imaginative graphic detail—everything he was going to do to her, but couldn't stop the smile when his zipper jammed.

Dead or not, no woman deserves to be slapped across the face.

A moment later the roles—and positions against the wall—were reversed.

The look of shock was still blooming in the skinhead's eyes when Allison's fangs cut an incision line under his jaw from ear to ear and popped his top.

Instant convertible.

But then she tossed it and got down to some serious feeding. Tossed it and didn't even bother to check where.

Damn! And she was trying to be so careful. By the time the police found the skinhead's final resting place, *if* they found it, she'd be—

Allison stopped and ran a cold tongue over her colder lips.

Where would she be?

Here? Somewhere else? Hook some inter-state trucker with promises of eternal life and find new hunting grounds before giving him the ol'"fuck-suck-see ya, shmuck" routine.

And splitting.

Like Seth had.

Allison kicked a broken wine bottle into a pile of cardboard boxes and felt the memory of a chill race beneath her skin. If she stuck around too long somebody was *bound* to connect her with the killings . . . even in Hollywood that sort of thing wouldn't go unnoticed indefinitely.

All they had to do was dust Buck's car for . . .

"My *purse!*"

She hadn't even thought about it until now, but in her hurry to leave the scene of the crime, she'd also left her purse—in which could be found her driver's license, MacDonnel-Douglas Photo-I.D. card, MasterCard and (presently useless) blood type card.

"Oh . . . fuck."

"He—steal your—purse, lady?" A low voice mumbled. "Guess that means you—don't have any—change. Huh?"

Allison turned slowly toward the sound as her fangs

slid into position and watched the largest of the cardboard boxes tremble while something crawled out of it.

The man was rail thin and stooped . . . hollow eyed and hollower cheeks. Years on the streets had taken more out of him than she ever could.

For the first time that evening Allison was looking at a man who didn't inspire even the tiniest pang of hunger.

Or maybe she was finally full.

Her stomach rumbled softly.

"Who asked *your* opinion?"

When the man finally stood as upright as he was going to get and faced her, Allison pulled in her fangs and quickly measured the distance between her and the narrow exit.

There was something about the bum . . . something just underneath the soiled clothing and skin . . . something that made her dead flesh crawl.

"Y-you hungry?" he asked, staggering toward her. Another scent wafted over to her: Cheap wine and even cheaper sterno.

This time her stomach took the hint and lay still.

"N-no. Thanks. I just ate."

"Yeah," he said, jerking his head toward the headless corpse and smiling. Three of his front teeth were missing—two up, one down. "I know."

Allison's body took over even as her mind was still recoiling from the shock of having been seen. In less time than it once took her heart to beat, Allison had the man by the front of his ragged, sweat-brittle flannel shirt and three inches off the ground.

"Anth wha are you goith t'do abouth ith?" she growled around fully extended fangs. *"Thith!"*

"Hey . . . no, it's okay," he said calmly. *Too* calmly for a man suspended five inches off the ground by a reanimated corpse that sucks blood from the living. Maybe he'd been an agent before the street caught up with him. "You're new in town . . . aren't you?"

He was trying to pick her up.

Jesus!

Allison let go and heard his jaw clink together as he landed. He didn't seem to notice.

"But it's . . . okay," he said, stumbling toward the body. Halfway there he fell to his hands and knees—and continued at a crawl. "I know what t'do. 'Kay? Just leave it all t'Big Mike. Big Mike'll do what needs t'be done. Just like the others."

The others?

Allison slowly began to move in on the hunched figure digging through the dead man's pants pockets.

"Oh, yeah . . . musta been plannin' a real hell of a party with this shit. You want any?" *Big Mike* glanced over his shoulder and held out a wad of cash that— *once upon a time*—would have made Allison reconsider denying him a date.

"Naw," he said, stuffing it into his own back pocket, "guess you don't need it anymore."

He laughed, then hacked up a glob of phlegm and shot it into the hole where the man's head should have been.

"His head . . ." Allison said.

"No problem," Big Mike said. "I'll find it and once it's

boiled down I can get maybe fifty . . . sixty bucks off those Devil Worshipers over on Franklin."

"And the—rest of him?"

Big Mike looked back at her and smacked his lips. Shit, he was a fucking ghoul! What the hell was this town coming to?

"So," he said, standing up, "you want some?"

She back-handed him to the ground. Big Mike landed flat out on the corpse's middle . . . their two bodies making a crude cross. Doubling over, Allison turned around and vomited nearly half her intake across the litter-strewn lot.

"Damn. Someone not agree with you?" She could hear him coming after her, the busted-out knees of his jeans scraping against the hard ground. "Gotta be more careful, little girl. Too many goddamned diseases goin' around. C'mon . . . it's okay. I get tested by the Red Cross all the time 'cause I give blood."

Again his laughter was cut short by a coughing fit.

"Give *blood* . . . get it?"

No . . . she didn't.

"Really, it's okay." He began fumbling with the cuff button on his sleeve and finally managed to tear it off. "Go on . . . have a hit for the road."

Allison felt the ground glide beneath her feet—the bloodless puncture marks on his wrists drawing her like a moth to the flame.

"Yeah . . . *knew* you were one o'em even before you did the guy. I can smell 'em, y'know."

Dropping heavily to her knees, Allison took the hand

gently between her palms as if it were a fragile flower. The points of her fangs were digging into her bottom lip—demanding action.

"Who. Did. Thith?" Allison asked as slowly as her need would allow. "Wath. Hish. Name. Seth?"

Big Mike's chuckle set his entire body trembling with the effort.

"I don't ask names, baby-doll. I just do what I'm told . . . and it ain't bad. All I gotta do is clean things up once 'n awhile and shred some juice t'keep things interesting and I got it made.

"How long you think a bum like me'd survive these streets without protection from the night. But you're the night . . . and I'm the day! And it all works out!"

He belched and her eyes started watering.

"So, go on, moonlight lady," Big Mike said, flexing his wrist. "I know you want to. Go on."

They both shuddered when she ran her tongue over the wounds—moaned in unison when her fangs pierced the thin scabs.

"Oh . . . God, yes! Just . . . umm . . . just don't take too much . . . oh . . . kay?"

Allison went on Auto-Pilot with the first mouthful. Somewhere in the back of her mind, almost buried by the memories flooding down her throat, she heard the occasional *ding* of a gas pump being emptied.

Real high octane stuff.

ding ding

SIX

"Breathing any easier now?" Gypsy asked as the tip of the toothpick danced in the corner of his mouth.

The swaying movement reminded Mica of the way Luci had moved on stage.

Closing his eyes, Mica nodded and exhaled as loudly as he could. Just to *prove* he still could.

"Yeah, my little lady really got to you tonight, didn't she, pal? Shit, that was a stupid question—half the *'verts* in there are shaking out their Fruit-of-the-Looms right now. 'Course she got to you. Got to me, too, and I only caught the tail-end."

When Mica finally opened his eyes, Gypsy shook his shaggy head and flipped the sliver of wood to the sidewalk.

"Christ, Preacher-boy, you gotta be more careful," he

said slapping Mica *lightly* across the shoulders. "The Lord can only forgive just so much."

"Yeah." It still felt like somebody'd dropped a hot iron down the front of his pants. "Thanks, Gyp."

"Not to worry, man, maybe one day you'll pull a thorn out of my paw."

Mica nodded and felt Gypsy's knuckles rake the top of his skull.

"I *mean* it, Preacher-boy. With Luci the best thing a man can do is look and drool from afar. And in *your* case I'd suggest long-distance field glasses. Now don't get me wrong," Gypsy said, finally smiling, "I would be more than willing to hump the lady until her legs fell off or I went blind . . . and I'm sure there's not a Furvert in the place that wouldn't do the same if the opportunity presented itself."

The smile disappeared somewhere in the depth of Gypsy's beard.

"But not you, Preacher-boy. You get too close and she'll fucking eat you alive."

Without really being sure why he was doing it, Mica balled his hands into fists and starting walking toward his best friend in the world. What the fuck did *he* know about Luci? All Gypsy saw was tits and ass and bush—he didn't see the *real* Luci. The Luci beneath the fur and grinding hips. The Luci whose soul was begging for redemption.

Just . . . *begging* for it.

"You don't know anything about it," Mica snarled. "Besides, *I* got all the protection I need."

68

"Yeah, right . . . Christ, sometimes you can be greener than grass in the spring. Don't you know you can't trust condoms one-hundred percent! Some got these little pin-prick holes in 'em and—"

"Lift your mind out of the gutter and see the light shining down on you. That's not the kind of protection I mean!"

"It's not?"

"NO! I'm talking about real Protection," Mica said, feeling lightheaded and angry and shaky all at the same time, a sure sign the Spirit was moving through him, and raised his fists toward the criss-crossing power lines overhead. "I'm talking about the Protection that comes from the Lord All Mighty."

"Aw, God."

"YES! Praise His name and feel the Glory of His—"

"*Mica.*"

Mica blinked so quickly he heard his eyelids pop. Gypsy never called him by his chosen Christian name unless things were getting out of hand.

Like now.

Mica shoved his hands back into the pockets of his jacket, where they couldn't get into any more trouble.

"The Holy 747 come in for a landing yet?"

"Yeah. Sorry, Gyp."

Gypsy folded his arms across his chest and scowled like the three-dimensional genie from Aladdin that Mica used to see through his View-Master.

"Sorry's for folks who don't think before they act," he growled. "Now get your sorry ass back to work before I kick it all the way to Santa Monica. You hear me, Preacher-boy?"

"Yes sir," Mica said, snapping to attention, "I hear you."

"Good!" The voice was still gruff, but Gypsy was smiling again. "You want to convert someone—start by converting the walking dead out there to the joys of fur."

He was just blaspheming to get back at me, Lord, Mica offered as the big man stalked back into the smokey darkness beyond the first set of curtains. *Forgive him.*

And me.

Knowing that they both would be, Mica stepped back behind the yellow line and nodded to the haggard looking man leaving the club.

"Hope you had a *furry* good time," he said, using the standard parting line. "And be sure to tell all your forest friends that we really know how to shake our tails here at the *Fur Pit*. Please come again."

You lecherous, voyeuristic—

"Oh, I will . . . you *know* I will," the Furvert said. "Man, you really got some show in there. Jesus!"

"Saves," Mica mumbled.

He'd already caused more than enough scenes for one night—and it wasn't even midnight yet. Like it or not . . . disgusted by the men (and *women,* may the Lord open their eyes to the damnation of their unnatural sexual preference) or not . . . the Lord had led Mica to this place and to this place he must stay until . . .

. . . until whatever the Lord had in mind for him happened.

Whatever that was.

At first Mica thought the constant exposure to naked women and their nightly invitations to get to "know" them better was a Divine Punishment because he'd walked out on (*left, dammit*) Piper.

But the Lord had made him see the error of that the same way He'd shown Mica the error of putting the love for a mere woman over the purer Love of God.

The job was a test of his Faith. Mica understood that. He just hoped he'd max the final when it came.

"Damn . . ." The Lord spoke through the Furvert's raspy voice, "Would you *look* at what's coming?"

Mica knew it'd been the Lord speaking, because—when he *saw* what the man was pointing at—he'd felt a great orgasmic shock rock his body.

It couldn't have been any clearer if the clouds had suddenly parted and the voice of his old high school Ethics teacher had intoned "Please remove all items from your desk and take out a Number 2 pencil, the final exam will begin momentarily."

"YES, Lord," Mica answered.

"*Amen* to that, brother," the Furvert agreed.

She was weaving in and out of the crowd—oblivious to the hungry stares from the men and envious glares from the women as she moved steadily up Sunset.

Toward the *Pit*.

Toward him.

Mica zipped the jacket all the way up to his throat and shivered. It was as if the steaming night had suddenly been put under attack by a freak arctic blast.

Dressed in short joggers and a dark leather vest, she paused briefly under a street light and ran a hand slowly through her hair. Another jolt raced up Mica's spine then did a quick U-turn. Even in the cat-piss yellow sodium glow he could tell her hair was red . . . the color of autumn leaves.

It was a little shorter than he remembered, only halfway down her back, but there was no doubt in Mica's mind that the woman lurching away from the light and staggering up the street was . . .

"She's drunk!"

"As a skunk," the Furvert said as he turned in the opposite direction. "Well, see ya tomorrow. Fur Forever!"

"Yeah. Right. Fur-ever, man." He mouthed the Furvert-Farewell without even hearing it.

Piper—drunk or on drugs. A woman of the streets.

And he'd done that to her because he'd walked out on her *(yeah . . . walked out)* without taking the time to sit down and try to explain . . . without trying to make her understand that it wasn't really *her* he was leaving it was just that . . .

. . . that what he felt for her scared the piss out of him.

Loving her left no room in his heart for God.

Mica knew the Lord had forgiven him.

Now all he needed was *her* forgiveness.

Mica took a half-dozen steps down the street and stopped dead. Piper was talking to a grey-haired man in black, laughing and shaking her head. When the man sidled up alongside her, Piper threw her head back and howled loud enough for Mica to hear.

Maybe she wasn't drunk or high . . . maybe she was just prone to the same "fits" as Mica's Grandmama had been. On more than one occasion he could remember the old lady lurching around the house singing at the top of her lungs. But since she was a devout teetotaler there was no reason behind her actions.

Mica suspected demonic posession.

His mama suspected the old lady was totalling more than tea.

The doctor came and said she'd just gone crazy after Mica's Granddaddy died.

Maybe Piper had gone crazy after he left.

Guilt twisted the bile in his gut while he watched the black-clad old man try again. This time Piper puffed out her cheeks and patted her stomach.

"Oh, God."

"Yeah, I heard you were talking to him again," Luci's voice said out of nowhere.

Spinning on his heels, Mica came face to face with the full-color cutout come to life. Only *this* one was furless. And dressed.

In knee-length cutoffs and an oversized man's white shirt with the sleeves rolled up to the elbows Luci looked more like everyone's kid sister than an exotic dancer. This was the *real* Luci. He preferred her that way. And she seemed to know it.

"So, what's the good word from above?" she asked. "Can we sinners expect another plague?"

Mica smiled and almost forgot Piper on the street behind him. *Almost*.

"No, ma'am."

"I'm so glad."

Smiling, Luci ran a hand slowly through her white-blond hair—*the same way Piper had*—then tossed it over one shoulder and began braiding it. Mica felt his own short hairs stand up when Luci's smile became an ugly smirk. But only for an instant.

An illusion.

When he blinked her smile was just as sweet and innocent as it always was when she talked to him.

Strange.

"So tell me," she said, still smiling, "how did you like my dance tonight? Have I corrupted you yet?"

Mica chuckled and shook his head. That had been a standard joke between them since he started.

"Guess I'll just have to try *harder* then." Luci poked him gently in the belly and let her hand slide down the front of his jeans before pulling it away. "Won't I?"

"You try any harder," Mica gasped, "and you might win."

She liked that answer. "Promises, promises. Now . . . one other question since I can't tempt you over to the *dark* side yet—you just taking a little break or are you running away from home. Again?"

"What?"

Luci jerked her head instead of answering and Mica looked past her. They were a good fifteen feet away from the club. His "office" unattended.

"Oops."

"Oops, he says. I'm probably losing twenties of dollars because you're not out there shilling and all you can say is *oops*."

Tossing the half-completed braid back over her shoulder, Luci laced her arm through his and gave it a quick hug, showing him she was only teasing. Mica could feel the coolness of her skin even through the jacket—one of the benefits of working inside an air-conditioned building.

"What *am* I going to do with you, Preacher-boy? Chain you to the door? Hey, that's not a bad idea. We could . . ."

Mica stopped listening the same way he had with the old ladies and glanced back down the street. *Piper* had stopped laughing and was trying to find her way back on to the crowded sidewalk. She stumbled and Mica caught his breath . . .

Piper

. . . afraid she'd go down and get trampled by the un-seeing herd. But she caught herself at the last moment and ricocheted off a kid in a Mickey Mouse T-shirt who looked like he'd just got a jump start into puberty. Especially after Piper reached out and patted him on the head.

The tug on his arm spun Mica around.

"You talking to the heavenly host again?" Luci asked, pouting candy-pink lips to let him know she was hurt he hadn't been listening.

"I'm—um, I'm sorry, Luci," Mica stammered. "It's . . . no, I wasn't . . ."

"Oh, I'm just teasing. Who's Piper?"

The question blind-sided him the same way a fast-ball had his first summer at Vacation Bible Camp. And done about as much damage. Mica's head was throbbing when he finally managed to look into Luci's fiery green eyes.

"What'd you say?"

"Piper," Luci answered. "You said that name a minute ago and I wondered who that was. An old girlfriend?"

"I—" *What's happening, Lord?* "—I really said Piper? Out loud?" *I couldn't have. Could I? Did I, Lord?* "Really?"

Luci nodded and sucked in her lips like a little girl standing up in Sunday School who'd been caught talking in class.

"Uh huh, you said it all right and I just wondered . . ."

"It's that girl right there," Mica said, turning around and pointing—just as *Piper* caught the toe of her running shoe on a piece of buckled concrete and went sprawling.

Luci didn't seem too impressed. "You mean the one on the ground?"

"Yeah."

"Piper?"

"Yeah."

"An old friend?"

"Yeah."

"Lover?"

The answer caught in Mica's throat with the tenacity of a chicken bone and wouldn't come out. A moment later, Luci's arm snaked around his waist and pulled him close. The coolness of her touch helped. A little.

"I understand, Preacher-boy, you don't have to go into details right now." Shaking her head, Luci let go of him and watched Piper's ass play tag with the sidewalk as she tried to stand up. "Looks like she's had kind of a rough time since you knew her, huh?"

"Yeah."

"Well, don't just stand there, Preacher-boy," Luci said, slapping him on the butt. "Go get her. Unless she's strung out too high for even me to deal with, I think we could find a place for her at the Pit. Sure as hell beats the street."

"The Pit?" Mica repeated. "You mean as a . . . *dancer?*"

"No," Luci said, hands on hip, "as a bouncer. Gypsy needs somebody who can take over for him when he goes on pee-breaks. Of *course* as a dancer. Why? Do you think what I do is wrong, Preacher-boy?"

Yes! You incite the evil in men's minds and fill them with wanton lust and desires beyond the scope of God's intent!

"No," Mica said out loud, "of course not."

"Well then," Luci said as she turned and started walking back to the club, "go get her. And who knows, Preacher-boy, between the two of us we might just corrupt you yet."

"Now, Luci you know that—" Mica glanced back over his shoulder but Luci was already gone . . . probably ran ahead to tell Miriam about Piper.

He'd talk to her later about putting an end to the joke once and for all. Right now he had to get Piper off the streets and back into the arms of the Lord.

Fetch!

SEVEN

She was dead.

Truly and honestly *dead*.

And God had forgiven her, because a golden-haired Angel was hovering above her. And lo, the Angel spoke:

"What the fuck do you think you were doing out there?"

She must have been an Episcopalian Angel.

Allison blinked carefully and squinted in the soft pink light. *Heaven* was certainly different than the pictures in her Sunday School books.

She was laying on an ebony day-bed, half covered by a rabbit-fur throw that had been dyed red to match the walls. A long row of makeup tables dominated one end of the room. Brass hooks were hung with feathered boas and satin scarfs . . . and whips and chains and leather straps. What looked like discarded, flamboyant costumes draped the two Mama-San chairs set up in one corner.

And instead of paintings that showed the Rewards of the Righteous—like her Sunday School teacher had promised—the flame red walls were hung with framed cartoons of large-eyed animal men and women engaged in many and varied (and humanly impossible) sexual acts.

Not even an Episcopalian Heaven would look like this.

Hell, maybe.

She was still damned. *Oh goody.*

Grabbing the sides of the day bed, Allison got as far as her elbows before the room and all its marvelous decor started doing laps around her. First clockwise, then counter clockwise, *then* diagonally . . . just to be different.

Allison managed to regain her prone position before the blood in her belly finished its migration up her throat.

"Then I'm *not* dead?" she moaned.

One of the "Angel's" snowy eyebrows rose as she giggled. "Well, of *course* you're dead," she said, "you're a fucking vampire."

Oh shit.

Allison braved another attack of vertigo and pushed herself up against the brass rails. Swallowing hard, she stared into the woman's deep green eyes and felt the room merry-go-around them.

How the hell does she know I'm a vampire? Oh, shit . . . what did I do while I was drunk?

"What do you mean *drunk?*" the woman asked as she reached out and slowly brushed a wayward lock of hair out of Allison's eyes. "You can't get drunk, baby-cakes. Don't you know that? And as far as the other thing . . ."

She smiled—and pearl white fangs gleamed in the soft light.

"You're a . . ."

"Vampire," the woman finished, "same as you. Guess you could call us *blood* sisters, huh?"

She chuckled again and Allison tried to join in, shutting her eye as the queasiness shot through her belly like molten lead.

"Stop it!"

Allison's head cleared instantly.

When she opened her eyes, the blonde nodded. Smiling through her fangs.

"Now, isn't *that* better."

"Yes ma'am."

"Yeah, I think we'll get along just fine," the woman said, taking Allison's hand in both of hers and patting it gently. "But there *is* one thing you have to remember . . . you lie to me or cause me or mine any grief whatsoever and I'll have that tight little ass of yours tossed out on the Hollywood Freeway at high noon. Understand?"

"Yes ma'am."

"And the name's Luci."

"Yes ma'am. Luci."

"And *you* are?"

Allison sat up and straightened her shoulders, just

81

like her mother always told her to do when she introduced herself to someone.

"Allison. Allison Garrett."

"Well, pleased to meet you, Allison Garrett," Luci said as she pulled Allison's hand into the baggy shirt folds laying across her lap and held it there. "But around here we don't use last names. *That's* part of the real world, not ours. We're free . . . free to do *anything* our cold little hearts desire."

Smiling, Luci reached out with one hand and slowly trailed it up along the inside seam of Allison's vest until it came to the safety pin.

"I'm sorry I yelled back there, Allison, I'm not really such a bitch when you get to know me. And I hope we'll get to know each other real well."

A low grumble, like a pit bull ready to attack, suddenly echoed through the room.

"What was that?"

"Oh, don't worry about *that*." Luci said, chucking her gently under the chin. "We're all friends here."

A throaty *HAH!* bounced off the walls. Luci ignored that, too.

"Now, why don't you tell me all about that little one-woman show you were putting on for the tourists."

Allison licked her lips and tried to move away without being obvious about it. There was *something* in that room that didn't like what was happening on the day bed any more than Allison did. "I . . . I didn't know about . . . not being able to get drunk." Allison scooted higher on the bed and managed to remove both her hand and Luci's from their previous locations. At least for the moment.

"I'm . . . kind of new at this."

This time, the empty room produced an exaggerated sigh.

"You're telling me." Luci clasped her hands and folded them, ladylike, in her lap. "Who the hell turned you, anyway? Probably some stuck-up, butter-wouldn't-melt macho asshole, right?"

"You know Seth?" Allison asked.

Luci giggled and slid across the fur until their hips touched. "Like I know every stuck-up, butter-wouldn't-melt macho asshole vampire in L.A." Shaking her head, Luci laughed like it was the funniest thing she'd ever heard. "You *hear* that, Gina? Our little Fledgy got done to by one of the *brothers*. Didn't I tell you they were nothing but bad news?"

" 'Specially the one what done *her*. Man, he musta been *really* runnin' on empty. Musta just done her tonight, too. Left her staggerin' an starvin'."

The woman's voice was as disembodied as the other sounds had been.

The back of Allison's head and spine made direct and immediate contact with the plaster wall as she pressed herself into a corner and scanned the room for the owner of the voice. There was nothing . . . *no one* there who hadn't been there a moment earlier.

"Naw," Luci said, apparently not concerned that she was talking to thin air . . . and having it answer her. "She got that way feeding on some drunk. Poor little thing thought since alcohol is absorbed through the blood that she'd get drunk, too. That's so *sweet*."

"*Shit* sweet, you mean," the voice snarled. "God-damned Fledgy. You shoulda left her for the sun . . . served her right! Don't know nuthin' 'bout nuthin'. Her Maker done right by leavin' her . . . hell, she's so dumb she don't know the first thing about bein' free."

Luci glanced back over her shoulder and continued talking to . . . nothing. "Oh, like *you* were all knowing when you first turned, right Gina?"

"I knew 'nuff t'stay away from folks less I was feedin' off 'em. *That* much I knowed!"

Luci turned back to Allison and shrugged.

"You have to forgive Gina," she whispered. "The guy who caught her collar tonight doesn't look like he has a full pint of blood left in him. She was aiming for this fat dude.

"Come on, Gina . . . come on over and say hello to our new little sister."

The pile of clothes that Allison had thought was nothing more than casually tossed costumes, suddenly stood up and walked over. Black as a starless night, her hair and eyes the color of a raven's wing, the woman tightened the sash on the multi-colored satin robe she wore and glared down at Allison.

"Little sister, m'black ass!"

"This is Gina," Luci said—the perfect hostess. "Gina's a natural chameleon . . . so you'd better be real careful about what you say or think, because you never know if she's around or not."

Allison almost thought about asking her about the skill then immediately sucked the thought back into the depths of her brain when Gina's eyes flashed red.

"Pleased . . . to meet you. Gina."

"Why don't you go find yourself some dumb Breather to live off and leave us alone?" Gina snarled, looking at the hand being offered like it was a soup bone and she was the pit bull Allison first mistook her to be. "We got us a nice little thing goin' here an' we don't need no brain-dead Fledgy who still thinks like a Breather to screw things up."

Gina took another step forward and stopped—sniffing the air.

Like a pit bull.

Gina's glare told Allison she'd heard that loud and clear.

"Who was that drunk you done, bitch?" she demanded.

"Oh, no, Gina . . . there must be hundreds of drunks out there." Luci smiled back at Allison, but there was a trace of worry in the green eyes. "What are the chances of her getting him?"

"What are the chances o'her endin' up *here*." Gina's face transformed into something that would have been more at home peering out onto a jungle clearing. "Talk, Fledgy . . . or I'll fuckin' tear out your heart and stuff garlic down your throat m'self!"

"Better tell her, kiddo," Luci said, taking her hand. This time Allison didn't mind. This time it almost felt comforting.

"I don't know what drunk," she said. "It was just this skinny guy in a vacant lot off the street."

"Damn it!" Gina yelled, spinning in a cloud of satin and sleek black fur. "DAMN it! I knew it . . . I fuckin' *knew* it! She did Big Mike. I can smell him all over her. FUCK!"

When she turned back, the ivory colored fangs were almost touching the point of her chin. Clenching her claw-tipped fists, Gina threw back her head and howled.

"MIRIAM!"

Allison tightened her grip on Luci's hand as the Angel-faced vampire turned and shook her head.

"Well, you done it now, Alley-cat."

It wasn't Piper.

Mica stood next to Luci's cut-out as if he were also made out of cardboard. Furverts came and went unnoticed; the uninitiated tourists got by without being verbally assaulted.

It wasn't Piper.

Gypsy had handed him a cup of coffee liberally laced with corn whiskey a few minutes after he'd carried the drunk woman—*who wasn't Piper*—into the dressing room and slapped him on the back.

Asked Mica to find one for *him*.

And laughed.

Mica finished the coffee before he got a quarter of the way through the club.

It wasn't Piper.

Then *why in Hell* did he feel so responsible for her?

EIGHT

"MIRIAM!"

If there'd been any glass in the makeup mirrors it would have shattered from the force of Gina's shriek. When the last echo died, Allison heard the heavy clump of boot heels coming down the hall.

Toward the dressing room.

I'm fucked, Allison thought.

"You can say that again, bitch," Gina snarled, pointing a talon at the door. "But you won't know *how* fucked 'till Miriam gets here."

Allison swallowed the dry lump that suddenly materialized in her throat and tried *not* to think about what to expect. If Gina and Luci were any indication of the kind of vampire Amazons she was up against, Allison would have been more than happy to put off meeting Miriam.

Indefinitely.

She was scanning the room for a viable exit—gazing longingly at the mouse hole in the corner—when the door burst open.

And a midget in a monkey-vomit green caftan huffed into the room.

Miriam.

Not *exactly* a midget, Allison decided, although without the heavy-heeled orthopedic oxfords she couldn't have been much over five feet.

If that.

Short, round, her permed hair rinsed to the color of a Robin's egg, Miriam looked like everyone's favorite old maiden aunt—

"So you called like maybe the place is on fire?"

—from the Lower East-Side.

"Miriam," Luci said, "this is Allison."

Miriam grabbed the pair of shocking-pink tortoise shell glasses that had been hanging around her neck and slid them on—glaring at Allison through the thick lenses. They magnified her tiny eyes a hundred fold.

"She really doesn't need those," Luci whispered to Allison, "she just likes the way they look."

"I can understand why," Allison whispered back.

Then burst out laughing.

Miriam's eyes completely filled the lenses.

"For *this* you called me?" she asked, pointing a mauve-painted fingernail at Allison. "If I want to see a laughing hyena I can turn on *Wild Kingdom*."

A mental swat across the backside from Luci—

although painless—was loud enough to re-establish Allison's priorities. These were the only others of her kind she'd met besides Seth, and if she was going to learn *anything* about her new after-life style it would be from these women.

Sitting up quickly, Allison tucked her legs up under her and tried to look repentant (as much as she was still able) when Gina pointed her own accusing claw.

"She did Big Mike!"

"Oh, like you don't think I see you and little-Miss-Innocence over there sneaking out between shows for a quickie," Miriam said, clicking her tongue. "Nah, nah, nah, there's still plenty around here that I know all about, thank you very much."

"No, Miriam," Luci interrupted, "Gina means she *did* him."

"Yeah . . . so she did him."

"No. She. DID. Him."

"She *did* him?"

"Yeah."

"Oh, you mean she *DID* him."

"Yes, Miriam."

"Oy."

Luci bowed her head and sighed. "Uh huh."

"This true?" Miriam asked, giant owl eyes shifting back to Allison. "This true what they said about Big Mike?"

"Um . . . well, I didn't know . . ."

"Ah, get your fingers caught in the sugar cookies and it's always the same. I didn't know. I didn't know you were saving that potato for dinner. I didn't know those rubles were for rent. *I didn't know* that bum was family."

Miriam pulled off the glasses and tucked them carefully inside the caftan, as if she were worried Allison might make a try for them as well.

"So tell me, Miss-Laughing-Hyena-I-Could-See-On-Television," she continued, "why'd you *DO* Big Mike? There's not maybe a million bums in this neighborhood that you had to go pick ours? He could barely handle *these* two and you have to come and shake those hot panties in his face. What? Like you couldn't smell our mark on him?"

"Mark?" Allison asked.

Three sets of eyes—green, black and piggy grey—stared at her in childlike wonder.

"Damn," Luci said, breaking the momentary silence, "you really *are* a virgin, aren't you?"

"Um . . ."

"Now look what we got," Miriam snapped, "from laughing hyena to hummingbird. Is this a vampire we got here or a whole *ferstinkena* zoo?"

Moving in. Luci tossed an arm protectively around Allison's shoulders and squeezed. Given the black looks she was getting from the other two, Allison put aside the discomfort she'd felt earlier and pressed close. She'd worry about clearing up whatever misconceptions the gesture might have inspired *later*.

Right now, Luci was the only thing sitting between her and possible dismemberment.

"Her Maker sucked her dry and left," Luci said. "I don't think he even gave her the basics. You know, the standard eat and run type. Probably didn't even show her how to leave her mark on a Breather . . . but that's a man for you, huh? Living or dead they only think about what's best for them. And if they're not fucking you one way, they're fucking you in another. Right Alley-cat?"

Allison nodded silently and tried to ignore the almost tangible waves of hate radiating across the room at her. *From Gina to Allison, with all my UNDYING love.*

Shit, what have I gotten myself into?

Whatever you want to get into, Alley-cat, Luci's voice whispered inside her head.

When Allison jumped at the mental invasion, Luci tightened her grip—chuckling.

"So now we got two laughers for the price of one? This is maybe a contagious disease?" Miriam snorted, walking back to one of the chairs and collapsing into it. The woven bamboo creaked under the assault. "So go ahead . . . laugh . . . don't let me or the fact that we now got no Watchman worry you. Laugh. And when the cossacks come with their torches and stakes we can just laugh in their faces. Big Mike was like family, but go ahead. Laugh!"

"Oh, for Christ's sake, Miriam," Luci said. "Big Mike was *meat*. I told you we should have just called him *Big Mac* and let it go at that."

"Oh . . . and now she's telling me my business?" Miriam groaned, sweeping the air in front of her with one hand. "Lookee here, Miss We-Don't-Name-Our-Food-Because-You-Get-Too-Attached, I've been doing this centuries longer than either *you* or the Queen of the Jungle over there so I know what I'm talking about.

"You take *care* of your Watcher and your Watcher will take care of you. Big Mike wasn't much . . . but he was our Watcher and we should show some respect at his passing."

Miriam dropped her three chins and the other two followed. Allison got the message after Luci's elbow smacked into her rib cage.

"He was a good breather, may he stay dead. Now, we got to find us a new Watcher right off and . . ." Miriam stopped talking and nodded her head at Allison—her eyes sparkling like a matchmaker. "I take it you want to keep this one, Luci?"

Luci gave Allison's shoulder another squeeze. "Sure do."

"What the fuck for?" Gina shouted, crossing the distance between them in one lunging stride. "We a'ready got us as many as we need. You get too many Suckers in one place and somebody's gonna notice. I say cut her loose!"

"Oh, *you* say cut her loose?" Miriam said as she stood—straightening to her full diminutive height. "And who died and made you Queen of the Jungle? What if I said *cut her loose* when you were still playing hide-and-seek with those men in white sheets? Huh?"

"But she's—"

"She's one of our own and that's all there is to that. Now, we got a room full of men out there wanting a little fur in their face. Gina . . . tone down the teeth and claws and get out there before they tear the place down."

"But?"

"Go. Everything's settled. Go."

Gina gave Allison one final long glare—*God if looks could kill and I wasn't already dead*—before sucking in her fangs and transforming from the *beast* into something that more closely resembled the cartoons on the walls.

Allison felt her jaw unhinge as she watched the sleek black-panther woman slip out of the multicolored robe and toss it over one shoulder. Tail twitching angrily from side to side, she moved with slow, deliberate steps to the row of hooks on the far wall and selected a spiked collar.

Turning, Gina growled at Allison and stalked to the door—nose and tail in the air.

"And tell Gypsy I want to see him," Miriam shouted after her. "I hate to do it—he so good throwing out drunks, but . . . considering the alternative."

Miriam twisted her hand back and forth in an exaggerated manner and Luci giggled. Allison wasn't sure she wanted to be let in on the joke.

"So, Allison is it?"

"Yes, ma'am. Allison Gar—"

"No last names," Miriam said quickly. "Last names only tie us to the past. Besides, I'll put something down on the W-2's later. Not to worry."

"W-2's?" Allison asked as she slipped out of Luci's grip

and leaned back against the wall. Regardless of what Luci had told her, she still felt a little dizzy. "You mean as in . . . income tax?"

This time Miriam's eyes grew without benefit of the coke-bottle glasses.

"Of course I mean income tax. What, you think I want the cossacks riding down here because I don't pay taxes. Sheeze, that would be a fine kettle of blood."

Allison shook her head until the room began spinning again.

"I don't understand," she said, "why do *vampires* need jobs? We're . . . dead."

"So being dead should stop a person from earning— if you should pardon the expression—an honest night's work? You think the electric company and liquor licensing board should care if we're dead or not? HAH! Those people'd dig down six feet if they thought there was a penny in a dead man's pocket."

"But . . . *working?*"

"Well, what else would you suggest, Alley-cat?" Luci asked as she leaned back on the bed and folded her arms back behind her head. "Hit the streets like we're hookers? Too much competition and *way* too many cops."

The word *cops* sent shivers creeping into Allison's belly.

"On the outside you could find yourself neck deep in shit before you knew what hit you. Here we have a Watcher and people who just think of us as nice, respectable exotic dancers. Besides," Luci smiled, running a pale pink tongue over paler lips, "*this* way the cattle come to us. Makes hunting a hell of a lot easier when its given of it's own free will."

Allison nodded, mulling it over. "Huh?"

Miriam mumbled something foreign Allison didn't catch and Luci started giggling again.

"You poor baby," Luci said. "Look, here's the bottom line, okay? Vampires feed off the living to survive, you understand that part, don't you?"

Allison nodded. And Miriam mumbled again.

"Good. Now think, in all the movies and books about vampires, what *traditionally* happens when this sort of thing occurs?" Luci didn't wait for Allison to guess. "Well, I'll tell you . . . large, angry villagers with torches and wooden stakes come knocking at your door.

"It might be fun in the movies, but it's not too pleasant if you've got the starring roll."

Luci jerked her head toward Miriam and Allison glanced over to see the tiny "woman" silently clawing splinters off the arm-rests.

"*This* way," Luci said, redirecting Allison's attention back to her, "the cattle not only round themselves up, but they *beg* us to brand them. It all works out *so* well, Alley-cat . . . trust us, we've been doing this for a long, *long* time."

Allison didn't even *want* to know how long.

"Yeah, yeah," Miriam looked at her watch and rolled her eyes. "So, Allison . . . Alley-cat, whatever, you want a job or not?"

"Maybe I should mention that I had a little . . . trouble and the . . . police are probably looking for me. Right now."

"Oy! *This* I need?" Miriam shouted at the ceiling. "It's not bad enough that You send me one of Your loud-mouth servants? Now I end up with a criminal fugitive? What, being *damned* isn't good enough for You?"

"Miriam gets a little carried away at times," Luci said to Allison. "Besides, *Miriam*, they're looking for a corpse, remember. Don't worry kid, even if they trace you here you can always change into someone else."

"I don't think so," Allison said, remembering the disaster in the car when she tried to *change* clothes. "I must have blown a fuse or something. I tried to put on something . . . clean and nothing happened."

Sitting up with a groan, Luci reached over and tugged on the blood splattered leg of Allison's shorts.

"Damn, I wish I could get my claws into that Maker of yours for just a few minutes . . . Look, baby, rule number one—blood keeps us going, but if we get any of it on us we can't transform. Got it? Good. Now slip out of those things and we'll have the new Watcher burn them. Evidence you know."

"Yeah." *Made sense.* "Good idea." *The faster they got rid of every trace of her victims blood the better.* "I'll do that."

Then why wasn't she?

This was stupid.

She'd been undressing in front of other females since the seventh-grade. In front of boys since the eight-grade. Besides, she was going to be an *exotic dancer* . . . and that meant she'd be bumping and grinding in the nude every night from now on.

So why couldn't she undress in front of *these* two?

More specifically in front of Luci?

Allison knew why the moment Luci stood up—naked, skin gleaming like polished pink marble. Just seeing her standing there made Allison feel the same way walking alone had once made her feel. An easy target. Defenseless. Vulnerable.

"No! It's okay, I can . . ."

"Shh," Luci whispered. "I'm just going to help. Don't get your back up, Alley-cat. Not *yet* anyway."

Allison gasped—a remarkable feeling since her lungs didn't work—when Luci suddenly darted forward and dipped her tongue into the patch of dried blood between her breasts.

"Humm . . . O-positive with traces of A and B-negative. My, my," she said as she knelt in front of Allison. "You *have* been a busy girl."

Allison kept the next gasp to herself as Luci slowly pulled the jogging shorts down past her knees to her ankles.

"Oh . . . you're a natural redhead," Luci giggled. "That means you have a HOT disposition, doesn't it?"

"I—I don't know. I . . . get a little cranky now and then but—" The pin snapped in half and shot across the room as Allison ripped the vest open.

Luci's smiled widened considerably.

"Now the question is," Luci said as she got to her feet—her shoulder *accidentally* brushing against Allison's crotch on the way up, "are *they* real or did you manage to figure out how to do some of this already?"

"Luci! Stop with the teasing already. You're making her nervous enough and she hasn't even started work yet."

Oh God . . . Miriam had been in the room all the time and while Luci was . . .

Allison felt the room take another turn for the worse and went along with it, sliding half-way down the wall before Luci strong-armed her back into a semi-erect posture.

"I . . . don't feel so good," Allison whispered, hoping they'd take the hint and leave her alone.

They didn't.

"Not to worry," Miriam said as a new set of footsteps thumped toward the dressing room, "you just need a little something. Fledgies are just like little birds . . . all the time hungry."

"But *I*—"

"Shush—first you eat *then* we talk."

And there's dinner now, Luci's voice whispered in Allison's ears. From the inside.

"Knock, knock," a booming voice called from the other side of the closed door, "anybody decent?"

"Lord, I *hope* not," Luci called back. "But hang on a second, Gypsy, okay?"

"I'll hang on to anything you want, Miss Luci," the strong voice chuckled, "for however *long* you want."

"That's what they all say, right Alley-cat?"

Before Allison could answer or even move, Luci was walking over the *real* pile of clothes on the chair and digging through them. When she returned she was carrying a flame red dressing gown lined in gold.

"Here," she said, helping Allison slip into it, "you're too weak to materialize anything right now. But don't worry, baby-cakes, soon you'll be able to do this without even thinking about it. Okay, Gyp . . . all the, all the, outs in free! Come and meet the newest member of our little family."

Luci was still naked when the knob turned and the door swung open; but the moment the man's boot crossed the threshold she was fully dressed. If one could call a vinyl thong-backed, chain-front teddy and thigh high patent leather boots being *fully* dressed.

She looked like the "Biker Bitch from Hell" . . . much to the newcomer's obvious delight. Winking at Allison, she walked up to the man and laced her arm through his: Mr. and Mrs. Harley-Davidson on their Wedding Day.

"Hey, Gypsy, come say *hi* to the new girl."

Luci walked him over and he nodded. Politely. Perfunctory. Not even noticing she was wearing less than Luci.

"Hello, new girl," he said then turned back to Luci.

A week earlier, Allison would have made some kind of venomous remark about his possible ancestry and walked away.

Four *days* ago, she would have slapped his face just to remind him that there really *were* such things as manners left in the world.

Her stomach grumbled in anticipation and Allison decided it was nicer living in the here and now.

So what do you think? Luci's voice whispered.

He's a real asshole, she answered, almost amazed at how easy it was.

We like to call it BUTT steak.

"Gypsy," Allison said as she took the man's free hand. "Pleased to *meat* you."

NINE

Mica checked his watch against the real Rolex the kid on the skateboard was wearing.

And frowned.

That made the fifth time in the last hour Mica checked his usually faithful timepiece to make sure it hadn't suddenly started running fast.

It hadn't.

And *that* made him frown all the harder.

It'd been fifty-two minutes since he carried the red-haired woman (*who wasn't Piper*) into the dressing room and Gypsy *still* hadn't come out to compare, contrast and just plain bullshit about her.

And that wasn't like him.

Mica pulled his sleeve back over the watch and folded the arm in against his chest. It didn't help much—he could still feel the case pressing into his ribs.

Dammit, what was keeping him?

Mica nodded absently to a sweating man wearing a fake-fur jacket and tie—a true *Furvert's Furvert*—then glared back at the constant shuffle of sidewalkers. Most of them probably thought he looked as ridiculous in his uniform as they did normally.

Two men in matching silver-lamé tights and fringed shirts walked by hand-in-hand . . . just *begging* for a lecture on their dangerous and evil lifestyle . . . and Mica let them walk by.

Even nodded.

Absently.

Sighing, Mica shifted the position of his arms and checked the watch for the *sixth* time. Another two minutes had ticked away.

What the fuck was Gypsy DOING back there?
And with WHO?

Gina had been on stage the last two "piss breaks" Mica had taken. The first time she'd been a black panther—snarling and growling at the cheering fur lovers. The second time she was "dressed" as a sleek otter . . . squirming and wriggling across the stage in such a way that made Mica decide he'd *better* use the facilities before he went back to the streets.

And she was up there again.

Mica didn't need to check personally, he could tell by the music. Luci preferred sixties Hard Acid Rock while Gina only danced to African music—full of bells and whistles and pounding drums and things that didn't have any meaning for Mica but still made him all nervous inside just from hearing it.

And it was *that* kind Mica heard pouring out of the club. Again.

Which meant Luci was back with the red-haired woman *(not Piper)*, too.

Also.

Still.

With Gypsy.

Maybe that's what they were doing. Since Gypsy had been a music promoter in one of his "past lives" it seemed reasonable that Luci would have asked him to help decide what kind of music the woman-*who-wasn't-Piper* would use in her act.

(for a FULL HOUR?)

At the Pit.

Mica felt his belly drop into his shorts just imagining what she'd look like under the spotlights, prancing around in little more than a transparent layer of fur . . . showing off her private parts to a bunch of screaming men who probably did unspeakable things to their teddy bears as children.

Maybe she'd dress as a long haired orange tabby cat. With a big pink bow.

Mica's belly moved into the *front* of his shorts.

"Lord," he said closing his eyes, "it's not what You think. I'm just concerned, that's all. It's been . . ." Mica opened his eyes and checked the watch again, although he knew the Lord had no need for such primitive methods. "*Shit* . . . excuse me, Lord, but it's been over an hour, Lord, and I was just wondering what might be keeping my friend, that's all."

Mica didn't like to lie to the Lord, but knew the Lord would forgive him when he asked later on that night . . . once Gypsy'd come out and explained his long delay.

In the dressing room.

With Luci and . . . the *other* one.

And Mica knew Gypsy was still back there because he'd asked the assistant bartender the *last* time he shoved his way to the "Little Furvert's Room." The man had nodded his stylishly moussed head back toward the dressing room and, even though Mica suspected him of being a homosexual, rolled his eyes and licked his lips when Mica asked if the redheaded woman was still back there as well.

"Oh, yeah . . . I would have noticed if she'd come out. Shit, did you see the legs on her? Damn! What'd they feel like when you carried her in?"

Mica had held himself back from punching the man's lights out right then and there. And actually felt bad about not having done it. Turning the other cheek was one thing, but the man needed to be taught a little respect for others with the proverbial jaw bone of an ass . . . this time with *him* being the ass and Mica's fist being the jaw bone.

It made Mica angry again just thinking about it.

"Show him the Truth, Lord," Mica whispered as another Furvert, this one in outdated Disco clothes, hip-hopped into the club. "Show him the only things he should really want to feel are Your Love and Forgiveness."

Her legs had been cold. As cold as if she'd just stepped out of a refrigerator.

Mica exhaled loudly and tried to shake the lingering sensation of her cold flesh off his arms. It wasn't as if he'd been lacking in opportunities to have his arms around beautiful women. He saw beautiful women every day, and Luci herself had made it resoundingly clear she'd be *more* than willing to stop over sometime and look at his religious etchings . . .

. . . but there was something about the redhead.

Something.

"Lord," Mica said quickly, "You've got to stand by me on this one. It's more than just the way she looks—" *like Piper* "—and You know that because You can see into my heart. But I feel there's *something* deep inside her that longs for the Knowledge and Understanding of the mysteries that surround her."

I should be taking notes.

Allison smoothed the red robe over her knees and tried to look completely at ease with what was taking place in front of her; although she'd never even *rented* anything stronger than a "R-rated" video before this. But here she was, calmly watching a live sex show . . .

. . . or as *live* as sex between a Breather and a vampire could get.

Will you pay attention, Luci's voice whispered in Allison's head. *Creating a Watcher isn't just like feeding . . . it has to be done slowly and carefully or you end up with something like Big Mike. Gina just got carried away on that one. Are you watching?*

Allison nodded although she doubted if Luci was in any position—physically or otherwise—to have noticed. Luci had been between the big man's legs for the last five minutes . . . her head pumping up and down like an oil well.

"Yeah . . . I'm watching," Allison said out loud—just to be different. Watching the Watcher being watched. What fun.

Hang on, Luci whispered, *the REAL fun's about to start.*

With a loud *smack* as she pulled away, Luci suddenly collapsed to the floor next to the jeans bunched around the man's ankles—panting, shoulders heaving, her face glistening with sweat.

Allison leaned forward in her chair and almost applauded the performance. Damn, she was good!

"Jeeze, Gyp," she panted, "I don't know how much more I can take. You're so *big!*"

Allison didn't bother to check. It was almost the same line—with respects to gender—that Seth fed her (Shit, baby, I don't know how much more I can take. You're so hot!) before *he* started feeding. She scrunched deeper into the chair and pulled her legs up after her, hugging them tight. First Rule of Vampirism: Do Unto Others.

Period.

"I . . . I'd better take a breather, Gyp," Luci said, allowing the man to help her onto the bed next to him. "But I think Allison might be willing to take my place . . . if you ask her nice."

Their eyes met and Allison wondered if hers looked as shocked as his.

He FORGOT I was here?

Luci smiled from across the room and began undoing the chains on the front of her teddy. The man almost broke his neck trying to look two places at the same time.

Oh, don't get your fangs out of joint, Alley-cat . . . he was occupied. Now stand up and walk over. Slowly. Give him something to look AT.

There was a definite note of challenge in Luci's nonverbal chuckle.

Standing slowly, Allison let the robe slip off one shoulder just enough to let the man see the firm swell of her right breast.

She'd taken off the bloodied running shoes while Luci was porking out . . . just to have *something* to do . . . now she thought of shoes—the kind of shoes her mother had always said looked trashy in late night movies: Five inch spiked heel red satin slippers with matching puffs of marabou at the toes.

Manually inflating her lungs, Allison let the robe fall open the rest of the way and managed to keep her wobbling down to a minimum as she crossed the room.

Nice, Alley-cat, Luci purred, *but you have to make him ASK for it.*

For what?

Luci frowned at her. *God, you really are one for the books.*

Allison stopped dead in her tracks. And almost fell over.

Book? You have books on all this? Can I read them?

They were both staring at her now: The man's eyes wide with anticipation . . . Luci's just wide.

When all this is finished, her voice promised, *we're going to have a LONG talk.*

"Aw," Luci said, pressing her lips against the man's ear—as if she was telling a secret. "I think our little Alley-cat is shy. Isn't that sweet? You're going to have to ask her, Gypsy. Ask her to come over here and give it to you.

"Ask her. Now."

"Come over here and give it to me," he repeated.

"What do you want me to give you, Gypsy?" Allison heard herself ask.

Then snapped her jaw shut and stared at Luci.

Neat trick, huh? Just relax and don't let Gina know I helped you out, okay. And at least TRY to look like you're enjoying yourself.

Allison shot the man a toothy grin.

Shit. "Come on, Gypsy," Allison's voice purred as her body lurched forward, "tell me what you want me to give you?"

"I . . . I want *you.*"

Luci stood up and stepped away from the bed, the vinyl teddy and boots dissolving into thin air.

"But what do you want *of* me, big man? You have to tell me. I won't know what to do unless you *tell* me."

Shit, *that's* the truth, Allison thought as her body shivered out of the robe and stepped into the man's waiting embrace. His penis was rock hard and the color of an over-ripe plum, jutting up through the salt-and-pepper thatch of pubic hair to brush against her own red bush.

He shivered and Allison's body responded.

Her fingers curling through his greasy hair, Allison watched her legs move to the outside of the man's and bend . . . vaginal muscles tightening as she slowly lowered herself onto him.

"Tell me," her voice whispered, "tell me what you want."

"I want . . . oh, shit . . . I want . . ."

His fingers dug into her ass as her body rose and fell with all the precision and excitement of a wooden horse on a Merry-Go-Round. Half-turning, Allison glanced over her shoulder at Luci.

What? You never used sex as bait when you were a Breather? I may have been on this side for a long time, but I thought that was one of the basics every little girl learned in high school.

A memory of herself at sixteen in the backseat of Biff (the Stiff) Taggart's Pinto suddenly filled Allison's mind. She hadn't wanted to go all the way, but every girl in school wanted the captain of the football team and *he* wanted sex, so . . .

So stop acting like the poor little virgin.

"Tell me what you want, Gypsy," Allison asked—back in charge. "Tell me or I'll stop right now!"

"NO! Please . . . no." He was getting close . . . and Allison didn't need any heightened vampire sixth sense to know that.

"Then tell me."

"I want to be with you," he gasped. "Always. I don't want to leave. Everrrrrr!"

His cum warmed her belly from the bottom-up while his blood warmed it from the top-down. But she only got a mouthful when Luci sank her fingers into Allison's hair and yanked her off.

"You Fledgies are all alike," she said, shaking her head at the dribbling wounds in the man's throat. "Go right for the pump without thinking. Look at that! Shit, what a mess."

Allison looked. And licked her lips.

Luci let go of her hair and rapped her one across the back of the skull.

"I said *think*. People don't go around with bite wounds in the neck unless they're making a movie . . . not even people in Hollywood. It's so fucking obvious. Now get up and I'll show you a better place."

Allison stepped back and watched the man flop back onto the rumpled day bed: Arms flung out to his side, hairy legs twitching every few seconds . . . his wasted cock just laying there like a misplaced and silent tongue.

He looked good enough to eat.

Allison shifted slightly as Luci moved closer to the

bed, smiling, with her shimmering white-blond hair falling over her naked shoulder and making her look like the Angel Allison had first mistaken her to be. She patted the man's fuzzy beer gut.

His rapidly shriveling penis stopped shrinking just long enough to reach for her hand . . . the world's ugliest seedling lifting its head toward the sun.

"You've *got* to be kidding," Allison choked. "I didn't even like doing *that* when I had to!"

Luci tossed her hair back over her shoulder and shook her head.

"Right . . . like *that* would be a real inconspicuous place to leave your mark. You plan on him dropping his pants every time you want a little sip? Shit, they'd raid this place faster than if we started walking around with our fangs hanging out. *This*," she said, cupping the limp organ in her hand, "is generally more trouble than it's worth anyway."

Luci flipped the cock to one side and slapped the inside of the man's upper thigh.

"But if you *do* get a Breather stretched out like this, go straight for the femoral artery right here." Luci patted the pale flesh and smiled. "You'll be able to suck them dry in less than three minutes. And it works just as well on female Breathers as males."

Females?

Allison nodded but stepped to the end of the bed *farthest* away from Luci.

"Now what are you doing all the way over there?" she said, grabbing the man's right wrist and hauling him

111

into a semi-slumped-upright position. "You plan to mark him by long distance?"

"Me?" Allison said. "You want me to bite him?"

Turning the hand palm up, Luci slapped the veins in the wrist to full attention and held it out to Allison.

"You destroyed the Watcher so it's up to you to make the first bite." She wiggled the limp hand at Allison again. "Of course if you don't *want* the honor I can always get Gina to do it . . . but then she might just rip your head off once she was finished."

The man smiled up at her, winking drunkenly when Allison took his hand and lifted it slowly to her lips.

"Bite deep," Luci said, leaning forward like a Home Economics teacher making sure the recipe was being followed to the letter. "Make sure you pierce the vein all the way through . . . but don't take too much."

Allison moaned as her fangs slipped into him—and the sound echoed back in a low baritone. They met in her mouth and caressed each other as they poured down her throat, filled the emptiness inside her with drinking, laughing, loving, fighting, talking with the Preacher-boy, chili . . .

Her head snapped back an instant before Luci pulled her off.

"I told you not to take too much, dammit! Now . . . open up."

Allison was about to ask what the hell she was talking about, when Luci's mouth clamped over hers.

Give it up.

Allison resisted only until Luci's fist slammed into her belly and sent the blood racing back up her throat.

And into Luci.

For one brief instant, while Gypsy's blood acted like a conduit, Allison tasted fragments of lives that had been in cold storage for so long they seemed to be little more than dreams.

Little more than nightmares.

"Humm," Luci said as she pulled away, licking her lips, "that was nice. You really have a talent for this sort of thing, Alley-cat. Okay . . . last step, so watch carefully. Who knows, one day you *might* leave our little family and have to do this all on your own."

Allison pretended not to hear the whispering laughter ringing inside her head as Luci cupped the man's face gently in her hands and lifted it until their eyes met. Although Allison was standing off to one side, it was almost as if she was looking at him straight on.

Neat trick, huh? Luci's voice asked. *Now quit being awed and pay attention.*

With one hand still under the man's chin, Luci moved the other to her right breast and, deftly . . . tore off her nipple. Allison cupped her own breast in sympathy and swallowed hard even though there was nothing left in her belly.

Thank God.

"You're such a *good* boy, Gypsy," Luci said softly . . . a Master speaking to a slow, but loyal pet, "I'm going to give you a little treat. Would you like that?"

It wasn't all that hard for Allison to imagine a tail waggling happily.

Luci lifted her nippleless breast to the man's mouth and he latched onto it like a starving calf.

"Drink us in, Gypsy," she said, scratching him gently behind the ear. "Taste us so you'll know us when you come to Watch. Protect us, Gypsy . . . and we'll protect you. *Won't* we, Alley-cat?"

Allison nodded.

Damn, I really should be taking notes!

TEN

Mica downed his second "freebie" beer to its half-way mark and stared at the full length portrait of Luci—in her Silver Fox costume—stretched out on a polar bear rug. Luci had told Mica she'd commissioned the same artist who'd done her cut-out to do the painting because she remembered liking the way they looked in old-time saloons.

Probably the ones at *Disneyland* and *Knotts Berry Farm*.

Mica set the half-empty bottle back on its soggy "Furverts Are Meat Eaters" cocktail napkin and glanced at the pale strip of flesh just below the knob of his left wrist . . . where his watch *had* been.

It was *now* in his jacket pocket.

He'd taken it off when the club closed at one . . . and Gypsy *still* hadn't shown.

What the hell was he DOING back there?

Mica closed his eyes and took a deep breath. He changed his mind . . . didn't *want* to know what Gypsy was doing. With Luci. And the woman who wasn't Piper. For almost three full hours.

Goddamn him!

Sorry, Lord . . . didn't really mean that.

Much.

Opening his eyes, Mica picked up the beer bottle and theatrically saluted Luci's pastel smirk—*this ain't over yet, lady*—then spun the stool around and turned his back on the painting.

And tried to ignore the feeling that her painted eyes were still trained on the back of his neck. Watching.

Mica shivered the feeling away and finished off the bottle.

The club was empty except for the assistant bartender, taking his time dragging a mop over the floor, and the three "Lucky Collar Winners" talking to Miriam. Three of them for dinner and drinks. One for Luci . . . one for Gina . . .

"—and one for the little girl who lives down the lane," Mica finished out loud. Although *why* she'd be invited to dine with the customers was beyond him. The only thing *she'd* done that evening was not throw up on anybody when Mica carried her in.

Maybe Luci thought an impromptu dinner would be a good way to introduce the woman to one of the "many benefits" working at the club had to offer. Mica looked down at his crumbled jacket and cap laying across the stool next to him and saluted them as well.

He could hardly wait to see her up there in the spot-light, shaking her fur-covered tits and ass.

And a sharp twinge in the front of his jeans told him exactly how *hard* that wait would be.

"Jesus," Mica said as he crossed his legs, "You know that's not what I meant."

Something sparkled in a far, unlit corner of the room and drew Mica's attention away from the trouble brewing in his pants.

Thank you.

It took his eyes a minute to separate her from the surrounding darkness. Still wearing the black velvet dressing gown she'd put on after her fifth and final consecutive routine, Gina was hunched into the narrow booth fiddling with the real diamond-and-jet ring Luci had given her last year at the Club's annual Christmas/Hanukkah/Winter Solstice Party.

Mica was used to seeing Gina play with the ring—it was her prize possession and she was always sticking it under people's noses—but the way she played with it tonight made him think of the way a cat's tail twitched right while it waited for a mouse.

A big *black* cat . . . and a *red-headed* mouse.

Twisting the stool around, Mica leaned over the bar and grabbed two more dripping bottles out of the ice-bin. Gypsy always kept a dozen bottles of the "good suds" on ice to unwind with after work. But tonight only two bottles and one bartender were missing.

"Screw you, Gyp," Mica said as he lifted out two

more bottles. "You probably got more than beer tonight anyway."

Luci's painting smiled down at him as he turned and walked across the empty room toward the club's resident jungle beast. He and Gina had never really hit it off, but maybe tonight would be different . . . maybe tonight she'd open up and lower her guard.

Maybe they could finally talk—just talk—about this life, the next and what the hell had been going on in the dressing room all night.

Maybe.

Mica increased the overall voltage on his smile and nodded when Gina finally turned and noticed him standing there. She growled.

Well . . . maybe not.

But, not being one to be put off by a little show of frayed nerves, Mica set the bottles down and slid into the booth across from her.

"Thought you might like to join me in a nightcap."

Gina ignored the bottle and growled again. This time it sounded as real as the one produced by the MGM lion.

Okay, he thought, I should take the hint and just leave her alone. She doesn't want to talk and she's obviously had a rough night. I should go.

Aw, what the hell.

Smiling, Mica leaned forward and clicked his bottle lightly against hers.

After all, what was the worse thing that could happen to him?

118

ELEVEN

"So, how 'bout it? Looks like you could use a nightcap."
Mica inched the bottles closer to Gina's hand—being
careful not to get too close to her long, red-lacquered
nails. Having seen the results of what those claws were
capable of, he wanted to have plenty of room for a
quick and strategic retreat if the need arose.

Which it could. In an instant.

He personally knew of at least one Furvert and three
hookers who would carry the scars of Gina's *hand*iwork
to their graves.

She could be a real bitch when she wanted to, Mica
thought, *just like now.*

He had to fight to keep the smile on his face when
she twisted around and glared at him. If looks could
kill, his ass would be *en brochette*.

"Aw c-c'mon, Gina. A drink'll do you good."

As an example, Mica picked up his bottle and downed half just to get rid of the sudden dryness in his mouth. It didn't help that much.

"Yeah," Gina said, leaning across the table in Mica's direction. "I think a drink'd do me *real* good, Preacher-boy."

Mica felt his body tilt forward as if the whole room had suddenly keeled over on itself. It was an interesting sensation. Mica giggled as Gina's face drifted in close. She was smiling . . . her lips so red . . . her teeth so white . . . her fangs so—

"GINA!" Miriam shouted from across the room. "Be *good!*"

Mica slammed back against the booth and instantly felt something wet and clammy at his crotch. He was afraid to look—*Lord, don't let me have pissed myself*—but when he did it was just as bad.

The rest of his beer was busily soaking into his jeans.

"Aw . . . *fuck.*"

Gina's giggle made him look up. "Now that's some nice language for a Preacher-boy t'be spoutin'. My ol' pappy hear you say things like that, he'd take a hick'ry switch t'your backside."

He just *loved* the way she put things. Brushing the worst of the puddle off his lap, Mica waved at the assistant bartender—and got a one fingered wave in return.

Shit.

Gina chuckled for no apparent reason.

"So . . ." Mica said as he shifted his butt to a drier patch of Naugahyde. "How was work?"

Gina stopped chuckling and returned to glaring. "Am I botherin' you?"

" 'Scuse me?"

"I asked if I was botherin' you by just sittin' here mindin' my own business?"

Mica cleared his throat and felt the dryness return. "Well, if you put it that way . . ."

"That's the onliest way to put it. You're all the time buttin' that Holy-Roller nose of yours into other people's asses. An' if you ain't careful, one o'these days that nose gonna get bit off. Like *that!*"

Gina snapped her fingers and Mica jumped— suddenly very happy he hadn't gotten another beer. He was even happier when Miriam waddled up, all smiles and wrinkles and blue hair.

A Munchkin come to life.

"So, you two having a nice chat?"

Gina just snorted and turned back to watch the door leading to the dressing room. Mica wanted to do the same—Where the hell was Gypsy?—but nodded instead. It wasn't like Miriam to leave anxious, *paying* customers to talk with the hired help. She must have thought that he was trying to convert Gina again.

Like that could be accomplished with a Holy sledgehammer.

Gina growled low in her throat and shifted farther back into the booth.

Following Gina's example, Mica leaned slightly to one side and glanced around Miriam's diminutive (but substantial) frame. *Anxious* was too mild a term to describe the three "dinner companions." *Frantic* was probably a better choice of words. Laughing, jostling one another, shooting nervous, jittery glances around the room . . . they reminded Mica of high school freshmen visiting their first whorehouse.

Or, at least, the first time *he'd* visited a whorehouse.

Sitting back, Mica looked up into shadows laying across Miriam's face and nodded.

"Yes ma'am," he said, "we've been having a real nice chat."

Gina huffed.

"Good . . . good. I like seeing my kindela getting along together. Makes things so much easier."

Her chubby, cold little hand reached out and patted Mica's. *His* eyes had already become accustomed to the dark booth, but Miriam had been able to find him without a moment's hesitation. Glasses or not, her eyes must have been a lot sharper than Mica thought.

"So why are you just sitting here in the dark like a mushroom?" she asked, patting his hand again. "A good looking boy-chic like you should be out seeing what kind of mischief he can get into."

"Or, least-wise makin' sure other people *don't*," Gina snarled.

Mica paid her just enough attention to forgive her *(again)*.

"I'm waiting for Gypsy," he said. "He and Luci sure have been back there a long time."

Was it his imagination or did the temperature in the room suddenly drop by thirty degrees? Mica hunched his shoulders against the chill and picked up the empty beer bottle. His fingers left dripping impressions on the frosted glass. It wasn't his imagination.

Lord? You working some kind of miracle here?

"Yeah, a long time," Miriam said, nodding her head. Mica half expected to see her breath plume out in front, and was surprised when it didn't. "But a real streak of luck for us. What you might even call a miracle—"

A shiver raced up Mica's spine as the cold settled down around him. A *miracle* . . .

"—you should excuse me for stepping in your territory, Mr. Miracle-Man. Okay, so maybe miracle wasn't the right word . . . so sue me." Miriam shrugged and batted the air in front of her. "Anyway, Luci finds out that girl's a dancer and needs a job—so what can I do? You know how big hearted our Luci is, she'd have all the dancers in Hollywood in here if she could."

The temperature dropped another degree as Gina's nails put four new scratches across the table top. Mica caught the scowl that passed between them and pressed his back tighter against the back of the booth. Getting out of the line of fire.

"*Anyway,*" Miriam said, all smiles and talking faster than usual when she turned back, "the big Gypsy is working out the arrangements . . . lights, music, whatever they do out here when I'm back in the office paying bills. You know."

Mica nodded and chuckled. It was the first time he could ever remember Miriam lying to him. She sounded exactly the way his mama had the day he came home early from school and found her and an Encyclopedia salesman sitting in the darkened living room . . . talking fast and trying to push her crumpled panties under the couch with her foot.

Stay close by, Lord, Mica prayed, *and best put on Your hip boots . . . it's running pretty high in here.*

Whatever Gypsy was doing in the dressing room, Mica was dead certain it had nothing to do with music and lights.

"So I tell you what, you go home and I'll personally tell the Gypsy you got tired of waiting."

"That's real tempting," Mica said, "but I think I'll just wait. I don't have anything better to do."

Do I, Lord?

Miriam's face went stony as she stepped back from the table.

"Like I should tell you what to do. Stay up all night if that's what you want. *Gina* . . . you be nice and don't give him any hassle, you hear? Now, I gotta get back to those three before they start peeling the wallpaper off with their teeth. Be good!"

Mica nodded even though he wasn't sure which one of them Miriam's parting shot had been directed at. Lord knows *he* was trying to be good.

Trying even though he kept seeing Luci and Gypsy and the Woman-Who-Wasn't-Piper rolling around the floor of the dressing room—naked, sweating bodies crawling . . . touching . . . sucking . . .

"Are you gonna fuckin' sit there all night?" Gina suddenly hissed, slapping the table with her palm.

Oh, Lord . . .

"Well, ain't this a cozy little scene."

Mica's head snapped around so quickly he was sure he'd heard one of the vertebra in his neck pop. Gypsy leaned up against the end of the booth, a shadow among shadows . . . one with a shit-eating grin stretching from ear to ear.

"Gyp?"

"What's the matter, Preacher-boy?" he asked, leaning over and punching Mica lightly on the arm. Only this time it *was* lightly. "You look like you've just seen a ghost."

"So what's so special about him?"

Dressed in the conservative starlet outfit that Luci had picked out for her: Slit-to-the-thigh hip-hugger jeans and a plunging-to-the-belly-button sequined top and shoes that would make a podiatrist cream his shorts, Allison folded her arms over her breasts and squinted at the man gaping up at Gypsy.

He didn't look like anything special. His dirt-water brown hair was too long for his thin face—his hawkish nose too long for his narrow eyes. His whole manner too young for the body that held it. All he needed was glasses and a pencil stuck behind his ears and he'd look like a grown-up version of the audio-visual nerds Allison and her girlfriends used to laugh at in high school.

"That's the Preacher-boy," Luci said. The little white dinner dress that she'd slipped into made a soft rustling sound as she stepped up behind Allison and ran a hand slowly down her back. "He works out front. But you better watch out for him. He's a real dyed-in-the-wool True Believer, always talking up the Big G and praying for our immortal souls."

Allison felt her skin crawl under Luci's cold hand.

"He's a *holy* man," she gasped, "and he can still come in here? Isn't he supposed to burst into flames or something?"

"Believe me, he's come close," Luci said, "but so far all he's done is smolder. A little."

Allison shook her head—shook off Luci's hand and pressed her back against the wall. What the hell was a preacher doing working for the damned?

"I already told you, Alley-cat," Luci said out loud, answering the unspoken question. "Besides, I like having him around . . . it's a challenge."

Allison watched the smile mold itself around Luci's fangs.

"What challenge? Everyone knows a Man of . . ." Allison pointed one finger toward the water damaged ceiling, ". . . *you know* is immune to our kind."

Luci's emerald greens blinked slowly, as if she were coming out of a deep sleep.

"Is that more paperback novel crap? Jesus, I wish you hadn't read all that shit. Look, no one is immune to us, baby. *No one.*" Luci grabbed Allison's shoulders and turned her back toward the far booth. "Sometimes the rules of the hunt change, but that's all. If we sucked him now, his blood would destroy us . . . okay, so that part's *like* the books. But all we have to do is make him lose his faith. And that's going to be a whole hell of a lot easier now that you're here.

"So come on," Luci said, looping her arm through Allison's and dragging her away from the wall. "Suck in your fangs and stick out your tits. I can hardly wait to introduce you two."

Allison let herself be herded across the room even though she could have waited.

Could have waited an *eternity* if she had to.

Too many things had already happened for one night. The last thing she needed was to make the acquaintance of a Fire-and-Brimstone Preacher.

But I don't understand? Why him?

Because, Luci's voice whispered against the inside of her ears, *I WANT to.*

TWELVE

Mica licked his lips and tried hard not to stare.

A ghost was *exactly* what Gypsy looked like. His face—or, at least the part that showed beneath his cap and above his dark stubble—hovered above Mica in the darkness like some disembodied spirit.

"You got a problem, pard?" the spirit face asked. "Don't think I ever heard you stay quiet so long and still be conscious. What's the matter? Gina get your tongue?"

The low, booming laugh sounded like Gypsy's . . . but there was something missing. Something.

It just *felt* wrong.

"Well, c'mon, Preacher-boy," Gypsy's voice chuckled, "say something or I really will think you and Gina were getting it on."

"Fuck," Gina groaned, "*that'll* be the day."

Mica scooted higher against the seat and cleared his throat.

"You look like shit, Gyp." *Lord, don't let me ask. It's none of my business. Please, Lord*. "What the hell were you doing back there all night?"

Thanks, Lord. I sure hope YOU know what I'm doing.

Gypsy thumbed the cap back on his head as the smile inched farther across his face.

If that was possible.

"Just talking to that little girl you brought in, man. That's all. Just talking."

Mica's belly cinched into a tight ball. Another lie. This one from his closest friend. Even Gina snorted her disbelief.

What the hell happened back in that room, Lord?

"Hey, they're coming over," Gypsy said as he reached into the booth and hauled Mica to his feet. "Stand up and act like a gentleman. And for God's sake *don't* get all sacramental, first thing, okay? Let Allison get to know you before you fall to the floor and start talking in tongues. All right? Comprende, amigo?"

Mica nodded without really hearing the question.

Allison. Her name was Allison.

The stage spots had been left on and they backlit her hair as she and Luci walked toward the booth. A golden-red halo surrounded her head. Mica swallowed hard and moved his hands to the front of his jeans—less concerned that they might think he'd peed himself than he was that they'd see the sudden bulge under his fly.

Allison.

Her pale skin glowed in the soft light, competed with the glimmering sparkles on her shirt. Allison . . . the woman who wasn't Piper. She looked even more beautiful—if that was possible—than when he'd first carried her into the club.

If that was possible.

It had only been three hours (*only* three) since he brought her in and she'd been dead drunk.

Or something.

". . . and this is the famed and fabled Preacher-boy," Luci was saying, pushing the glittering, radiant, *sober* creature toward him. "Preacher-boy . . . this is Allison. Alley-cat, for short."

Mica nodded and forced the corners of his mouth into a smile.

"Hey," he said.

She sneezed.

Long.

Loud.

And hard.

"Bless you!"

He would have said the same thing even if he hadn't signed up for a life-time hitch in the Army of the Lord, anyone would, but by the looks on all their faces— Gypsy's included—you would have thought he'd suddenly pulled out a gun or consigned them to the everlasting flames of Hell!

"I'm outta here!" Gina snarled as she slid out of the booth and stalked away. "I don't gotta put up with this— not for you, not for nobody! I been here too long t'let

some uppity Fledgy come 'tween me an' what's mine an'
I sure as fuck don't gotta listen t'no white-assed, psalm-
singin', Bible-humpin' . . ."

She was still muttering when she got to where Miriam
was standing with the three men—any of whom looked
capable of tearing off major portions of Mica's anatomy
without breaking into a sweat.

"*Shit,* Preacher-boy," Gypsy growled, "what'd I just tell
you not more than two minutes ago?"

The booth lights came on before Mica could answer.
Although it seemed as if he was the only one who noticed. Or blinked in the sudden glare.

"That's okay, Gypsy," Luci said softly, as if she were
calming an attack dog. "Preacher-boy was just doing
what comes natural. He didn't mean anything by it."

Mica got the impression that the last statement had
been directed to Allison.

"Poor Alley-cat's just getting over a cold," Luci said,
patting the woman's bare arm. "In fact, she took one too
many of those little time-released capsules before . . .
that's why she was acting a little loopy tonight. Gypsy
and I spent the last few hours pouring coffee down her
throat, then holding her head over the john when she
poured it back up. Isn't that right, Alley-cat?"

The woman—Allison—nodded from behind her
hands, her golden-brown eyes wide and staring. But
Mica couldn't tell if the expression in them was embarrassment or something else. Luci's explanation covered
all the bases. Just one cold tablet left him sleepier than
hell. If she'd accidentally taken too many under the "if

one works, more is better" delusion, she probably would have looked drunk. *And* helping her get rid of them *would* have kept Luci and Gypsy busy.

For three hours.

Without one word of explanation.

It all made perfect sense.

It just gave Mica a creepy feeling that all his questions were answered *before* he said anything. Out loud.

"I hope you're feeling better now, Allison," he said. "And I hope I didn't say anything to offend you just now. You know . . . about blessing—"

"Preacher-boy!" Gypsy's face and body suddenly eclipsed Mica's line of sight. "What the fuck am I going to *do* with you?"

Gypsy smiled.

Mica had seen the smile before. Usually it came right after Gypsy asked obnoxious drunks if they wouldn't mind joining him outside for a little air. He'd always come back smiling that particular smile. And rubbing the knuckles on his right hand.

"S-sorry. I didn't mean anything by it. Honest." Mica stood on tip-toes and nodded to the women. "Sorry."

"Oh, shoot," Luci said, running an arm over Gypsy's shoulders, "I've been blessed by worse. Hey, Alley-cat, why don't you come on over here and sit a spell with the Preacher-boy? Get to know each other a little better while I go over and chat up our dinner guests. I'll call you when we're ready to start."

Luci's sudden smile flashed as bright as her white dress. "And I don't think you have to worry. Looks like the boy's already off loaded once tonight. You should be safe enough."

Mica wondered what the hell she was talking about until he followed her gaze—down to the front of his pants.

"N-no . . . that's beer." He sidestepped back into the booth quickly and crossed his legs, barely wincing when his knee slammed against the underside of the table. "Ummm—I just spilled my beer."

Luci took a deep breath and winked. "If you say so, kid. Come on, Alley-cat . . . curl right on up here."

When the woman didn't move, Luci reached back without looking and dragged her to the table. Then sat her down like a mother forcing a child to sit with unloved relatives. And nodded.

Mica looked at the woman . . . at *Allison*.

And grinned.

Allison looked at the scar on his forehead.

And shuddered.

"Oh," Mica said, running his fingers over the puckered flesh . . . trying to pull his hair down to cover it. "Sorry."

She wasn't the first woman who'd seen the scar and been repulsed by it. Piper hadn't even noticed it until he mentioned it. Then she claimed it looked more like a lopsided *X* than a cross. But Piper had never been able to see any of the miracles he'd tried to show her.

"Sorry," he said again.

"Do you *believe* this guy?" Luci said as she walked over and planted a cold kiss on the scar. A very cold kiss. It felt like she ran an ice-cube over his skin. "He goes around with the Big G in his pocket all day and night . . . then forgets that *vanity* is one of the Seven Deadly Sins.

"Well, I think your scar is cute." She kissed it again and this time Mica couldn't stop the shiver. "And so will Alley-cat when she gets used to it. Right?"

"*Right*," they both answered.

Giggling, Luci patted Mica on the head and began walking toward the group near the stage, her snow white dress and hair swaying in time to the movements of her hips . . . Gypsy trailing after her like a puppy.

Leaving the two of them alone.

Together.

"Hey, *Gyp!*" Mica called out, grabbing the beer Gina had pointedly ignored, "how 'bout a night-cap? I know the bartender here personally."

Mica waited for the usual slow chuckle and eye-roll and got neither. He even doubted if Gypsy would have turned around if Luci hadn't stopped and nodded. And when he did turn, it was like looking at a full-sized oil painting—flat and two dimensional. *Dead*.

"No thanks, pard. Gotta make sure these guys act like gentlemen tonight." Winking, Gypsy tapped the brim of his cap with two fingers and turned. The whole thing reminded Mica of a movie he once made in his high school audio-visual class.

A soft giggle, followed by an even softer sneeze, brought his eyes back across the table. At her.

Allison.

God, she was beautiful, more beautiful than Piper ever was or ever could be . . . yet there was something in her golden eyes . . . something that reminded him of Piper. Mica lifted the beer to his mouth and tried to wash away the desert that was covering his tongue.

So beautiful. And so . . . lost.

Is that it, Lord? Is this the way You've chosen so that I may fully redeem myself in Your sight? Please, Lord . . . just give me a sign.

Allison sniffled, wiping her nose off on the back of her hand—and in that sniffle Mica realized that not even a bolt of lightning shooting through the ceiling and ending at the feet of the Archangel Himself could have shown him God's purpose more clearly: He was to lift Allison off the street of Self-indulgence and Pride and set her firmly back onto her spiritual feet.

Much the same way he'd scooped her up off Sunset . . . when he thought she was just a drunken whore.

"Hey, again," he said, lowering the bottle, *"Alley-cat."*

Mica had hoped that using the nickname would help cut a path through the tension. It didn't so much as nick it.

"Preacher-boy."

But at least it was a start.

"It's really Mica," he said, setting the bottle aside and holding out his hand to her.

She just looked at it.

"What's really Mica?"

"My name."

"Mica?"

"Yes ma'am . . . a name as strong as the ancient Prophet who foretold the doom of Judah. Praise God!"

Allison scooted closer to the end of the booth. "I though mica was that flaky mineral we tried to set fire to in science class."

"Yes, but it didn't burn did it?" The spirit was moving in him now and Mica wasn't about to stop it. The hand he'd offered her now closed into a fist—ready to fight anyone who would challenge the Word. "You tried to burn it but it didn't burn . . . because it was impervious to the flames, wasn't it? And that's why my name is Mica—because I'm impervious to the flames that have destroyed other men. Sing His Glory!"

Mica was panting when he finished—the fine sheet of sweat already drying in the cool air as he lowered his hand and smiled.

"Then you *really* are a preacher."

"Oh, yes." *The Truth, Mica!* "Well, sort of. I don't have any kind of church or anything . . . nothing like that. I just praise the Lord whenever the Spirit moves me and try to lend a hand to those who have fallen by the way."

A small half smile touched Allison's lips as she dipped her finger into the water ring the bottle left behind.

"Well, as *one* of the fallen . . . literally . . . I just want to thank you and your lending hand."

"Just part of the job . . . like listening and not making judgments if somebody wanted to unburden themselves."

He reached across the table and took her hand without thinking—it just seemed like the natural thing to do.

For some reason. Allison's flesh was as cold as Luci's had been. She snatched her hand back so quickly it left freezer burns on his palm.

"Don't!"

Mica didn't answer. *Couldn't* answer. He was too busy waiting for her to explode. Face screwed up tight, back rigid, one hand clamped onto the edge of the table, the other pressed over her nose—her whole body trembled as the sneeze built to escape velocity.

Mica prepared himself—a *Bless you* already on his lips—when one watery eye opened and glared at him. Warned him off.

The sneeze died silent and unmourned. *I'll catch her the next time, Lord . . . I promise.*

"Oh, G—eeeze, I'm sorry. This stupid cold . . ." She shrugged and sniffed—her nose as pale as the rest of her face, her eyes clear and shining again. The lie about having a cold was going to stand fast.

Mica nodded and forgave her. He would wait and keep waiting until she felt comfortable enough to tell him the Truth about what had driven her to the streets. *Because waiting's part of the job, too. Waiting until the sinner is ready to confess and accept Your Forgiveness, Lord. So I'll wait, Lord, then, just as Jesus reached out to Mary Magdalene and lifted up her soul so am I sent to this woman to lift up her skirts and fuck her legs off.*

SHIT!

Mica prayed he hadn't said it out loud . . . but wasn't sure when he looked up—ashamed and repentant— into Allison's eyes and saw the smirk.

"A *preacher,* huh?"

"Yeah. That just means somebody who preaches the Word to whoever'll listen . . . even if the *who* is just the image staring back at you from a mirror."

All traces of humor faded from her face.

Allison.

God, she was beautiful.

THIRTEEN

God, he was pathetic.

A Born-Again-Nothing-Can-Harm-Me-Because-I've-Been-Saved-But-You're-Still-Up-Purgatory-Creek-Unless-You-Part-Those-Legs-And-Accept-the-Lord-Holy-Roller *hypocrite!*

Allison's nose twitched and she ran a finger under it. *Shit.* The holy man's scent was all over her and it burned her nose worse than cayenne pepper.

He blessed her again—in his mind—and Allison's belly cramped up on itself. Damn, she wished he'd stop doing that. If Luci hadn't mentioned that his blood would probably destroy her, she would've ripped his head off and been *done* with it.

Right here and now.

The last comment about the mirror had gotten to her more than it should have. *Maybe he KNEW.* But even as the possibility blossomed Allison was cutting it down. No. The guy was too self-important not to miss the once-in-a-lifetime opportunity to rid the world of a flock of vampires.

A *covey* of vampires?

A *tooth-full?*

Allison brushed her hair out of her eyes and looked across the table. Smiled. He smiled back and "saw" her wearing an orange tabby-cat costume—complete with long silky whiskers and fluffy striped tail—working on his engorged cock like it was the world's largest bowl of cream; while he prayed for her immortal soul.

You fucking, Bible-humping, sanctimonious—

"You sure you're okay?"

Allison blinked him back into focus and nodded. He was just what he seemed—a perverted overzealous ass-hole.

She could handle that.

"Yeah." She sniffled for effect. "It's just this cold thing . . . you know."

He nodded and took another pull off the bottle. She could have told he didn't believe her about having a cold even without supernatural powers. His eyes told her. Normally a soft blue-grey, they darkened to the color of a winter storm each time she mentioned it.

The windows to the soul.

Allison sniffed again and leaned back against the booth—watching the storm gather strength. It would be so easy . . . cayenne pepper or not . . .

The sound of laughter near the stage made her turn.

One of the three dinner guests was wearing Luci's rhinestone collar and doing a first-class bump-and-grind down the silent runway. Luci and Miriam were clapping and Gina was giving one man just enough attention to keep him happy. In fact, *all* of the . . . *What did Luci call them?* . . . the *Breathers* looked happy.

Except for the one Allison was sitting with.

Naturally.

"Well," she said, scooting out of the booth and inching toward the stage. Her stomach began to rumble again. "It was really nice meeting you . . . Preacher-boy, but I've got to—"

He stood up right along with her. "Yeah, the *dinner*. Well, how about if I stick around and walk you home when you're finished."

Home.

Home was a tiny one-bedroom condo in Sylmar she bought back in '92 when she still thought being a single, independent woman meant something. It meant shit somewhere in a galaxy far, far away.

"No. Thanks, anyway," Allison said, her inching away becoming full steps. "I don't know how long this thing will last and I . . . wouldn't want to keep you from anything."

"No, it's okay. Really." He followed her like the Blind Date from Hell, refusing to take the sugar-coated "leave me alone, you creep" hint. "One of the good things about working nights is I can sleep till noon if I want."

Allison's retreat picked up a little more speed. As did his pitiful advances.

"But what about your . . . *flock?* Won't they miss you?"

He shrugged and stuck his hands into the back pocket of his jeans—the movement was just enough to showcase the bulge pressing up against the stain at his crotch. Both the stain and bulge were bigger than Allison had first guessed.

He looked even bigger than Seth.

Her stomach grumbled angrily. *Feed me! Now!*

"Look, Mica, I'd love to stand here and talk but I *really* have to go. Okay? And don't wait. Please."

Allison could feel Luci's eyes crawling over her as she got closer to the stage. The preacher was still following. *Shit . . . maybe I should just sprout fangs . . .*

Then he'll never leave, Alley-cat. Chill out and use some of your NATURAL talents. Things aren't all that different.

You're telling me.

"Look," Allison whispered, leaning forward until her nose started twitching, "I'm just on probation here, okay? I don't want to get into any trouble . . . you know."

He looked over her shoulders at the group and nodded. His eyes were slate grey.

"Think I might be able to see you again?" he asked.

Lifting her chin, she reached out and flicked a straggly curl off the cross-shaped scar on his forehead. The tips of her fingers suddenly felt like she'd stuck them into a vat of hot bleach.

"Yeah, you can see me again," she said, jerking her thumb at the stage, using the gesture to curl her throbbing fingers into the coolness of her palm. "I'll be dancing right up there tomorrow night."

"Oh . . . oh, yeah. Yeah, I'll be here, but what I meant—"

"Great! I'll see you tomorrow night then." Tossing her head, Allison spun on the stiletto heels and began the slow, hip-grinding walk to the stage. "Be sure to look for me . . . I'll be the orange tabby cat."

She didn't have to turn around—she could feel the shock radiating off him like light from an atomic blast.

Nope, some things didn't *have* to change.

FOURTEEN

Mica frowned and flicked his jacket at a scrawny weed growing in a crack of the sidewalk. Seemed like nothing grew in the smog-filled L.A. basin but weeds and palm trees . . . and he was getting sick of both.

When the jacket missed its mark, Mica changed directions and stomped the dandelion into mush. It didn't make him feel better.

Allison.

The woman who wasn't Piper.

The woman who somehow managed to reach right down into his brain and snatch out the sinful image he'd conjured of her.

Allison.

Mica's frown worked the scar deeper against his skull and made it itch.

"Yeah, I know You're there, Lord," he muttered. "I know."

But somehow that didn't help as much as it normally did.

Shaking his head, Mica scraped the weed mush off his shoe and tossed the jacket over one shoulder. It was still too sultry a night to put it on and, of course, there were *other* things to consider. He once made the mistake of wearing the pink satin monstrosity home and had every Butt-Boy on Selma Avenue

". . . prancing after me like I was the fucking Queen of Sheba!"

Damn.

Mica glanced skyward and grinned sheepishly.

"Sorry, Lord. I guess I'm too tired to hold my tongue."

"I'll hold your tongue for you, mister," a soft voice said from the shadows. "For twenty-five I'll hold anything you *want*."

Mica kept walking—eyes straight ahead. He didn't want to see how young the boy was . . . didn't want to see the evil that already lay like a mantle over the small body. If he did, he might feel compelled to take matters into his own fists.

"Mister?"

"For the Love of God, kid," Mica said, quickening his pace, "isn't it past your bedtime?"

"If you got a bed it is." The child's voice had took on an excited "Christmas morning" edge. "I'm real good in bed."

Dear Lord . . .

Mica stopped and took a deep breath of exhaust

fumes. He could feel the child stepping around him as dawn began lightening the sky over Cahuenga Blvd. The boy didn't look any older than twelve. Smiling, he reached up and laid a hand against Mica's arm.

His skin felt so hot it almost burned.

"I'm *real* good," he whispered.

"Are you? Are you *real* good? Because only the *good* go to Heaven. Are you *that* good, kid? Are you *really?*"

The jacket lay crumpled at his feet as Mica grabbed the boy's T-shirt and lifted him to his tip-toes. The yellow lights made the terror on the boy's face almost comical. Almost laughable if it hadn't been so damned pitiful.

"Because if you are I could send you to the Lord right now. It would be so easy . . . you being so good and all . . . I snap your scrawny, ass-fucking little neck and *wham*—" Mica shook the kid and heard his teeth click together. "—you're an Angel. If you're as good as you say you are.

"But if you lied to me and meant it some *other* way, you're going to be bent over spreading it for demons that have harpoons for dicks. You understand?"

Tear-spit splattered across Mica's knuckles when he straightened his arms (he'd have to remember to wash with cleanser . . . God only knew what diseases the kid already had). Mica held him there while he whimpered and tried to get away.

"No, you don't understand. You *can't* get away until you turn your back to this sin—" *Bad choice of words, Lord. Sorry.* "—until you *renounce* the sin you've chosen and accept the Lord back into your heart. Do you?"

Mica snapped him like a dishrag—just to remind him of the Power behind the Spirit.

"Do you accept the Lord?"

"Y-y-y-y-"

"Do you renounce your sin?"

"Uh-uh-uh-h-h-h-"

"Do you ask the Lord to Forgive you?"

"YES!"

Mica pulled the sobbing child to his chest and hugged him.

"Praise the Lord," he shouted at a blinking airliner as it passed overhead. "Another lost sheep has found its way back to the flock. Now, get the hell home, kid . . . and if I ever see you doing this again I'll tear you a *new* asshole. God hates backsliders almost as much as I do."

The kid took off at a dead run, heading back up Selma to Highland. Bending to retrieve the jacket, Mica hoped he wouldn't run into the pervert in the dress . . . a newly saved soul was so fragile.

So easily broken.

Allison.

Mica fumbled the jacket back to the sidewalk and almost followed it down. What the hell did *she* have to do with anything?

Grabbing the jacket, Mica wadded it into a ball and pressed it against his belly as he broke into a slow jog. Dawn was soaking the darkness out of the sky and for some reason that bothered him . . . made him think about the night and hair the color of autumn leaves.

"Hey, man," someone wearing a black plastic garbage

bag shouted as Mica rounded the corner to Cherokee, "slow down 'fore you bust the sound barrier."

But he *didn't* stop running until he collapsed against the side of the Crazy Croatian's Coffee Shop—established 1969, bankrupted 1970.

"But what a year it was," Mica panted, repeating the litany he'd heard at least once a day, every day, for the last eight years since Mrs. B had found him preaching at the Farmer's Market and brought him home.

Home.

Taking a deep breath, Mica scooted his back along the loose boards and listened to the age-blistered paint crinkle under him. The city had been threatening Mrs. B for years to get the place (1) brought up to code or (2) torn down. Neither of which she would do.

Her husband—*may he rest in peace*—had enclosed the front porch of their 1930s bungalow and turned it into the thriving business with his own hands and she would be in her grave before she let the city change so much as one broken light fixture!

Mica suspected that it wasn't so much her husband's memory that made her so adamant about keeping the eyesore as it was to spy on the group of hookers who plied their trade directly across the street from it. Sometimes she'd even cook up a batch of popcorn and invite Mica to join her.

Tossing the wrinkled jacket over his shoulder, Mica stood up and walked to the mailbox marked 1611 1/2—and smiled at the collection of *Occupant* mail he'd received that day. His parents had long ago given up trying to persuade him to come back to Tulsa, and Piper . . .

Piper wouldn't have known where to even start looking for him.

Mica pulled the envelopes out of the box and tapped them against his chin. Smiling. Mrs. B hated to think that he was so alone in the world that he only got junk mail, and try as he would, Mica still hadn't convinced her that he *wasn't* alone: He had the Lord. And if *that* still wasn't enough, he had his Calling, his Ministry, his job, his . . .

Allison.

"NO!"

A moment later Mica heard the creak of ancient bedsprings through the security-barred window behind him. *Dammit.*

"Mica?" a low voice asked. "Is that you, dear?"

Mica looked down the rutted drive to the tear-drop shape emerging from the shadows. The little trailer was the "1/2" of 1611 . . . *home sweet home* with shower privileges every Monday, Wednesday and Saturday in the "big" house.

And, *Lord,* how he wished it was Monday, Wednesday or Saturday. His skin felt like it was covered with grease and his crotch kept sticking to his jockey shorts.

Allison.

"No . . . I mean, *yes!* Yes, it's me. Sorry if I woke you, Mrs. B. I—I just stumbled. A little."

The bed creaked again. He could hear the slow, uneven shuffle of her bare feet against the worn carpeting as the old woman walked to the window. When the frail, hunched figure appeared at the window, Mica accepted the consequences of awakening his landlady/surrogate mother and wrapped his fingers around one of the wrought iron bars.

It jiggled in his fingers. Just because an old lady living alone has to put up iron bars like a prison doesn't mean she has to bolt them down and die in a fire like you read about in the papers—she said. Often. Every time Mica offered to fix them.

As a Cradle-Catholic she was of the firm belief that if someone *thought* they couldn't get in they wouldn't try—a philosophy that undoubtedly cut down the Mackerel-Snapping population in Heaven by half. Mica, on the other hand, knew that all men were sinners looking for redemption.

Or anything else they could lay their hands on.

"Good heavens, it's almost morning," Mrs. B yawned and Mica joined her for a quick one. "Oh my . . . Did you have a date?"

There was so much *hope* in the old lady's voice that Mica couldn't help smiling. Having no children of her own, she'd recently begun looking at him to provide for her grandmotherly needs.

"No, ma'am," *Sorry.* "Just met a new dancer, s'all."

Mrs. B's next few questions came as fast as a chicken going after a June bug.

"Is she pretty?"

She was beautiful. An angel. "Yes, ma'am."

"Smart?"

"Yes, ma'am."

"Are you going to ask her out?"

The June bug went down kicking and screaming.

"I—I just *met* her tonight, Mrs. B."

"That's what you said. Are you going to ask her out?"

Mica was suddenly aware of how light it was getting. Another couple of inches and the sun would crest the horizon of roofs and the old lady would be able to see the blood-red blush on his cheeks.

"Yes, ma'am," he said, "I think I will."

"Good! Too much of anything, even *God*, isn't healthy." Spoken like a true Papist. "But it's way too early to give you the third degree now . . . plan on dinner tonight and I'll beat the details out of you. All right?"

"Yes, ma'am."

"Good, I'll make big salads and we can watch the hookers." Her pale outline left the window and disappeared back into the dark bedroom. "G'*morning*, dear. Sleep tight."

"You, too, Mrs. B," Mica said, turning toward the trailer and his unmade but comfortable pull down bed— images of dreams not yet born already forming on the back of his eyes. "And don't let the bed bugs bite."

"Oh sure." Her voice followed him up the narrow driveway. "I have so little blood left who'd want to bite me?"

Allison.

FIFTEEN

Allison opened one eye and moaned. The effect—considering she was in a closed coffin—was enough to send shivers down her own spine.

She'd thought being dead would make getting up easier.

It didn't.

If anything it made it more difficult. Once—three weeks ago—all it took was a decently good cup of coffee to get her blood pumping. Now, not even Draino would do the trick.

God, she hated being dead and Seth and being a vampire and having to sleep in a coffin and—

The noise that "woke" her came again. Three gentle rappings . . . *rappings at my chamber door. Quote the Raven*—

"Go the fuck away!"

Wakey, wakey. Luci's voice sounded disgustingly perky for someone who had spent the better part of the pre-dawn hours draining a man from both ends.

"Ah, shit."

Well . . . we really don't have to anymore. But whatever turns you on.

Allison unclasped her hands at her chest and thumped a knuckle against the pale pink satin lining. She was glad she'd chosen pink instead of the red Luci had suggested—to match her hair. Shit, imagine waking up to your own personal retina hernia test every night . . . for the rest of eternity.

Luci knocked again and Allison pretended not to hear—pretended not to notice old feelings of claustrophobia by marveling at the workmanship of the coffin.

Her coffin.

One phone call to the Dream Away All Night Mortuary (The Embalmer to the Stars since 1923) and a VISA number and she not only had all the comforts of home, but a twenty-five-year written guarantee against seepage.

How thoughtful.

tap tap tap

"Hey, sleepy-head," Luci shouted through the polished mahogany lid. "You getting up or what?"

"*What,*" Allison yelled back and immediately regretted it. One of the features the hollow-eyed salesman *hadn't* pointed out was the acoustical value of the coffin. Of course, Allison doubted if *many* clients normally took advantage of it.

"Go away," she moaned, "and let the dead rest in peace, will you?"

The sterling silver hinges made a nails-on-the-blackboard squeal as the viewing lid rose. Luci smiled down at her and wiggled her fingers.

"No rest for the wicked, Alley-cat," she whispered, "I thought you knew that. Come on, up and at 'em. It's a beautiful day."

Day?

Allison sat up slowly, hands folded across the *Furverts Like 'Em Hairy* nightshirt she was wearing. If any Breather saw her now it would take a few full years' growth right out of them—*Dracula Rises From the Grave, the Next Generation*.

The club's storeroom "boudoir" was dark and silent. Of the four coffins laid out dormitory-style, only Luci's white "Snow Queen" model and hers were open. Gina's ebony black casket shuddered violently but didn't open when Luci reached out to smooth down Allison's hair.

"What do you mean *day?*" Allison asked as she blinked into full consciousness.

"Day," Luci answered, "You know, the opposite of night? The bright stuff Breathers like to lay out in during the summer. Blue skies, sunshine . . . *day*."

Allison scooted her rump over the cushiony soft padding and was about to say "ha, ha, really funny" when she noticed the shimmering golden light oozing around the room's heavy velvet drapes.

*Day*light.

Allison grabbed the coffin's side and jammed herself back in. "Close the lid!"

"Who do I look like—Señor Wences?" Tossing her head, Luci snapped open the remaining clasps and propped the lid up the rest of the way. "Now, get your little ass out before I dump it out."

Luci lifted the coffin a foot off its twin saw-horse dais and rattled it. Proof she could do exactly what she threatened. Not that Allison needed proof. After the coffin was dropped off by two sweating men in Greatful Dead tee-shirts, Luci had picked it up and tucked it under her arm like a pocketbook.

"But . . . Look, okay, I don't know a whole hell of a lot about all this, but you *can't* tell me that vampires can go out in the daylight." Allison sat up as the coffin came to rest. "Every fucking legend maintains the fact that one of the known ways to destroy a vampire is to expose it to the cleansing rays of the sun."

Luci stepped back and played with the marabou trim on her black satin nightgown.

"What *were* you—a lawyer? Forget it. And forget what all the fucking legends *maintain*. Just get up and I'll show you how the *real* undead behave."

Mumbling under her breath, Allison threw one leg—gracelessly—over the side and proceeded to half-fall, half-slither to the floor.

"Ah . . . the dead rises from her tomb," Luci said—smiling as she watched Allison's nightshirt ride up past her hips. "But you *do* know you can just levitate out of those things you know."

"Now you tell me. Why didn't you mention *that* a minute ago?"

"Because you aren't wearing panties. Now, get changed. We got things to do and people to do them to." Turning in a swirl of shimmer and feathers, Luci walked to a small cupboard at the far end of the store-room and opened it.

"Oh, and while you're at it, goose up the back door a little. Your tits are knockouts but they make your ass look too small and we don't want you to look lopsided." Luci giggled while she rooted around. Allison could hear bottles clinking. "T and A, Alley-Cat . . . all juicy and ripe, that's how you catch a Breather. Non-breathers, too . . . sometimes."

Allison still wasn't used to hearing a woman talk like that . . . about her. While Luci's back was still turned, Allison dematerialized the nightshirt and "slipped into" something far less comfortable but much more familiar—jeans, boots and a rose-colored western shirt with black piping. It was almost exactly the same thing she'd been wearing when Seth noticed her.

A million and a half years ago.

When things *were* different.

"Well, yippee-ki-yo," Luci said when she turned—one hand on her hip, the other holding what looked like a mayonnaise jar. "And for your information, *real* cow-boys never wore shit like that. Catch."

Allison amazed herself by snatching the jar in mid-air. A second before it smashed into her face. Luci just smiled.

"Now, slap some of that on all exposed body parts and we'll get this road on the show."

Allison unscrewed the lid and immediately felt her eyes water. "What the hell *is* this stuff?"

"Sun block." Luci's black negligee reformed into white hip-huggers and a Gold's Gym muscle tee as she walked over to Allison and stuck two fingers into the thick white goop. "SP 95. Not a hundred percent protection . . . your ears will buzz and it'll feel like your skin's shrinking, but you won't go up in smoke and that's all that counts, isn't it?"

Allison cringed as Luci smeared the viscous lotion on her cheek and—slowly—began massaging it in. Gina's coffin trembled again.

"I'll do you then you can do me, okay?"

"Yeah-right-sure . . ." Her skin already felt like it was two sizes too small. "Where did you *get* this stuff?"

"We have this crack-head chemist who makes us a new batch every month. He thinks he's going to be bigger than Coppertone." Luci's fingers smoothed the cream down the front of Allison's shirt. "Too bad he doesn't know how limited his customer base is, huh?"

When Luci's fingers continued to descend, Allison scooped out three fingers worth and pushed the jar into Luci's hand.

"It's okay . . . I can do myself," she said quickly—

probably too quickly considering the look on Luci's face. "You . . . go ahead."

If looks could kill . . .

But it's already too late for that, Luci's voice growled. *Isn't it?*

Shit.

Setting the jar down on the top of Gina's rumbling coffin, Luci walked over to the plain pine box that held Miriam and tapped lightly on the lid.

"Miriam? I'm going to take Alley-cat window shopping. Yeah, there are a couple of things I want to expose her to. Don't wait up. Ready, Alley-cat?"

Allison nodded and followed Luci to the double-bolted, steel-reinforced door.

"Okay, Gypsy," Luci said suddenly. "Time to earn your keep."

The army cot moaned under the big man's weight as he rolled slowly to his feet and stood up. Gypsy's eyes were wide and staring as he walked to the door and fumbled with the locks.

"Is he okay?" Allison asked, watching the zombie-like movements. "Aren't *Watchers* supposed to gibber and eat spiders?"

Luci's drawn-out sigh told her they weren't.

"He's asleep," she said, "but if a Breather so much as leaned against the other side of the door he'd be wide awake and swinging. Yeah, this one's a *lot* better than the last one. Big Mike had this real aversion to soap and water . . . that's why we had to keep him outside. Never could housebreak him."

Luci turned as Gypsy opened the door, and kissed Allison full on the mouth.

"That's for helping with him last night. Thanks. He should do real well until the next one."

Allison fought the need to wipe Luci's kiss off her lips by sticking her hands into her back pockets.

"You got someone in mind?" she asked, just to have something to say.

"Never know, Alley-cat. Come on . . . the day's getting away from us." Nodding to Gypsy, Luci tucked Allison's arm through hers. "Don't worry, sweet-cakes, you'll catch on. It'll just take a little time."

Oh yeah, Allison thought as she followed Luci out of the storeroom hidey-hole, every day and every way . . . I'll get better and better.

SIXTEEN

"... like you were blind. Only by allowing yourself to witness the true miracles of our Lord, Jesus ... *CHRIST*—"

Mica's stack of Open Your Eyes to HIS Light pamphlets—printed on the old fashioned ink-drum copier in his trailer—slipped out of his suddenly numb hands.

Stumbling up the driveway after leaving his landlady, all Mica had thought about was the couple of hours of sleep he'd get before hitting the streets and saving souls. When he splashed himself with handfuls of luke-warm water from the cistern on the trailer's roof, all Mica thought about was putting his brain on hold and letting Angels sing him to his rest.

But when he laid down all he saw was her face.

Allison.

And the next four hours alternated between tossing and turning and praying and pacing and begging and finally hating himself for masturbating into the tiny chemical toilet while her face danced behind his closed eyes like a dream that wouldn't fade.

Like a nightmare.

And now, suddenly, there she was.

Reality in dark glasses. Standing near the curb. Smiling.

Allison.

It took Mica another minute to realize she wasn't alone. Luci, also in sunglasses against the summer glare, waved and pointed down. He thought—*knew*—she was pointing at the swelling in his pants . . . until he looked down and saw the scattered pamphlets. One had fallen open to the crudely drawn cartoon Mica had done of a man holding a bottle in one hand and an overly voluptuous woman in the other. The bold-faced caption read: "How much are you REALLY willing to risk your soul on?"

Mica gave Allison one last glance before bending down to collect his self-published guide to Salvation.

Yeah, Lord . . . how much? Anyone ever have the nerve to tell You that You don't play fair?

"Well, well, well," Luci said as she and Allison reached his side, "out saving souls before noon after having been up all night. Now *that's* dedication. I'm impressed, Preacher-boy."

Mica stood up and attempted to fumble the pamphlets back into some sort of order while trying not to look directly at the two women.

"Luci . . . Allison. You're up pretty early yourselves."

When the pamphlets proved to be more of a hassle than they were worth, Mica bunched them into his small nylon daypack and grabbed the worn zipper tab. All this without looking up. "Considering the party was just getting started when I left."

"Ah, well you know entertainers," Luci said, "we have this *marvelous* liquid high protein diet. You really should try it."

It was a joke—Mica could tell that by the way Allison suddenly giggled. *Well, at least they're happy, Lord. But help me to show them what REAL Happiness is.*

Allison's face shifted back into neutral when Mica finally looked up. If it hadn't been for the way her nose twitched he would have thought she'd been carved from white marble.

"Hope your cold's doing better. It could get real serious if—*Shit!*" While he was busy being polite he'd managed to snag the hem of his *Jesus is my BEST Friend* T-shirt into the daypack's zipper. "I'm sorry . . . I—sometimes my tongue gets away from me."

Luci's laughter sent shivers up Mica's spine. Allison didn't so much as crack a smile.

"Right. You'll have to watch this one, Alley-cat. I bet he says that to *all* the girls."

Even though he couldn't see them through the heavily smoked lenses, Mica could feel their eyes burning into him.

"We were just out window shopping," Luci said as she reached out and brushed Allison's hair away from her face. "Doesn't she have beautiful hair, Preacher-boy?"

165

"Beautiful," he heard himself answer. It was just like the night before. When he was talking to Gina about . . . about . . .

"What color would you call it, Preacher-boy?" Luci asked—stepping to one side until all Mica could see was Allison. "*Red* sounds too ordinary. What do you think?"

Piper's face looked back at him.

"Autumn leaves," he said, "at sunset. Her hair was that color."

"*Was?*" Luci gasped. "You mean it's not?"

Mica blinked and saw Allison. Allison. Not Piper. Piper was long gone—somewhere back in another life. Back when he made the mistake of thinking he could love a mere mortal more than he could Love God.

Allison's sneeze brought him back to the present tense.

"Bless y—Sorry." Mica yanked his shirt free and slung the bag over his shoulder. "You know, you might want to see a doctor if that doesn't get any better. Might turn into something serious."

"Oh, I wouldn't worry about it," Luci said as she walked up to him and took his hand. "Maybe our little red-haired Alley-cat is allergic to something. Or maybe she just *thinks* she is."

Then, without any warning, Luci stood on her tip-toes and pressed her lips against Mica's. Had the kiss happened any other time it would have had him on his knees.

Praying.

Any other time, if Allison hadn't been standing there

watching, he would have wondered why Luci's lips were so cold.

Any other time, Lord.

"Well," Luci said, bumping her hip—*accidentally*—against Mica's, "I don't know about you two, but I sure could use something to drink."

"Luci . . . !"

Despite the emotion (Fear? Anger?) in that single word, Allison's voice was as sultry as Mica remembered it from the night before.

"Oh, hush, Alley-cat," Luci said, lacing her arm through Mica's. "I'm just *dying* for a good cup of coffee. How about you, Preacher-boy? Hasn't a full morning of pious devotion dried out the old tonsils?" *bump bump* "So how 'bout it? My treat."

Mica had never seen Luci act like that before—and didn't mind one bit. Maybe she was trying to make Allison jealous. Part of him hoped so . . . and was ashamed.

Within reason, Lord.

"Well, sure . . ."

"No, Luci," Allison interrupted, "it's okay. I'm *not* really thirsty. Honest, *Luci.*"

Luci leaned against him—as cold as a high mountain spring—and sighed. Allison looked as nervous as a penitent facing her first dunking. Poor little thing.

Lord, it's going to be up to both of Us to help this poor child. To set her feet back towards the Glory Everlasting and Life Eternal.

Allison sneezed.

Bless her, Lord.

167

Then growled.

"Coffee sounds good to me," Mica said as he tried to ease his arm out of Luci's cool grasp—without any luck. "But only if you let me pay for it."

Luci brushed her head against his chest. "You can pay for whatever you want, Preacher-boy. *Anything*."

An image of the three of them—naked, sweating, squirming like snakes on a giant unmade bed—instantly redirected all the blood that had been pooling in his cock back up into his cheeks.

Where it belonged.

"Now *I'm* sorry," Luci said, giggling, yanking him into a slow walk and heading south. "What must you *think* of me?"

Mica glanced over his shoulder to see if Allison was following. And smiled. He could tell she wasn't thrilled about being a tag-along, but she was coming.

"I think of you . . . of *all* of you as lost lambs who've just slipped the fence and need a little help getting back into the fold."

Allison bleated. And he burst out laughing. *Could have been worse, Lord . . . she could have told me to go to hell.*

We'll get her yet.

"Baaah."

"Now *that* gives me an idea," Luci said as she picked up the pace. "What do you think if Allison and I wore these little lamb outfits and sheared each other on stage? Think it would work, Preacher-boy? How 'bout it, Alley-cat?"

This time the *baaah* had teeth in it.

A werewolf in sheep's clothing.

Smiling—trying hard *not* to think about what they'd look like—Mica let Luci drag him down Vine and began humming "Jesus, Lamb of God."

Allison sneezed.

Allison watched a no-see-um do the backstroke across the surface scum of her cup of café au lait and wrinkled her nose. There wasn't even enough blood in the insect to make her want to drink it.

Straightening her arm, Allison emptied the cup all over Cecil B. De Mille. The coffee ran down the sides of the weather gray marble like a bad case of diarrhea.

"You didn't like it?" Mica asked.

Allison tossed the cup into a rusted wire litter basket (circa 1932) and turned around—concentrating on not sneezing. The Preacher-boy was standing next to Mrs. De Mille's monument, his own cup of coffee stopped just below the narrow point of his chin.

"A bug got in it," she said. "Ugh."

"Oh. Well, you can have mine if you like," he started around the graves, holding his cup out to her. It was all Allison could do to control the burning itch racing along her sinuses. The morning had already gone *so well* she was afraid another "sneeze-blessing" would finish her completely.

"NO! No, that's okay." Taking a step backwards, Allison patted her belly and smiled. "I'm really still full from last night. But thanks anyway."

He nodded and lowered the cup without taking a drink. "Yeah, I guess it's kind of hard eating so late."

"I'm getting used to it."

He nodded and she nodded. He looked out over the cemetery and she looked out over the cemetery. He took a deep breath and she looked out over the cemetery.

It had been Luci's idea—just like the coffee—to pay a visit to the world famous Hollywood Cemetery and she wouldn't take no for an answer . . . despite the obvious lack of enthusiasm from *both* her captive traveling companions.

"Sooooo . . ." Allison said, "come here often?"

"Yeah. As a matter of fact, I do."

"Really?"

"Yeah."

A shallow blush worked its way up his throat and into the hollows just below his eyes. Allison couldn't help watching the slow filling of tiny blood vessels any more than she could stop her stomach from grumbling or her mouth from watering.

Holy man or not, he looked good enough to eat.

Allison swallowed and casually folded her arms across her chest. "Why?"

The Preacher-Man's face darkened—and it had nothing to do with the fact that he suddenly turned and walked beneath a drooping cypress limb. Allison tried to listen in on his thoughts the way she could with Luci and the other . . . *women*, but all she got were jumbled words and phrases:

. . . left . . . . . . the right thing to do she didn't . . . the Lord would have Forgiven her . . . Allison . . . not the Lord . . . she's not Piper . . . Piper's gone Lord help me to see Thy Light

Allison

"Mica, look," she said, breaking contact, "if you don't want to talk about it . . ."

He looked at her, shaking his head. "No, no it's okay, I don't mind. You called me Mica."

"I'm sorry." *Shit . . . what sin have I committed now?* "Isn't that your name?"

"Yeah," he said. "Yes it is, but usually everybody just calls me Preacher-boy."

Allison fumbled with the sunglasses and shrugged.

"I'm not like everybody else." *And that's the truth,* "Well . . . are you going to tell me why you hang out in graveyards or should I start worrying?"

Not that Allison was really interested. He could get off on preaching to the dead for all she cared. All she wanted was for him to get so involved with the story he was about to tell that he wouldn't notice her doing a mental mind-sweep for Luci.

The sunscreen wasn't living up to Luci's glowing account and just being within praying distance of the man was giving Allison hives. *What the HELL kind of sick, mid-warped game was Luci playing—throwing them together and then splitting for parts unknown?*

The subliminal echoes were silent . . . almost as if Luci had really left them alone.

171

Together.

SHIT!

"... then, when we made love ..."

Allison wasn't sure if it was the scent of blood filling the blush in Mica's cheeks or the sentence that caught her attention.

"Excuse me?"

The blood deepened as he tossed his cup into the trash.

"Piper," he said softly, "the girl I was telling you about. After we walked out on the debate, we came here and talked ... Lord, it must have been hours. Then it just sort of happened."

The blood scent pulled at her.

"You made love to her." Allison felt the tips of her fangs tingle as they elongated. "That was nice."

But Mica was shaking his head—moving away from her, back out into the direct sunlight.

"No. No it was wrong and I *knew* it! The Lord put her in my path as a test ... and I almost failed it." The color faded from Mica's face as he talked—going back to its normal unappetizing pasty-white. "I almost let her into my heart."

Allison's fangs snapped back so quickly they almost gave her whiplash.

"What's wrong with that?" she asked.

"My heart only has room enough for the One True Love. Anything else ... any *other* kind of love is indulgent and self-serving and—"

"So you sucked her dry and left—*shit!*" Allison spun

around and slapped the corner of Cecil B.'s tomb. The corner exploded into grey dust.

"You're no better than Seth."

"Seth?"

Allison watched him step back into the shadows—his hand lifting toward her, instant concern replacing the self-pity in his eyes.

"Did this man Seth hurt you? Do you want to talk about it, because I'll listen. I'll listen and help you. With the Lord's help I swear I will—"

Piper.

Allison heard the name as clearly as if he'd said it out loud. Piper . . . the girl who had threatened to push God from his heart.

Mica took another step toward her. Allison felt her belly twist inside.

"I would . . . rather not talk about it," she said, a limb brushing against her head as she backed away. "Maybe later. Okay?"

"You sure?" He didn't seem to mind when she didn't answer; just shifted into another mode—this one of Tour Guide. "You want to see something really neat? Come on."

Mica's fingers closed around her wrist and Allison waited for the fiery pits of Hell to open beneath her undead feet and suck her down like a grape.

The ground didn't so much as heave.

But she did.

SEVENTEEN

"I still can't believe I did that," Allison said as she followed him through the mausoleum's muted light. "It must have been some . . . *thing* I ate last night."

When their hands touched it was as if a cherry bomb had gone off in Allison's stomach. She could no more stop the gelatinous, ruddy fluid from gushing out her mouth than she could have sprouted wings and flown away. Which, during the five-minute regurgitation, she had tried to accomplish with the utmost zeal; while Mica stood by, like a plaster saint, and prayed for the Lord to give her strength.

But the session had done one thing, Allison no longer had the urge to sneeze when he got close. Now she just wanted to puke.

"Don't worry about it, I do the same thing after one of Gypsy's late night to-dos." A shadow flickered past his eyes

175

but it disappeared too fast for even Allison to second guess its origin. "Oh, we're here! Come on, Allison, I want you to meet someone."

Allison watched as he skipped off into one of the side rooms that lead off the long central hall—Mondo Condos for the dead—and rubbed her gurgling stomach. Luci was in here with them. *Somewhere.* Allison had felt her the moment they entered the mausoleum, but so far Luci was still happy with her little game of Hide-n-Seek.

Bitch!

Allison waited for the scathing mind-to-mind rebuttal. Nothing.

"Damn."

"You say something, Allison?" Mica asked, poking his head out from around the corner.

"No. Nothing at all."

"Good," he said, crooking his finger at her, "come on."

"Right . . . like whoever it is, is going to get up and leave."

"What?" his voice echoed to her.

"Nuthin'."

When she got around the corner, Mica was running his hand slowly along one of the brass name plates halfway up the wall. White silk rosebuds adorned the two plastic vases that flanked it.

"This is Peter Finch," he said.

Allison walked close enough to get a good look (and feel her stomach turn over on itself) and nodded.

"Yo, Pete."

Mica laughed, taking no offense, and patted the actor's final resting place again.

"I remember seeing him . . . I mean *really* seeing him in *Network*. That was such a powerful movie." He glanced back over his shoulder at her without moving his hand. "Did you see it?"

"I think I saw it on cable."

"No, then you missed a lot. You really needed to see it on the big screen to get the full impact of what he was saying." Mica shook his head and turned around. "The character he played, Howard Beale, wasn't the Mad Prophet of the Airways that Faye Dunaway's character said he was . . . he was a *real* Prophet. He was telling people the Truth and that's why he was killed."

"I thought it was because of bad ratings," Allison said. Mica looked hurt.

"No, that's what the producers *wanted* you to believe, but if you pay attention you'll start hearing the Voice of the Lord actually speaking through Peter Finch."

Allison pulled her dark glasses down on her nose and stared over the frames at him. She was suddenly glad she was already dead. If she were still a Breather, the thought of being alone with a man who made saints out of actors would have frightened the shit out of her.

"You know," he said, finally laying the actor to rest and turning away, "I have a copy of it over at my . . . place, if you'd like to see it. I could point out the Prophetic passages for you."

Shit, was he THAT lonely?

"Gee, you know I'd love to," she said, returning the

glasses to their original position, "but I think I'm going to be pretty busy for the next couple of—*(centuries)*—weeks . . . at the least. You know with the new job and all . . . learning the routines and stuff."

The excuse even sounded weak to her. But what the hell.

"But, maybe after things settle down a bit." Allison shrugged, lifted her hand to stare at the gold-and-onyx Chronograph that hadn't been on her wrist a moment before and frowned. "Gee, look at the time. I think I'd better find Luci and—"

Allison's body suddenly stopped moving . . . with the exception of her chest which rose and fell as if she just ran the L.A. Marathon.

"Allison? Are you okay?"

Mica was coming straight at her and she could do about as much to stop him as she could to stop her cowgirl shirt's pearlized snaps from popping open. *What the fuck—?*

Relax, Alley-cat. I'm just giving the Preacher-boy something else to think about when he gets down on his knees tonight.

The last snap parted and her naked breasts (she hadn't *thought* about underwear) surged into full, bouncy view.

"My . . . *God.*"

His fingers burned her nipples as he caressed them.

"Mica. Please—don't."

"It's not too late." His voice was hoarse as he lowered

his face to her breast. She felt his tongue—a tongue of fire—slide down over her flesh. "I can help you. Whatever happened to you I can help. Believe and it will happen. Just ask the Lord to help and He will. Just one word can restore your soul, just—"

one bite and Life Eternal can be yours.

His lips found her nipples and closed around them. Psalms and seduction. Whoever Piper was she was damned lucky to have gotten away when she did.

"You fucking hypocrite."

Without anger or emotion of any kind, Allison shook off Luci's control and hurled the Preacher-boy back first into the wall of tombs. One of the plastic vases fell to the floor and bounced, disgorging its white silk rosebud.

"Oh!"

Luci appeared in the hallway, sunglasses in hand, blinking those great, green eyes of hers.

Alley-cat . . . I'm shocked!

Any particular reason you did that? Allison refastened her shirt.

Take a look.

Mica was peeling himself off the brass name plates slowly, gingerly . . . his face and neck flushed bright red, but not from embarrassment. Dead or alive, Allison knew lust when she saw it.

I don't believe him.

Oh, you can believe it, Alley-cat. Breathers are about as dumb as cattle when you get right down to it. I've seen bulls follow a cow straight into a slaughter house . . . and this little bull is going to do the same. A couple more sessions and I think he'll be ready, ELSIE.

Fuck you, Luci, Allison thought as she spun on her heels and stormed out of the room.

"And fuck you, too—*Preacher-BOY!*"

EIGHTEEN

"Idiot!

"Asshole!

"Blind, *arrogant* bastard! What the hell did you think you were *doing?* God!"

Mica glared at the hang-dog eyes staring back at him from on the trailer's wall. He slammed his fist hard against the countertop.

"You fucking prick. Her soul was troubled and in need and all you could see was the package it came in. She *needed* your strength and guidance and all you could think of was humping her legs off! It was the same thing you did to Piper . . . I fucking don't *believe* you."

Without breaking eye contact, Mica swept his hands over the clutter until they found the large Reference-sized Bible he kept there.

Make it a GOOD one, Lord.

Glancing down just long enough to open the worn pages to Matthew 5:28, Mica scooped the heavy book into his arms before glaring back at his reflection in the mirror.

"And *Jesus* said . . . *anyone who looks lustfully at a woman has already committed adultery with her in his thoughts*."

Mica skipped the part about gouging out your own right eye, but made it a point to rake his knuckles against the side of the printing press as he set the Bible down. The pain helped—a little—but it wasn't enough.

He needed to suffer for his sin.

He *needed* plagues and boils and the Angel of Death to come creeping all green and fog-like up to his front door to pay him a little visit; sit a spell and talk about redemption.

He needed . . .

Allison

Hunching his shoulders, Mica leaned forward and pressed his forehead against the mirror's cool glass. It was the same temperature as *her* breasts. Cool and firm and trembling against his tongue.

NO!

Mica smacked his head against the mirror and felt the rattling vibrations deep inside his ears. *Lord, what are you doing to me? Please . . . take this cup away from me. I'm not as strong as You think I am*.

ARE YOU NOT?

He stood up, throwing back his shoulders and nod-

GET UP TO
4 FREE BOOKS!

You can have the best fiction delivered to your door for less than what you'd pay in a bookstore or online—only $4.25 a book! Sign up for our book clubs today, and we'll send you **FREE* BOOKS** just for trying it out...**with no obligation to buy, ever!**

LEISURE HORROR BOOK CLUB

With more award-winning horror authors than any other publisher, it's easy to see why CNN.com says "Leisure Books has been leading the way in paperback horror novels." Your shipments will include authors such as RICHARD LAYMON, DOUGLAS CLEGG, JACK KETCHUM, MARY ANN MITCHELL, and many more.

LEISURE THRILLER BOOK CLUB

If you love fast-paced page-turners, you won't want to miss any of the books in Leisure's thriller line. Filled with gripping tension and edge-of-your-seat excitement, these titles feature everything from psychological suspense to legal thrillers to police procedurals and more!

As a book club member you also receive the following special benefits:

- **30% OFF all orders through our website & telecenter!**
- **Exclusive access to special discounts!**
- **Convenient home delivery and 10 days to return any books you don't want to keep.**

There is no minimum number of books to buy, and you may cancel membership at any time. See back to sign up!

*Please include $2.00 for shipping and handling.

YES! ☐

Sign me up for the Leisure Horror Book Club and send my TWO FREE BOOKS! If I choose to stay in the club, I will pay only $8.50* each month, a savings of $5.48!

YES! ☐

Sign me up for the Leisure Thriller Book Club and send my TWO FREE BOOKS! If I choose to stay in the club, I will pay only $8.50* each month, a savings of $5.48!

NAME: _____

ADDRESS: _____

_____

TELEPHONE: _____

E-MAIL: _____

☐ **I WANT TO PAY BY CREDIT CARD.**

☐ VISA   ☐ MasterCard   ☐ DISCOVER

ACCOUNT #: _____

EXPIRATION DATE: _____

SIGNATURE: _____

Send this card along with $2.00 shipping & handling for each club you wish to join, to:

**Horror/Thriller Book Clubs
20 Academy Street
Norwalk, CT 06850-4032**

Or fax (must include credit card information!) to: 610.995.9274.
You can also sign up online at www.dorchesterpub.com.

*Plus $2.00 for shipping. Offer open to residents of the U.S. and Canada only.
Canadian residents please call 1.800.481.9191 for pricing information.
If under 18, a parent or guardian must sign. Terms, prices and conditions subject to change. Subscription subject
to acceptance. Dorchester Publishing reserves the right to reject any order or cancel any subscription.

JOIN NOW!

ding. *Yes, Lord, I am. Mica is my name and like mica I shall resist the flames of temptation. With Your Love and Understanding I shall prevail.*

I shall face my enemies and embrace them in the true meaning of the Spirit.

Sure you will, his reflection said, just remember to let go afterwards.

His sigh fogged the mirror—obliterating the pathetic-looking man that stared back at him.

Taking a deep breath, Mica turned and walked the half-dozen steps back to his unmade, fold-out couch and collapsed onto it. A whole new set of rattles shook the tiny trailer. Mica ignored them the same way he ignored the damp briefs cutting into his crotch. He hadn't dried well enough after the last shower.

Mrs. B had fussed around him like a mother hen the second time he'd asked if he could use the shower. The third time she offered to call the doctor. The fourth she simply handed him a new towel and smiled, saying something about how her late husband, Frankie, had been the same way when they were first "stepping out."

After that, Mica had washed off (cooled down) in the sink.

But still felt dirty.

The clock on the VCR read 5:56, which meant he still had plenty of time to grab dinner, re-read a few selective passages, throw on some clothes, run off another hundred pamphlets and go out to save a few souls or slit his wrists before it was time to be at the club.

To face her.

To apologize.

Again.

Wrong.

Mica threw one arm over his eyes, trying to block out the stuffy yellow glow that filled the trailer. He kept confusing Allison with Piper and that had to stop. It wasn't fair to either of them.

It wasn't fair to *him*.

He lifted his arm just enough to see the red blinking numbers above the television. 5:58—Nothing on but sitcoms, news and kiddie shows. He didn't feel worthy enough to put on one of the televised Evangelical programs recorded days, weeks . . . *months* earlier.

What he needed was someone who'd trod the same ground and would listen without passing judgement.

He needed Gypsy. The big man might rant and carry on for a time about being woken "so goddamned *early*," but Mica knew he'd calm down once he heard what the problem was.

Sometimes sinners could be just as understanding as *real* people.

"Sorry, Lord," Mica said, sliding his arm back over his forehead and gazing up at the water-damaged ceiling, "but You're just too perfect to be dragged into this. And it was written that You help those who help themselves, so I know You'll understand."

Turning onto his side, Mica grabbed the cordless phone off the orange crate end table/nightstand and punched in Gypsy's home number.

And listened to it ring.

And ring.

And ring . . . ring . . . ring . . . ring . . .

He watched the blood red numbers turn to 6:04 as the phone kept ringing in his ear. Where the hell *was* Gypsy?

"Come on, man," Mica whispered between rings, "pick up the phone. I need to talk to you."

He took a deep breath and felt his fingers tighten their hold. Gypsy should be home. One of his hard and fast rules, unless there was booze or women involved, was to always get at *least* twelve hours of sleep a day.

. . . unless there were women . . .

A mental snapshot of Gypsy helping Allison slip into one of the slinky, form-fitting costumes twisted Mica's belly into a hard knot.

No. Not him. Not Gypsy.

The phone rang another three times before Mica could get the picture out of his head.

Then where the hell *was* he?

Where the hell *was* he?

Allison tightened her grip on the flame-red dressing gown and batted at the smokey air that drifted into the backstage wings. Her new incarnation might have given her perfect predatory night vision but it still didn't allow her to see through walls or around corners . . .

. . . or where ever the *hell* Gypsy was hiding when he was supposed to be standing right there next to her, offering immoral support and an open vein. Just like Luci had promised.

185

But Seth had made promises, too.

"None of this is working the way it's supposed to," Allison muttered as she tugged back a corner of the stage drape and watched Gina—this time a smokey black otter—slither across the stage on her belly.

Allison couldn't remember if real otters had fangs or not, but *this* one did and none of the clamoring Furverts seemed to notice.

Or care.

"Shit."

She let the curtain fall back into place when her stomach grumbled. Where the hell was that stupid breathing Watcher, anyway?

Gypsy!

"Yeah, I know," he said, stumbling out of the shadows behind her, "I'm late. Sorry. I just couldn't seem to wake up. You won't tell Luci will you?"

He didn't look so much worried as he did terrified—and it would have been a pitiful sight if she hadn't been so hungry.

"Left wrist," Allison said . . . *commanded* as she held out her own hand. "Now."

The big man instantly unbuckled the studded leather wrist band and held his arm out to her. Smiling. Like he was handing her a beer.

"There you go, ma'am . . . on the house."

The blind obedience part she could get used to.

On an impulse, Allison let the robe slide down off one shoulder. It produced the desired effect. She could see the veins in Gypsy's wrist swell . . . and could care less if any other portion of his anatomy was similarly inclined.

It was the first time that Allison could remember being so totally and completely in charge.

Power. Total and absolute.

It was another thing she could get used to.

Gypsy's entire body quivered as her fangs punctured the soft scabs on the feeding holes from the night before.

The first rush of blood splattering against her tonsils made her light-headed. The second swallow turned her hunger into a raging need. She could drain the man in less time than it would take to drain a beer . . . and he wouldn't have noticed.

Or cared.

Just like the other Breathers watching Gina strut her stuff as a saber-toothed otter.

Allison forced herself to stop after three—her usual limit back when Tequila had been her drug of choice—and licked the swollen flesh clean with the care of a child cleaning out a bowl of cookie batter.

Not that she could really remember what cookies tasted like.

Closing the robe over her naked breasts, Allison straightened up and tugged the man's beard gently.

"Thanks, Gypsy," she said softly, "it was great."

"Wrong attitude, Alley-cat." Luci stood near the dressing rooms, "dressed" in a silver-white snow leopard pelt and matching rhinestone collar. "Didn't your mother ever tell you not to play with your food?"

"Luci!"

"Gypsy," Luci said as she walked toward them, "tell Alley-cat what you are."

"I am food," he answered. Immediately. Mechanically.

"See," Luci said, taking Gypsy's hand and turning it over. And frowning, the silky whiskers bristling. "Sloppy, Alley-cat . . . really, *really* sloppy. Didn't your Maker even tell you this much?"

When Allison didn't answer, Luci shook her head.

"We *do* have an image to maintain, you know," she said. "One thrust in to pop the cherry and then just let it flow. You don't have to *gnaw* out a whole new excavation every time you eat . . . especially on a Watcher who still has to be able to toss drunks. Watch and *learn*."

Luci's fangs curled downward as she lowered her head over the swollen flesh. Gypsy's sigh was lost in the thundering applause coming from the direction of the stage.

"I didn't *gnaw*," Allison mumbled as Luci fed.

I'm not going to argue with you in front of a Watcher— it's bad for morale. Besides you don't have the time.

"What do you mean?"

Luci lifted her head—blood glistening on her lips and staining the curved incisors—and blinked.

"What do you mean what do I mean? In case you hadn't noticed, Gina's number just finished. This is it, kid, your big break into show business."

"You know, I'm still not real sure about all this," Allison said. "I mean, I never even learned to dance *normally*. Maybe I should just watch tonight."

188

Wishful thinking.

"Tol' you she'd be more trouble than she was worth. I still say we should cut 'er loose 'fore she gets us all staked."

Gina walked into the light that spilled through the opening in the curtains, collarless, dark fur shining— glaring daggers at everyone backstage. Allison in particular.

Luci coming in a close second.

"Chill out, Gina," Luci said as she tossed Gypsy's hand and threw an arm around Allison's shoulder. "Alley-cat's one of *us*. Understand?"

A low growl, more suitable to a lion than an otter, was the only answer Luci got as Gina stormed past.

"Oh, don't let that old bitch scare you, baby," Luci said, running a finger slowly along the front opening of Allison's robe. "Her bark's a *lot* worse than her bite . . . unless you're a Breather.

"Now come on, sweet-cakes, it's time to get *dressed*."

Allison pictured a long haired tabby with a fluffy tail and big pink bow—the same picture she'd seen in the Preacher-boy's mind—and felt the robe lengthen, molding itself to her as the color and texture shifted into soft orange fur.

With bands the color of *autumn leaves shining in the sun*.

Damn him.

"Very nice, Alley-cat," Luci said, kissing her coppery-pink nose pad. "You'll have those fur lovers pussy-whipped for sure. Do us proud and try to aim your collar at one of the bigger 'verts. Those thin guys aren't worth the trouble."

Allison let herself be turned toward the stage and even patted on the butt just above the tail.

Don't let us down, Alley-cat. I'd just HATE it if Gina was right about you.

Allison didn't fail to hear the threat as she parted the curtain.

But she *did* miss seeing Mica standing in the shadows near the stage door as she stepped into the spotlight.

Watching.

NINETEEN

Lord

He'd seen them.

Dear Lord, save and protect Your servant.

He'd REALLY seen them.

Vampires.

Mica leaned back against the mottled gray-and-black wallpaper and pressed his hand over his mouth. Allison and Luci . . . vampires . . . feeding off Gypsy like he was some kind of giant walking Slurpee.

"God!"

"Man, you got *that* right, pard."

The back of Mica's skull cracked into the wall as he jerked toward the voice. But the beer-drinking Furvert wasn't paying attention to him anymore. The man's eyes, as well as every other eye in the SRO crowd was riveted on the stage where a slinky, woman-sized tabby cat slashed the air with her tail.

Allison.

Mica's heart kept pace with the heavy metal beat as he looked around. Somehow he'd managed to find his way back into the club's lounge. He couldn't remember leaving the backstage area . . . couldn't remember much except the way the blood had glistened on Luci's fangs and how Allison had *transformed* herself into the abomination that was currently bumping and grinding up on stage.

Vampires.

Feeling the bile cauterize his lungs while he swallowed, Mica grabbed the beer-drinking Furvert standing in front of him and spun him around.

"Hey, man . . ."

Mica sank his fingers into the man's shirt front and yanked him close.

"They're vampires."

The man shrugged and pointed to his ears. The music was so loud. *Damn them, Lord! DAMN THEM!*

Mica closed the gap between them and shouted directly into the man's ear.

"I. Said. They. Are. *Vampires!* They'll suck you dry!"

The 'vert's eyes gleamed when he stepped back.

"Shit—you *think* so?"

Mica was about to request another damnation when he *felt* someone staring at him.

And turned.

Gypsy was about twenty feet away—the only man besides himself who wasn't watching the stage. The dark eyes that had always radiated warmth and kindness looked as hard and cold as cut glass.

And as dead.

When he smiled the hardness slid down from his eyes until it masked his entire face.

"Oh, sweet Jesus, Gyp."

As if he could hear the whisper over the gut-numbing blare, Gypsy lifted two fingers to the brim of his cap and winked back at Mica. There was a wide black band digging into the flesh on Gypsy's wrist that Mica had never seen before . . .

. . . *where they bit him! Dear Lord, where they FED on him.*

Luci and Allison.

Vampires.

He had to get out.

The crowd of Furverts growled and shouted physical impossibilities as Mica clawed his way to the door. The full impact of what was going on waited until he stumbled in front of Luci's poster, shivering uncontrollably.

When Mica stood up, the emerald green cardboard eyes followed him. Laughed at him.

"Suffer not a witch to live," Mica whispered at the haughty face staring back at him. "Lord . . . I *understand* why You brought me to this place now. Like Your only begotten Son, Jesus, destroyed the temple in John: 3.19 . . . I was sent here to destroy this bastion of evil. Praise be Your name!"

Mica stepped past the yellow line on the sidewalk in front of the club and looked up into the smoggy night sky.

"I have preached Your Words as a child preaches, safe and secure and protected from danger by Your True Love. But I'm ready, Lord. I'm ready to fight this face to face . . . hand to hand . . ."

. . . fang and claw . . .

Mica licked his lips and nodded. Accepting.

"Whatever you say, Lord."

"Yeh, thought I'd find you out here, Preacher-boy," Gypsy said as he stepped out from around Luci's cut-out. "Talking to the Big G again, huh?"

Mica looked down and edged toward the street—shrugged . . . tried to look relaxed even though his belly was doing back flips beneath his peace sign belt buckle.

"Yeah," he said, "just like *E.T.* . . . always calling home."

Gypsy's chuckle sounded as phoney as a sit com's laugh track.

"Don't feel like working tonight?" he asked, nodding to the demarcation line.

"No," Mica said quickly. Although he was ready to fight the Creatures of Darkness and his ex-friend *right now,* a little prudent research on the matter couldn't hurt. "I'm not feeling too well. In fact, I thought I'd go home before I . . . infected anybody."

"I really don't think you have to worry about these gals," Gypsy said, taking a step toward him. "They're unbelievably sturdy."

A police car came and went so quickly—all sirens and flashing lights—that Mica didn't even have a chance to see it swerve around the corner. *Not that I need their help, Lord. WE can handle this.*

"Yeah, well," he said, sidestepping into the pedestrian flow, "tell Luci she can dock me a night's pay if she wants to. I think I'll just head on back to the barn,"—*sprinkle a little garlic salt around*—"take a couple of Rolaids,"—*paint crosses on the door and windows*—"pop an ol' vid into the VCR,"—*sharpen some stakes*—"and say my prayers."

And say my prayers!

"Shit, sounds just like my old man's idea of a *fun* evening." Gypsy took another step. His smile was so cold it sent shivers down Mica's back. "Why don't you come back in. You barely got a chance to see Allison. She's really hot for you, you know. Luci told me."

Allison.

A cramp sucker-punched Mica's colon and he doubled over.

"I can't, Gyp," he moaned. "I really don't feel—"

Mica looked up to discover he was talking to Luci's poster and nothing else. Gypsy had gone back into the club . . . gone back to *them.*

Pressing his elbows into his twitching belly, Mica took off running—ignoring the looks and snide comments he was getting.

There was so little time . . . so little time to fill the hole he'd left in his soul when he walked out on Piper.

Yes, Lord, WALKED OUT . . . but it's okay now . . . because I can fix it . . . I can make up for the evil I did her by destroying REAL evil in her name's sake and Your's and
    Allison's.

TWENTY

Allison closed her eyes and let the images conjured from Alice Cooper's *Trash* take control of her body. It was almost like being back at a slumber party—shocking, then *impressing* the other girls with the latest "go-go-girl" moves.

It had been fun back then.

But it was *more* fun now.

Allison opened one eye and smiled. And fed the howling mob a quick series of pelvic thrusts.

And the fans go wild!

She could feel the rising heat from their collective blood pressures lap across the runway like a warm sea. They wanted her . . . they *all* wanted her. So what else was new?

Seth had wanted her, too—as a self-serve refueling

stop on the eternal damnation highway. Breathing or dead, men were still only interested in the package.

What did you expect, Alley-cat? Luci's disembodied voice whispered to her over the throaty shouts.

Power.

Careful, thinking like that is the surest way to get a pointed stick up the old aorta.

I'm not afraid of THEM, Allison thought back as she did three slow pirouettes *(if mama could see me now),* ending in a split that brought the crowd to its feet. *What the hell could they do? Really?*

You've got a lot to learn, Alley-cat. A whole HELL of a lot.

Breaking the contact as easily as hanging up a phone *(I'm learning enough, thanks),* Allison lay back against the stage and arched her spine, until she'd gotten enough curve to toss her legs up over her head. Landing on her toes, she grabbed her tail and flicked it in the face of a well tanned twenty-something guy in a Long Beach University T-shirt. College man—majoring in surfing and pussy.

Well, *she* was the pussy tonight.

Squatting, Allison gave the kid a quick glimpse at the flesh beneath the fur before flicking her tail back over what her mother had called "no man's land." Standing, she moved slowly, running long-nailed fingers up over her belly and breasts until they came to the pink bow at her throat.

Mica's face settled over Joe College's.

Damn him.

She chose the tabby "costume" to get back at the

Preacher-boy for that afternoon (sanctimonious bastard)—to give him an unhealthy dose of reality and then sit back and watch him squirm.

revenge

And he'd been there . . . at the club . . . somewhere. Allison was sure of that. Her stomach did back flips just like the ones she'd had at the cemetery. Right before she went on. And she knew it wasn't because of butterflies.

Mica *had* been there. But he wasn't there now and for some reason *that* bothered her.

"Aw, c'mon, honey! Give it to me!"

Allison looked down at the college student—violet eyes, black hair, billboard smile, clipped moustache, and muscles large enough to make their impression on the shirt—and stifled a yawn. She slowly untied the bow around her throat.

Go for it, girlfriend, Luci's voice whispered to her. *This one looks like there'd be enough for leftovers.*

Stomach grumbling while Alice Cooper's chuckle ended the song, Allison leaned forward and dangled the end of the ribbon just beyond Mr. Long Beach's reach. An updated version of the old Cat-and-Mouse game that had the mouse d'jour elbowing other rodents out of the way.

I knew you were a natural exhibitionist the moment the Preacher-boy hauled your ass in here.

Allison dropped the ribbon without actually seeing which of the combatants had grabbed it. It really didn't matter—O, A, or B . . . it tasted the same.

Only the memories were different.

Only the lives were different.

But she'd go on and on and . . .

When she got to the curtain, Allison turned and glanced over her shoulder. Joe College waved the bedraggled looking ribbon over his head like a banner. He must have ripped it out of another man's hand—there was a blood smear down along one side.

Whimpering at the stain, Allison ran her tongue slowly over the bristly fur touching her lips. She could already taste the Preacher-boy's blood.

NO! Not the Preacher-boy . . . the college-boy . . . what the hell am I saying?

The crowd was still cheering, congratulating the *COL-LEGE-BOY* on his quick hand-eye coordination, as she ducked through the curtain.

If Allison's heart had still been capable of movement it would have torn its way out of her chest.

TWENTY-ONE

Allison ran her hand along the tabby-striped fur on her arm and watched Miriam direct her "date" and the two other men to the dressing room.

"Just let the girls slip into something more appropriate," she said, nodding . . . shooing them forward like children.

Or chickens.

And she always *loved* chicken.

By the time the door closed on the evening's entrees, Allison had already traded her fur for a jade-green silk, cinched-waist wrap dress—the kind that was always put on the "wishful thinking" list every time she got paid.

Gina and Luci were already waiting inside. Allison heard their piercing giggles followed by testosterone grunts and felt her mouth water to the point of over-flowing.

"Be seein' ya, Miriam," Allison said as she headed for the door . . . only to have Miriam's pudgy little fingers take hold of her wrist and yank her to a stop.

"No, this time we *talk* first . . . knosh later. Come on."

Allison didn't have much choice as Miriam dragged her back down the hall toward the office. The whole thing reminded her of the *countless* times her mother would drag her downstairs to "perform" for guests when she wanted to be somewhere else.

Anywhere else.

Just like now.

Allison dug the four-inch heels of her snake-skin pumps into the thin carpet and shuffled into the room.

"Oh . . . so now she's mad at *me*, like I did something so terrible."

Muttering out loud, Miriam walked to the chair facing the massive oak desk . . . and picked up what had to be the *ugliest*, flea-bitten cat this side of Santa Monica.

Not even the world's loneliest Furvert would find it appealing.

"Shit, Miriam," Allison said as the tiny woman pressed her face into the bald patches along its spine, "how can you stand touching that? It's so . . ."

"So *what*, Miss-Now-That-I'm-Dead-I-Know-It-All?" Miriam tossed her head and settled herself *and* the cat onto the desk's executive booster chair.

Allison could hear the animal's thin purr. It even *sounded* ugly.

"Besides," Miriam added, "old ladies are supposed to keep cats and since I'm an old lady I keep a cat. It's part of the picture. And in case you forgot, missy, we're in the illusion business here. Play your part and everything will be hunky-dory."

Hunky-dory? "Yeah, right, thanks, Miriam, I'll remember, now I should really be—" Another series of giggles crept through the open door, curling around Allison's legs like her very own personal, ugly cat. "—going now, but thanks for the reminder, I'll—"

"Sit down right now, if you know what's good for you, Miss Impatient-pants." Miriam hooked the animal over one shoulder and began kneading her fingers through its thin fur. "Luci just wanted me to tell you that there might be a little trouble with the Preacher-boy. Nothing to worry about . . . just keep your eyes open. Okay, that's it, you can go to dinner now."

"Wait a minute," Allison said as she walked to the chair the cat had been sprawled in, "what kind of trouble?"

Miriam planted a prune-lipped kiss on top of the cat's head as she lowered it to her lap.

"Like I'm suppose to know what kind of trouble? You think I can read the Preacher-boy's mind like he was a regular Breather?"

"You mean you *can't?*"

"Oh, now she thinks I have powers far and beyond what I should." This time Miriam spoke directly to the animal. When she looked up, the wrinkles around her eyes and mouth had deepened into gullies. "Why? *You* can read him?"

"No," Allison said quickly. "No, I can't. I'm just worried."

"Like we should—so don't." Shrugging, Miriam lifted

her hand and popped something into her mouth. "Gypsy said he thought something might have happened . . . but, who knows from Breathers? The Preacher-boy could have constipation. Anything's possible."

Her hand moved to her mouth again.

"Luci's taking care of it, so, like I said . . . don't worry. Just be aware."

Miriam winked and sucked a tiny, black spot off her fingertip. The flea was quickly followed by another. It's body made a tiny popcorn sound when Miriam crushed it between her molars.

Allison gulped. Thoughts of filling the gnawing emptiness in her belly with hot, steaming blood took a back seat to the all too human desire to puke. Was *this* what old vampires did for fun?

"Miriam? What the *hell* are you doing?"

The next flea stopped just short of her lips.

"What? You mean *these?*" Miriam tossed it into her mouth and swallowed. "It's a bad habit I got back in the old country. I know . . . it's like eating too many barley-sugar drops but. . . ."

Miriam jiggled her head from side to side and popped in another flea.

"My Maker was this Cossack general . . . and so handsome it made your heart want to stop beating. Here I am, this old widow living alone and what do I find one night when I go out looking for firewood—this beautiful man half frozen in the snow."

She flipped the cat onto its back and snagged three fleas off it's chin without missing a beat. *pop pop pop*

"I couldn't just leave him to die out there, could I? So I bring him in and lay him out in front of the fire. Ah, so beautiful . . . eyes as blue as river ice, hair like corn silk, skin as white as the snow. And the way he made me feel when he *woke* up . . . hoo, hoo, hoo . . . just like a young girl again.

"Then he left and I had to look for more than firewood. Times were hard enough back then . . . the Great Czar was bleeding the peasants more than *our* kind ever could! And sometimes they were so stiff I almost broke my fangs trying to find a vein.

"You want to know how *hard* it was—don't *ask* how hard it was, *that* was how hard it was. There were no peasants . . . but there were cats. And even when I came to this country—almost a virgin like you—there were *still* cats.

"There still are, may the Humane Society never get its wish to make spaying mandatory."

Lifting the cat under the front legs, Miriam nuzzled its head out of the way and tore open its knobby throat. It took all of a minute before the slurping took on a "straw in an empty bottle" quality.

Allison watched Miriam toss the empty into the wicker wastepaper basket behind the desk and dab at her mouth with a lipstick-stained Kleenex.

"An indulgence," she said, "but, I figure at my age what's the harm of a before dinner snack? Now, go enjoy and don't worry about the Preacher-boy. Like I said, Luci's taking care of it. Go . . . *go*."

So Allison went—rocking slightly side to side as if the room were on a storm-tossed ocean liner.

"Such a good girl we got," her cat-draining sister purred. "You're gonna do just fine."

Right, Allison thought—keeping it to herself, I'll be just fine. Besides, what the hell can the Preacher-boy *do* to us anyway? He's nothing but a hypocritical, sancti- monious—

Mica's thin face appeared in her mind's eye.

And she sneezed.

Violently.

Mica wiped his nose off on the back of his hand then gen- tly polished Jesus's silver-plated belly with the dish towel. He'd bought the crucifix for $5.00 American—a real bargain—the weekend he and Gypsy spent in Tiajuana.

A year ago Christmas.

When Devils and Demons existed only in the pages of his Bible and Gypsy had still been within reach of redemption.

And the living was easy.

Outside, the metal garbage can next to Mrs. B's back door hit the asphalt drive and rolled. Mica wouldn't have given it a second's thought if the night had been windy.

But it wasn't.

They were out there. Mica knew that as certainly as he knew the Lord was watching over him.

Use BOTH eyes tonight, Lord, okay?

Mica tightened his grip on the crucifix and did an ab- breviated version of the Twenty-third Psalm.

"The Lord is my Shepherd and I will fear no evil.

Amen." Taking a deep breath, he traced the death agony cast into Jesus' face and nodded. "*He* knew what He had to do to Save mankind . . . and so do I, Lord. I really do."

When the garbage can smacked against the side fence, Mica jumped and pressed the crucifix into his belly. Things like this weren't suppose to happen. Not in *real* life.

Once the blood stopped pounding in his ears, he heard the slow rhythmic shuffle of feet heading toward the trailer.

They were coming.

Mica stood up and faced the poster-paint cross he'd hastily drawn *(Why the hell did I use RED?)* on the trailer's only door the moment he got home—pressed Jesus' visage into his skin hard enough to leave a negative impression, and squared his shoulders.

The scar on his forehead tingled like it was on fire.
Ready, Lord.

But he still almost peed himself when the knock came.
"Mica, dear? Are you there?"

Mrs. B! Thank GOD! "Yes ma'am . . . yes, I'm here!"

The busted door latch rattled but didn't open.

"Oh, good. Can I come in?"

"Sur—"

Mica's hand stopped a half-inch away from the knob. In the eight years he'd lived there, Mica had never seen the old woman up past nine o'clock unless he accidentally woke her coming home . . . or on New Year's Eve, when she allowed him to drag her up to Hollywood Boulevard to toot horns.

Yet here it was—Mica glanced over at the VCR—2:48 in the morning and she sounded wide awake and full of vinegar.

The knock was a little louder . . . a little more demanding this time.

"Mica, dear," Mrs. B said through the door, "aren't you going to invite me in?"

invite me in

Mica backed away from the door until his butt ran into the opposite wall. He'd squirmed through enough B-grade horror movies to know a vampire had to be *invited* into a person's home.

The first time.

Whoever . . . *what*ever it was knocking on his door, it wasn't Mrs. B.

"Dear? Hello?" *knock knock knock* "Are you all right?"

Mica turned the crucifix around until Jesus faced the door and held it out at arm's length.

"I'm fine, Mrs. B. I was . . . asleep. I really don't feel very well right now."

"Oh, you poor thing. Let me in and I'll brew you a nice cup of tea."

Liar!

Mica raised the crucifix until it overlapped the painted cross on the door.

"You can't come in," he whispered, "I refuse you entry to this place. Begone unclean spirit and trouble the Lord's servant no more."

Mica heard what sounded like the rushing wind sweep over the trailer, rocking the worn stabilizers from side to side . . . then heard nothing else. Still holding the crucifix out in front of him, Mica pressed both it and his ear up against the door.

Nothing . . . no sound.

He couldn't even hear the traffic out on Cherokee. It was as if the trailer had been wrapped in cotton batting.

"Mrs. B? Are you still out there?"

A perfect imitation of the old woman's off-key twitter filtered through the thin door and sent an icy shiver racing down his spine.

"Well, of *course* I'm still here, dear. Where would I go?"

"To hell," Mica answered. "You can go back to hell."

"I'm originally from Jersey," the voice corrected. "I told you that."

Mica closed his eyes, squeezing out the inappropriate tears and twisted his face into the still damp paint. *Lord . . . protect Your servant in his hour of need.* The scar-cross sizzled.

"*YOU* didn't tell me anything!" he shouted. "Get the fuck out of here you soulless blood-sucking demon! In the Name of the Father! And the Son! And the Holy Spirit I *command* you!"

He could hear gentle applause coming from the other side.

"Very impressive, dear." It *was* Mrs. B's voice . . . the same voice that had offered him lemonade on hot days and hot cocoa with marshmallows on cold ones and croaked out a honky-tonk version of *Happy Birthday* for him each November. "Now why don't you stop acting like God's personal ass-wiper and let me the fuck in?"

It was Mrs. B's voice—only the spirit inside had changed.

Something hit the door with the force of a jack-hammer, hurling Mica back across the room. Wisps of smoke rose from the wood surrounding the painted cross, sending the smoke detector on the ceiling into a shrieking fit.

"Make haste, O God, to deliver me—" Mica shouted over the alarm . . . over the frenzied pounding . . .

. . . over the sound of claws shredding laminated wood.

The crucifix felt like a steel bar in his hands.

"—make haste to *help* me, O Lord. Let them be *ashamed* and *confounded,* that seek after my soul! Let them be turned backward and put to confusion, that desire to do evil to me!"

The pounding stopped so abruptly that if it hadn't been for the smoke alarm Mica would have thought he'd gone deaf.

Taking a deep breath, Mica licked the running sweat off his lips and let the weight of the cross drag him to his knees.

"I am Yours, Lord . . ." He took another breath and raised his head, preparing himself for what might happen next. "Mrs. B? Are you still out there?"

When nothing answered him, Mica got to his feet with all the grace of a newborn foal and flat-handed the alarm into silence. Blessed silence thumped almost painfully against his eardrums. He didn't even notice the crucifix slipping from his fingers until it thumped against the carpet.

"Thank you, Lord," he whispered. "Praise and Glory to the Father and the Son and the Holy Spirit."

"And let's not forget the Avon Lady, Preacher-boy. Glory don't mean diddly if you're uglier'n sin."

"Gy-Gypsy?"

"None other." This time the knock at the door was accompanied by the sound of bottles clinking together. "You got me worried when you split tonight, so I thought I'd come over and see how you were feeling." The bottles rattled again. "Even brought some medicine. The *malted* kind."

Mica looked down at the crucifix laying at his feet and shook his head . . . remembering the way Luci and Allison had fed off him.

"Oh shit, Gyp."

"Nope, just Coors . . . but I could try and score some shit if you think you're up to it." The low chuckle that followed was so familiar it tore Mica's soul in two.

Gypsy.

"That's the name, Preacher-boy," he answered as if Mica had said the name out loud, "don't wear it out. C'mon, man, the night's taking the chill off the medication. Open the door and we'll toss back a few too many."

"Get out of here . . . Gypsy. For the love of *God*, leave me alone!"

"No can do, Preacher-boy." Mica heard the bottles rattle as they were set down on the wooden stoop outside the door. "We really got to talk . . . just like old times, man. Come on. Open up."

Open up . . . just what Mrs. B had tried to get him to do. Ice formed along the sweat stains in his T-shirt.

"What'd you do to Mrs. B?"

"You mean the old bag in the house? Luci had a real nice talk with her a while back . . . why, she been bothering you?" He chuckled again—and the hinges shook like castanets. "You want me to go punch her out? Oops, that's right . . . I can't harm the hand that bites me. Sorry, pard."

"Bastard!" Scooping up the crucifix, Mica slammed it into the door right where he pictured Gypsy's head to be. "You've let them seduce you! You made the *wrong* choice, Gypsy, and you're gonna burn in Hell's everlasting fire!"

"Promises, promises."

"Begone, foul creature," Mica croaked around the spiked lump that had suddenly formed at the back of his throat, "this is consecrated ground . . . you have no power here. Praise His Name."

"You sound tired, man," the creature with Gypsy's voice said, "you sure you don't want to talk? *I* can't do anything to you. Scout's honor, Preacher-boy."

It was all so ludicrous—Mrs. B spouting off like an octogenarian sailor . . . his best friend damned for all eternity by choice and talking like there was still hope. *Lord, pardon my French, but You gotta be shittin' me.*

Mica turned his back to the door and rode it down.

"Go away. *Please.*"

"You got it, pard . . . this time. But just remember, *we* got time on our side. Be seein' ya."

Mica pressed his forehead against his raised knees—and listened to the sound of Gypsy's motorcycle boots as he walked away.

Mica wiped his nose off on the faded jeans and took a deep breath.

"Goddamn you, Gypsy," he whispered.

"Not if you don't believe, Preacher-boy," Gypsy shouted back, his voice getting more and more indistinct—echoing slightly when he hit the drive. "And I only believe in things I can touch or drink . . . or *feed,* man. Only that and *nothing* more."

Mica stayed hunched over his knees for another ten minutes, trying to control both his heart rate and un-questioning faith. When neither seemed to be cooper-ating, he threw the crucifix into a pile of dirty socks next to the sink and jerked his face toward the ceiling.

To what lay *beyond* the ceiling.

"No *offense,* Lord . . . but what the fuck do You want me to do?"

The need to destroy *something* was too great—and he gave into it. Grunting wordlessly, Mica kicked out at the rickety plant stand Mrs. B had given to him as a "trailer-warming" gift . . . and in its destruction was given his answer.

The four legs—one inch wide, three feet long—lay perfect and unbroken amid the shattered base and pot-tery shards. As sure a Sign as if the Lord had suddenly appeared as a burning bush in the middle of the room.

Getting to his knees, Mica carefully picked up the ta-pered lengths of wood. They felt warm and alive in his hand. All he had to do was cut them in half and whittle them into stakes . . . just like in the movies. Then he'd go after each and every one of them:

Gypsy.

Gina.

Miriam.

Lucy.

Mrs. B.

Allison.

Oh God.

"Lord," he prayed, clasping the wood to his chest, "I am Mica . . . make me as hard as you made Peter when You cast him as the Rock on which to build Your Church. Harden my heart against these creatures, make my blood as ice, strengthen my arm so that I might fashion these to aim straight and true.

"And destroy the memories in me, Lord, that I may destroy Thy enemies."

amen

Nodding, Mica walked on his knees to the sink and fumbled through the cold scummy "soaking" water for the only decent (i.e., sharp) knife he had. The small paring knife looked remarkably unimpressive when he finally fished it out—and the soggy, brown carrot curl probably didn't help the effect—but he reminded himself that Jesus had fed the multitude with nothing more than an almost empty basket and a whole lot of Faith.

"Ready, when You are, Lord," Mica said as he carried it and the legs to the bed.

ready

"Then let's go."

Mica took one leg and cracked it against the bed's metal frame. It broke in two effortlessly—*another Sign*. Setting them aside, Mica picked up another leg and glanced quickly over at the VCR.

It was already 3:25 in the morning . . . that gave him less than three hours to prepare for his own Holy Crusade.

Mica ran a finger over the pale wood and thought about the woman who gave it to him. Mrs. B would be the first . . . he owed her that much for all the kindness she had shown him.

Besides, she was the closest—less than thirty feet from where he was now sitting—and if things *didn't* work out like he expected

(signs or no signs) he could always book it up Highland to the Hollywood Freeway and head north . . . or south . . . or . . .

"You made me Mica, Lord," he said as he broke another leg in half, "but You didn't make no fool."

Amen.

TWENTY-TWO

"You were fantastic," Allison's dinner . . . *date* purred. "Think I could see you again sometime?"

Allison glanced over his still bare shoulders and saw Luci shake *her* head as she drove her own date toward the door.

Three time's the charm, remember, Alley-cat? And that IS just like the movies. And there's no need unless you want to be a Maker. Think of Breathers like walking fast-food joints . . . you don't want to keeping going back to the same one, do you?

Allison heard Luci's sigh brush past her inner ear.

So many veins—so MUCH time.

Nodding, Allison batted her lashes and tossed the man—*what did he say his name was?*—his shirt.

"Never can tell," she purred, smoothing down the wrinkled hem of her dress. Allison had discovered, purely by accident, that if she just laid there and let him hump her like the Energizer Bunny, she could feed without having to apply suction.

It wasn't much different from other dates she'd had . . . all things considered.

When he yawned and glanced at his watch, Allison got another taste of retro-view. *Wow, look at the time. I gotta—FILL IN THE BLANK—I'll call you.*

"Wow, look at the time. I got a seven o'clock class." He looked up, apologetically. "I'll call you."

I should have torn his throat out while I had the chance.

"I'd like that," Allison said and walked him to the door. It was all she could do to keep her stiletto heel from implanting itself into his ass. "Do. Call me." *Unless you accidentally get run over by a bus or something.*

She wouldn't have even noticed the quick kiss he planted on her if it hadn't been for the fact that he lifted his hand to brush back her hair. The warm, inviting scent was still seeping from the inflamed wounds on the inside of his wrist.

Allison nuzzled his hand—running the tip of her tongue over the puncture marks. Groaning, he sank his fingers into her hair and pulled her close.

"Do me again," he moaned, "please."

Allison licked off the gummy scabs and shot a glance toward Luci. She was on the other side of the room, sprawled across the daybed with Gina. Both of them were giggling like schoolgirls.

"Please."

Allison looked up at the hunger in the man's eyes and felt it echoed in her belly. *Why the hell not?*

Lips curling away from her fangs, Allison held him steady and—

—found herself sucking air.

"Hey!"

"Hey, *yourself,* Alley-cat."

Luci had the college jock by the shirt collar, dangling him two inches off the ground. He looked as stupid as Allison felt.

"Tol' you she wouldn't do," Gina said, glaring at her from across the room. "I still say we'd be better off dumpin' her lily-white ass in the nearest salt pit."

"Can it, Gina," Luci growled, then shook the man like he was nothing more than a rag doll. "Look, Alley-cat, you keep pulling stunts like this and I'll leave you high and dry. These things"—She shook him until his teeth rattled—"are strictly sustenance feeders. *One* bite. One time. Understand *now?*"

Allison nodded and looked down, scuffing the toe of her shoe across the linoleum.

"Yes 'um."

"Good." Satisfied, Luci set the CSULB-BMOC back on his feet and patted him gently on the cheek. "I'm *so* glad you had a good time. Now, you be sure to tell all your furry little friends about us."

Then she slapped him hard enough to spin him around and flat-handed him out the door. Allison watched him go, and suddenly realized why Seth hadn't wanted to associate with his own kind. Become part of a group, and you have to play by their rules.

It was almost as bad as being alive.

Almost.

Allison folded her arms over her chest and walked to the mirrorless dressing tables. A couple more nights of this and she'd think about leaving and striking out on her own. Hell, there were other cities . . . other *states*. Hollywood, California, wasn't paradise.

And if she decided to stick to the "exotic dancer" gimmick she'd do a solo act—answer to no one—follow her *own* goddamn rules for once in her . . .

. . . death.

Allison slumped into one of the chairs, tucked her palm under her chin and watched Gina begin a whole new series of snarls and curses over something Luci was whispering. Now what, she wondered, more fun and games with the Butch Boss?

Turning, Allison stared at the cracked plaster wall behind the mirror frame and fluffed her hair—pretending she could still see the tiny lines that had sent her into a cheesecake binge-and-purge depression.

How long ago had that been? A month ago? A year? The night before she wandered into the Silver Spur where Seth was waiting.

For someone just like her.

Anyone just like her, it wouldn't have mattered.

If she'd been a little less desperate she'd be home right now . . . watching the Late, Late, Early Late Show and forcing down a full gallon of mint-chocolate chip ice-cream.

The slam of the dressing room door snapped her back.

Turning around, Allison saw Luci shaking her head at the still vibrating frame.

"Gina's a little miffed," she said. The white dinner dress reformed into tight jeans and a midriff length, spaghetti-strapped top as Luci opened the door. "So, you full or does a nightcap sound good to you?"

Allison looked down at her wrist—and smiled as the pale watch silhouette disappeared. She *had* to stop thinking like a Breather . . . time didn't *mean* anything anymore. It was just something that happened to the living.

But *still*—

"Isn't it getting a little late," she asked, trying to sound as casual as Luci looked. "Dawn should be coming up soon. Shouldn't it?"

Luci's firm skin went slack as her jaw dropped open. "You can't even do *that?* Shit, Alley-cat, we're creatures of the fucking night . . . can't you *feel* how dark it is out there? Can't you taste how far away the goddamned sunlight is?"

Allison smacked her lips. All she tasted was the college kid's blood . . . with traces of Old Spice. Luci leaned back against the door frame and shook her head.

"Maybe Gina's right about you, Alley-cat," she muttered, then shrugged as if it didn't matter. But it mattered . . . Allison knew *exactly* how much it mattered. "Not to worry, as our dear little Miriam would say, the sun's still a long way off. So, you want to come with me or not? I have this craving for Chinese."

"Sure," Allison said. Quickly. It seemed to please Luci. Somewhat.

"Good, I'll go get the car and meet you out front." Luci pushed away from the door and gave Allison a slow once up and over. "We are the things of desire and lust, Alley-cat . . . so for Christ's sake will you try and *dress* the part, okay? Vampires aren't supposed to look like the farmer's daughter unless they're going after the farmer."

Luci didn't say another word as she spun and walked out of the dressing room, hair billowing out behind her like a silver mist. It was probably just as well, Allison decided. If she asked why a vampire needed a car Luci might have given up all together and called Gina.

"Now wouldn't *that* be fun?" she said out loud. Her voice echoed in the empty room. She didn't like the sound.

Allison stood up and walked slowly to the door—the basic black leggings and matching lace tunic replacing her dress before she'd gone a yard. Black leather slippers dropped her three inches . . . but they felt so *good* after those damned heels. The outfit might not have been what the typical Hollywood vampire would wear to go out for Chinese food . . . but *SHE liked it!*

Adding a blood red Isadora Duncan scarf—complete with fringed tassels—as an afterthought, Allison turned back to the dressing tables and struck a pose.

And a lot of nothing stared back at her.

shit

I've just GOT to get the hang of this!

Allison had never liked coming to Chinatown even during the daylight. Somehow venturing into the heart of L.A.'s own little DMZ just didn't seem like the most prudent thing for a round-eyed, red-haired woman to do.

But that was then . . . this is NOW!

And she pressed her head down against her shoulder and spun in circles before the carved stone lions guarding the entrance to General Lee's restaurant.

God, it was great to be dead!

Nothing was open and no one was wandering around. Except the two of them. And that was fine with Allison. Too many things had happened in too short a time. She needed a little R-and-R time to think and sort things out. To work out what she was going to do next.

Allison kept spinning until she felt the blood in her belly start to churn. Letting the momentum wrap her arms around her, she stopped and giggled—waited for the tickle down deep inside that she remembered from her childhood. When nothing happened, Allison lifted her head and watched Luci across the wide court yard play in the Wishing Grotto.

Wondered if the ghost-pale vampire still felt *anything*.

And hoped not.

Having fun, Alley-cat?

Allison nodded and wiggled her fingers. *Sure am. I always loved this place.*

"And it's even better at night!" Luci shouted as she

223

sloshed through the shallow, multi-layered Oriental tourist trap. Less than a moment later, she'd vaulted the iron security fence and tossed the handful of coins she'd picked up back over her shoulder.

The money made *ping pang think thonk* sounds as they struck the plaster deities overlooking the water.

"Ah," Luci said, clasping her hand against her cheek, "a soothing Chinese lullaby."

"Hah, hah," Allison said, although she really didn't think it was all that funny. "You're all wet, you know."

Luci looked down at her soaking jeans and overacted a shiver.

"I'd better do something," she said, "or I'll catch my death. Again."

The *something* was simply to lose the jeans. Luci's skin was so pale it seemed to shine under the sodium-yellow street lights.

"See anything you like, Alley-cat?"

Allison shrugged instead of answering. It seemed the lesser of two evils—both of which were staring her straight in the eyes when Luci's top went the way of her pants.

"Luci . . . what if a *cop* sees you?"

She reached out and traced Allison's bottom lip with her thumb.

"He'd either come in his Fruit-of-the-Looms or not believe what he was seeing. Breathers are horribly dull for the most part . . . if they can't touch it or taste it, *it* just doesn't exist." Finished with Allison's lips, Luci's thumb made a slow southerly descent down the front of the black lace tunic. "But once they know it's real . . . watch out because *anything's* possible."

But not THIS!

"Why not, Alley-cat?" Luci said, keeping pace as Allison backed up into the paws of one of the stone lions. An ugly smirk curled the left side of her mouth. "You can't tell me that after killing all those men in *cold* blood that *this* makes you squeamish."

The ugliness slowly covered the rest of Luci's carved marble features. Try as she could, Allison knew she hadn't been successful at keeping her thoughts to herself.

"Goddamn it . . . you *do!* You fucking think I'm disgusting. Well, then let me tell you *this,* girlfriend . . . we're more fucking alike than you think. *I'm* just not afraid to be myself."

Luci pinned Allison's arms against the statue so quickly she didn't have time to react, let alone move out of the way.

"Poor little Alley-cat, my ass!" Luci snarled. "Your Maker didn't dump you, sweet-cakes . . . he *escaped.* Gina saw through your act the minute she laid eyes on you—*dammit*—so you can just cut the poor little virgin shit any time now, 'cause we ain't buyin' them eggs no more."

"I'm *not!*"

"The HELL you're not. And the worst thing is that you don't even know *what* you want. C'mer, bitch!"

Luci attacked before Allison knew what was happening—smearing her cold lips against Allison's slack ones while her slug-like tongue poured down Allison's throat.

While Luci's mind force-fed images of women crawling over one another . . . licking, sucking . . . their faces buried deep between the other's open legs.

NO!

I told you to cut the shit, ALLEY-CAT. Luci's fingers sank into Allison's hair like a vice. *Whatever you WERE died when you did, baby, so just let go and start enjoying THIS side. If you don't, you won't have any fun.*

One of Luci's hands left Allison's scalp and dropped to her crotch. Something cold and slimy scurried across the pit of Allison's stomach.

A *real* feeling . . . the first she'd had since Seth had sucked her dry.

Revulsion.

"Just let go, sweet-cheeks," Luci murmured, her hand sliding up toward the leggings' waistband. "You won't *believe* how nice it can be. You've already forfeited your chances at wings and a halo . . . so why not just enjoy what you got?"

"Sure," Allison whispered, wrapping her arms around Luci's back. "Why not?"

She pulled Luci in at the same time she kicked the woman's knee out from under her. Luci's naked ass hit the ground in front of her with a satisfying *smack*.

"You goddamned bitch," Luci growled as she dragged herself to all fours, fangs gleaming, "I'll tear your fucking heart out!"

In the instant before she charged, Allison saw Luci's face and body transform into something so old and wrinkled it seemed impossible that the thing could move as quickly as it did.

But move it did. And fast.

Allison just barely managed to duck to one side as Luci's gnarled talons slashed the tunic.

"Yeah, man . . . a *cat* fight."

Allison spun to the right and *felt* Luci do the same. The "disagreement," though not over by a long shot, would have to be postponed. For a while.

Two Chinese men in their early twenties stepped out of the shadows at the far end of the court. Both were smoking cigarettes and smelled like they'd been swimming in beer. Allison closed her eyes and tried to mentally eavesdrop. All she got was a smattering of words she didn't understand and a sense of ultimate good fortune. If they'd seen Luci nude and . . . *changed,* it hadn't registered.

Just like she said it wouldn't.

"Hmmmm," Luci said out loud—all palsy-walsy as she tossed an arm over Allison's shoulder and began walking her toward the men. She was dressed again. This time in a shimmering silver catsuit. "Looks like our dinner companions have arrived. Smile pretty, Alley-cat . . ."

. . . and I might let you survive another night.

"You boys looking to party?" she asked when they got within striking range.

One of the men, the taller of the two, flicked the cigarette out of his mouth and looked at Allison like she was a slab of half-priced beef.

"You two pros?"

Luci wiggled her hips against Allison's and inched the tunic's front zipper half-way down her breasts.

"Don't we look it?"

The men exchanged glances and knowing nods. Their eyes glinted in the semi-darkness like the switch-blade knives Allison knew were in their pockets.

"How much," the shorter, more pragmatic of the two asked.

"One hundred," Allison said—hoping that by entering the game she could start to defuse the feud she'd stupidly begun with Luci.

There were still too many things she needed to know before she went solo.

"One-fucking-hundred?" the short man growled. "You do something *special* for that, bitch?"

"Honey," Allison said, "you won't know what *hit* you."

Luci forgave her.

TWENTY-THREE

"Strengthen my spirit that I may not fall victim to the temptations of the mind.

"Strengthen my heart that I may not fall victim to the temptations of the flesh.

"Shield my eyes with Sights of Your Glory Everlasting that I may not fall victim to the . . . the . . ."

What? . . . to the memories and million kindnesses Mrs. B had done for him over the years? That didn't seem fair.

Even if he had to destroy her body to save her immortal soul it didn't seem fair to just forget all the good times they shared together—just so he could jam a stake through her heart.

"You don't make it easy, Lord, do You?"

Nope . . . He sure didn't.

Mica took another long swig off the *Stolichnaya* he

kept for medicinal purposes (when he had trouble sleeping) and slumped back against the headboard. He ran his thumb over the sharpened point he'd carved on the makeshift stake—testing it—and took another swallow.

It wasn't fair.

"But then it wasn't fair for Jesus to get nailed to the cross either," he said, tipping the half-empty bottle at the black-velvet portrait of The Son hanging above the refrigerator. "But He saw His duty and did it without question. Just like me, Lord, don't you worry.

"I know I'm weak and a backslider, Lord, I know it and I'm ashamed that You had to see me like that. I *know* I should have gone out there and faced them down . . . faced my enemies the moment they tried to get in. But I was afraid, Lord. Even with Your Love and Glory protecting me."

I was afraid.

The look in Jesus's painted amber eyes hardened to Holy disgust.

"Yes sir," Mica whispered, hugging the stake and bottle to his chest. "I'm sorry . . . I failed. Maybe if I hadn't waited, Mrs. B would still be—"

Stop it, he told himself, *feeling sorry for something is just another way of admitting you screwed up.*

Again.

"Forgive me, Lord?"

And the eyes softened. Forgave him.

Again.

"Thank you, Lord. I am Forgiven." Mica squirmed off

the mattress, scattering wood chips to the floor, and stood up—raised both the bottle and stake toward the picture . . . then thought better of it and tossed the bottle away. "I am Mica, Your servant, Lord, do with me what You will. Into Your Hands I commend my spirit.

"Now let's go kick some vampire ass."

Stumbling to the small window over the sink/range top, Mica used the sharpened point of the stake to lift one corner of the dusty curtain. The early morning sun was sparkling across the rutted black-top like diamonds. Mica ducked down and squinted at the almost-blue sky and nodded.

It was the kind of day Mrs. B loved.

Mrs. B

Gypsy had kept him busy talking while Luci had . . .

Mica's hands tightened on the stake. The undead bitch had corrupted the old woman instead of killing her to taunt him—to lay down a challenge against his Faith.

Good against Evil.

Mica could feel himself smile as he picked up the hammer from the counter. Just finding it, buried beneath the other crap in the "catch all" drawer, had taken him almost an hour—but what good were stakes without something to pound them in with?

It was another of Mrs. B's gifts . . . thin handled, pitted striking surface, chipped left claw and a passionate purple *Hooray for Hollywood* handle.

The smile tipped downward as Mica wrapped his fingers around the plastic grip—and wondered if driving a stake through the old woman's chest would feel the same as pegging a *Jesus Saves* flyer to a wooden telephone pole.

God, he *hoped* so.

"Mrs. B?"

Mica had come through the *unlocked* back door like one of L.A.'s finest—back to the wall, stake low on his left side, hammer cocked and held high at his right shoulder, ears straining, heart thumping.

If anything jumped out at him, he planned to stake first and ask questions later.

"Mrs. Berkovich, are you awake?"

Mica slid his rump along the edge of the kitchen counter, then darted the last yard to the wall next to the door leading into the rest of the house. It was too dark to see anything and all he heard was the Felix the Cat clock ticking away in Mrs. B's front room.

"Mrs. B? I thought we'd go out for coffee and muffins. My treat."

Nothing.

Taking a deep breath (and saying a silent prayer) Mica stepped out into the open doorway and followed the sounds of the clock deeper into the curtained gloom.

"You left the back door open, Mrs. B," he said as casually as he could through the constriction in his windpipe. "That's real dangerous, you know . . . especially in this neighborhood . . ."

Where any ol' Undead critter can just wander in for a late-night snack.

Mica lifted the tip of the stake a degree higher as he passed the closed bathroom door and licked the sweat off his top lip. Part of him wished he'd finished off the vodka—part of him wished he hadn't started drinking in the first place.

He'd walked the narrow hallway a hundred . . . a *thousand* times before—but not knowing what was waiting for him made it feel like he was trespassing into uncharted territory.

Lucky he tucked the small, pocket-sized "map" into his back pocket before leaving the trailer.

I'm still ready, Lord . . . but if there's ANY way to take this cup away from me . . . I'd be more than grateful.

Something thumped in the cozy, mildew-scented living room just ahead of him.

Yeah, okay, Lord . . . Gotcha.

Squaring his shoulders, Mica tightened his grip on the stake and inched forward into the possible *valley of death*.

"Mrs. B? Is that you? C'mon . . . answer me. Please?"

There was another thump, then the sound of a rocker slowly being put into motion—back and forth, back and forth against the worn carpet. Mrs. B's big maple rocking chair.

The stake angled itself toward the rhythmic creaks as if another hand was controlling it.

Which it probably was. *Praise be to His Name!*

Mrs. B's throaty giggle almost made him wet himself.

"Mrs. B . . . shit, you almost scared me to—"

The old lady's giggle dropped into a low predatory

growl as Mica stepped into the curtained living room. Mrs. B was a dark lump hunched low into the ruffled cushions—the rocker keeping time with the steady beat of the clock.

Mica lowered the stake slowly, tucking it and the hammer behind his back—as if it were a surprise present. *Surprise, surprise . . . Happy RE-birthday, Mrs. B!*

"You—you . . ." Mica cleared his throat and forced himself to relax . . . reminded himself he was still under Protection. "You left the back door open."

"Oh, dear. Isn't that just like a silly old lady . . . I'd probably forget me head if it wasn't nailed on."

It was still Mrs. B's voice—*Oh God*—but it was the memory of that voice from the night before that hardened Mica's heart.

Finding the edge of the wall with his heels, Mica sidestepped deeper into the room—keeping his eyes trained on the rocker and feeling her eyes trained on him.

Hungry eyes.

The hammer and stake felt as slippery in his hands as if he'd dipped them in motor oil.

Mica shook off the need to wipe the fear-sweat out of his eyes and concentrated on where to take his next step. Like every other old lady he'd ever known—his own aunts and mother included—Mrs. B had enough "collectibles" littering the floor to make walking a hazard. And the one thing Mica didn't want to do was take his eyes off her for even a moment.

He'd grown up reading Famous Monster magazines.

He *knew* how fast a vampire could move when it wanted to.

"Sure is dark in here," Mica said. The rocker was still a good ten feet away . . . too far to try and lunge. He *had* to get closer. "I thought you *loved* sunlight."

An embarrassed laugh floated up to him. "Oh, I was up late last night watching *Casablanca* again—you know how much I love Bogie—and I sort of strained my eyes. Silly of me. Just like leaving the door open. Real silly."

"Yeah," he said, "real silly."

Mica could see her now—frumpy old pink bathrobe, fuzzed out slippers, thin hair wrapped so tightly around curlers it made his head ache. Mrs. B looked just like she did every morning.

Nice.

Normal.

A little old lady vampire in a rocking chair, waiting for her breakfast to take one false step so she could tear his throat out.

Give me strength, O Lord. And put it all into my right arm.

But he still had to be sure. Gypsy could have been lying . . . *wanting* Mica to think they'd done something to the old woman just to get a rise out of him.

Maybe.

99 and 9/10 percent of him *prayed* that was so.

"So . . . I guess you don't want to go out for coffee and muffins, huh?"

Mica saw her smile. She wasn't wearing her false teeth, but that was okay . . . the two long, curving fangs more than made up for her lack of dentures.

"No, thanks . . . *Preacher-boy,* I think I'll just grab something here."

The magazines had been wrong. Vampires moved a *lot* faster!

Mica managed to get off one startled gasp when Mrs. B sprang out of the rocker and dug ice-cold *(dead)* fingers into his throat.

"I've been eating my Wheaties," she whispered, jerking Mica's head to one side . . . exposing the veins in his neck. Her breath smelled like raw sewage that had been cooking in the hot summer sun for a month. "See what a little fiber can do?"

Mica could already feel his blood spilling down the front of his *Jesus is my BEST friend* T-shirt . . . could already hear the Heavenly Choir singing him Home. Could already feel the wooden stake sinking into her chest.

Mrs. B forced his head back into a semi-upright angle and glared at him.

"Now *that* wasn't a very nice thing to think," she said. "Who the fuck do you think you are? One of the *Fearless Vampire Hunters?*"

Mica expected to die at that moment, instead he found himself tossed across the room like a used Kleenex.

His left shoulder shattered the glass front of the old woman's beloved china cabinet. Mrs. B had told him it once belonged to Carol Lombard—even though he couldn't imagine the one-time Movie Queen owning *anything* as gaudy as the six-foot high, red-lacquered and gold-leaved monstrosity he'd just reduced to kindling.

Brass baby-shoes, blown glass trinkets, the few *good* pieces of wedding china and the full set of Elvis commemorative dinner plates tinkled around him as Mica tried to sit up.

His hands were empty.

Mica groaned at the sharp pain in his back as he swept the debris immediately in front of him. The hammer and stake weren't there.

Lord . . . this is now getting serious.

"Problem, dear?" Mrs. B asked as her slippers scuffed along the carpet toward him. "You look worried but you shouldn't be . . . this is real kick-ass stuff. I haven't felt this good since back in '69—but what a year that *was*."

She came at him cackling like a chicken that just laid an ostrich egg. Mica made a blind grab and snagged something hard and round. He saw what it was the instant it left his fingers. It was the Snow Globe he'd bought Mrs. B last Christmas . . . their *last* Christmas.

Mica watched the plastic snow swirl around the Baby Jesus as it flew across the room.

She caught it without breaking stride and crushed it like a soap bubble.

"Strike one, *Preacher-boy*."

The dust-layered pair of baby shoes went next. These she just batted out of the way.

"Strike two . . . once more and I'll have to bench you. For *life*."

Mica's fingers found something long and hard and grabbed onto it like it was a life-preserver.

"You can't fucking *do* anything to me, you god-damned old *bitch*" he growled. "I have the Lord's Protection. You can't harm me . . . you can't fucking even touch m—"

She not only could, but she did.

Mica could feel the flesh tear behind his left ear as the dead woman wrenched his head back. *Now or never, Lord—*

"PROTECT ME!!!"

The cylindrical object in his hand practically flew forward on its own—burying itself into the hollow between Mrs. B's sagging breasts.

A geyser of cold blood accompanied her ear-shattering scream and hit Mica full in the face.

The feet of the hand-carved, wooden statuette of the Virgin Mary Mica had brought back from his trip to Tiajuana sizzled in the dark blood like a hamburger cooking.

Mrs. B's scream rose another octave as she lurched backwards, taking five strips of Mica's flesh along with her. She got as far as the slabbed redwood coffee table before going down.

It was only her body that writhed on the floor—screaming, thrashing like a catfish in the bottom of a boat—*only* her body. Her soul was already making the slow journey back from the edge of the Pit. Mica *knew* that . . . but he kept reminding himself as he crawled over to her.

"Lord . . . this *was* a good woman," he said as he

kneeled just out of range of the jerking legs and raised his hands to the ceiling. "Welcome her back into the fold once she has passed beyond the sin that was forced upon her. She has sinned mightily, Lord, but it was *forced* upon her. She was a victim, Lord, and if You can Forgive the meanest of backsliders then I *know* You'll Forgive her. Bless her, Lord."

The shriek sat Mica down on his rear. Hard. Human or animal he had never heard a sound like that before. Mrs. B's body was putting up one *hell* of a fight.

Literally.

"I'm not going to let them win, Mrs. B," he shouted at the contorting corpse. "I'll fucking *bless* the sin right out of you!"

The old woman's face was a parody of what it had once been—the deep-set brown eyes bulged from their bruised sockets while dark, smoking mucus boiled out of the gaping mouth. The Holy Mother's wooden feet were doing a silent tap-dance deep in the heaving chest.

Lord, she doesn't deserve this!

"LORD! Bless this woman and Prepare a place for her at Your table. She was wronged, Lord . . . Take her back. Bless her."

The screaming rose to a frenzied level as Mica leaned over and cupped his hands over the protruding statue.

"Get ready, Lord," he said softly, silently offering his own blessings, " 'cause here she comes. In Your name and in Your Son's name and in the Holy Spirit's name."

The scream cut off in mid-shriek—almost as if Mica

had hit the old woman's *On-Off* button when he rammed the statue in the rest of the way. Silence . . . blessed and sanctified . . . throbbed against the inside of his ears.

"Amen."

Standing, and feeling every ache, bruise and scrape from the encounter, Mica stepped over the old woman and walked to the window. The sunlight was so bright it hurt his eyes. It was a beautiful morning . . . a *Mrs. B* kind of morning that once meant hotcakes and sausage at McDonald's.

Mica turned and smiled down at the still, frail form spread-eagled on the floor. It was still a Mrs. B morning . . . but now she would be having nectar and manna with the Host Almighty.

"Eat hearty," he told her.

The old woman's face was back to normal—smooth except for the wrinkles, and peaceful. The hideous Evil that masked it a moment earlier was gone now.

She'd been Blessed and Welcomed Back.

"Thank you, Lord. You judged her and brought her home to the Glory Everlasting."

Mica hugged himself and shivered. The house suddenly seemed too quiet. Too empty.

Too *dead*.

"I have seen Your wonder and am blessed with the Miracle that has just occurred. Thank you, Lord, for allowing me to . . . to . . ."

Mica raced down the hallway back into the kitchen

and made it just in time to watch his stomach try to squeeze itself out of his mouth.

He wasn't worried though. Miracles often had that effect on mere mortals.

Just like Alien Encounters.

"Praise God."

TWENTY-FOUR

Allison's forehead slammed into the thin satin draped lining as she came "awake." *Shit, damn low ceiling.* She was going to order the optional dome lid first thing in the morning. First thing.

It was morning.

Allison lay back against the styrofoam pillow and chewed her bottom lip. Somehow she knew there were forty-six tufts radiating out from the satin-covered button above her left eye and forty-seven over her left; forty-two at her forehead and a measly twenty-two at her chin.

Which made a grand total of one-hundred and fifty seven . . .

That she could remember. That and the way she and Luci had taken the two men in the deserted courtyard—

taken them and drained them and stuffed them into the Dumpster behind a restaurant.

Allison remembered Luci licking the blood off her fingers and winking—calling them "Blood Sisters."

But she couldn't remember what had sent shock waves racing through her system.

pain

Allison pressed her hands against the hollow between her breasts. And flinched. The whole front of her chest felt as tender as if someone had . . .

. . . had . . .

Allison squeezed her eyes shut and tried to slip back into the nice, quiet, dreamless trance she just left.

escape

Her mother always said if you couldn't see the monsters under the bed they couldn't hurt you. *But I'm the monster now, mama—does that mean I don't exist?*

You fuckin' WON'T if you don't shut the fuck up!

Gina's lilting voice pried Allison's eyes back open. The pain was still there—a dull, aching throb that seemed to go to the very core of her being.

Luci?

Shit, bitch! I thought I tol' you—

I'm here, Alley-cat.

Allison spread her fingers out over the pain, felt the narrow limits . . . like someone had jabbed her right over the heart. A chill she shouldn't have even noticed raced up her spine.

Something's wrong, Luci.

Oh, like she just now figured that out. I'm tellin' you—

Gina, quiet! Then softer, *It'll be okay, Alley-cat. I'll explain later. Rest now.*

But Luci . . .

Bitch don't even know how t'listen.

Later, Alley-cat. Go back to sleep. You're safe. Listen . . . the Watcher's on the prowl.

Allison cocked her head to one side and heard the slow, muffled sound of boot heels circling the coffins. And something told her he'd be doing that until nightfall.

When they could get up and take care of themselves.

But the pain in my chest.

Matches the pain in m'ass you're givin' ME! Dear sweet Gina.

Later. Luci said. *Now go back to sleep . . . we're going to have a busy night.*

Allison wanted to press the issue until she got some real answers, but let it drop. Cupping her hands gently over the tender flesh, she began recounting the tufts.

Still one hundred and fifty-seven

". . . beers on the wall, one hundred and fifty-seven. If one of those bottles should happen to fall, one hundred and fifty-six beers on the wall. One hundred and fifty-six beers on the . . ."

Alley-cat! It's the middle of the morning!

Will you shut the fuck up?

Oy, so now we got a nightingale as well as a hyena?

The not-so-gentle tapping on the coffin lid ended the impromptu concert.

"Best do like Luci says, Alley-cat," Gypsy's low voice boomed down at her through the satin and wood.

"But I'm not sleepy," she answered and heard the man chuckle.

"Excuse me for saying so, Alley-cat . . . but you're dead. Maybe it'd be easier if you just started acting like it. Luci'll explain everything later. Okay?"

Allison refolded her hands in the proper "good little corpse" style and closed her eyes.

It was going to be a *long* day.

Mica squinted up at the sun—already a couple clicks past its zenith—and felt a cold sweat replace the natural perspiration covering his back.

The day was already half over and the police still just stood around picking their goddamned asses.

"Sorry, Lord," Mica mumbled, letting the handcuffs jiggle between his legs, "that just sort of slipped out. I didn't mean any disrespect."

The officer standing next to the patrol car bent at the waist and scowled at Mica over the rims of his mirrored sunglasses.

Just like the ones Allison and Luci had been wearing. In the daylight.

An unnatural cold, like the sweat, suddenly replaced the humid air locked in the backseat with him. Even if Luci and Allison were vampires (which he knew they were) and even if they had been out in broad daylight (which made him re-evaluate his comics-gleaned knowledge of the creatures) and wore mirrored sunglasses . . .

. . . there was still no reason to assume the policeman

glaring in at him that very moment was anything but a human being.

No reason at all.

"Did you say something?"

Mica lifted his cuffed hands and laced his fingers together. "Just praying, sir. No law against that yet, is there?" He'd meant it to sound like a joke, but it didn't come out that way. Mica squirmed around on the plastic-coated seat and faced the window.

"Would you like to join me?" he asked. "Offer up a prayer of Thanks that the Good Lord has taken Mrs. B back to His bosom."

"Mrs?" The scowl deepened on the officer's face. "You mean that poor old lady you killed?"

"No, you don't understand. Let me explain."

Mica scooted to the window and saw the man back up quickly, his hand dropping to the gun at his waist. Mica eased back against the seat slowly, fingers up and spread. Which, he discovered a moment later, was probably not one of the wisest thing he'd done that morning.

That . . . and dialing 9-1-1 to report Mrs. B's miraculous departure back into the Arms of the Lord.

And then *waiting* for them so he could explain.

The officer pulled off his glasses and stared directly at the dried, rust-colored blood on Mica's hands.

"You don't need to explain anything to me," the officer said as he moved back to his position next to the car, "but I'd love to be there when you explain it to the judge. Goddamned bastard . . . I hope they gas your ass."

247

"No, please, it wasn't like that." Mica licked his lips and gagged at the taste he found there. *Blood* "Wait, *please,* I didn't kill her . . . I released her soul from the evil bonds that would have confined it to everlasting torment."

Taking a deep breath, Mica closed his eyes and mentally chose a passage at random. *Make it a good one, Lord.*

"And Jesus told His Disciples . . . 'Do not think that I have come to abolish the law and the prophets. I have come not to abolish them, but to fulfill them.'" *Perfect, Lord. As usual.*

Mica opened his eyes and watched the man's face drop into a look that would normally have been reserved for the discovery of dog shit on a shoe.

"You fucking hypocrite," the officer said as he stood up and turned around. "Why don't you give the state a break and go for my gun? I promise you'd die a lot faster than that old lady did."

Mica folded his hands slowly back into his lap and refused to give the mirror-eyed officer a reason to even look back into the car. The cop had called him a hypocrite—the same way Allison had.

Allison.

The memory of her face and the way she'd looked under the spotlight the night before blended with images of long sweeping capes and yellowed fangs.

Allison. A vampire.

If he got the chance he'd drive a stake through her heart as well. But he didn't think he'd have the strength to bless her. Not after everything that happened.

The sound of shoe leather on asphalt made him look up. A tall black man in a suit and tie was walking toward the car, nodding the uniformed officer away. When he got to the patrol car, he thumped the roof just above Mica's head.

It sounded as if a bomb had gone off.

Undoubtedly what it was supposed to sound like.

When the door swung open, Mica's backbone was already ramrod straight.

"I'm Detective-Sergeant Moran of the Los Angeles Police Department, assigned to the Hollywood division—" All nice and formal to tighten any technical "entrapment" loophole Mica might have hoped to slip through. "—Would you mind stepping out of the car, sir?"

"No, sir," Mica said as he swung his legs out and felt the man's broad hand protecting the top of his head as he stood up. "I don't mind."

"Good." The detective actually smiled. "I like it when people cooperate. It makes things so much more pleasant, don't you think?"

The man's voice was a deep and soothing baritone— the kind Mica'd always thought Jesus would have. He took it as a sign.

"Oh, *yes,* sir."

"Very good. Now, if you'll just confirm a few things for me," the man said as he pulled a small spiral bound notebook from his jacket and flipped it open. "You are Mica Poke?"

"Yessir . . . but my real name's Milo," Mica said, leaning closer to the detective so the mirror-eyed-possible-vampire cop wouldn't hear. "I changed it to Mica when I got my calling."

"Your . . . *calling*." The man took out a gold Cross pen and added that to the other *facts* scribbled across the page. "No problem, I know how that goes. My first name's Jerome but I go by Jay."

"But you shouldn't—Jerome is a *Holy* name. You should be proud of it, Jerome."

Jerome cleared his throat. "Yeah. Anyway, *Mr.* Poke, according to your initial statement, you told the arresting officers that you alone were responsible for the death of—" Jerome checked the notebook again. "—Mrs. Anna Berkovich, 84."

"And a half," Mica added. He wanted to cooperate as much as he could and was mildly surprised when the man didn't write it down.

"Okay . . . but you *did* kill her?"

"I sent her to Glory, yes sir."

"Interesting term," Jerome said, tapping the pen against the paper, "for murder."

"But I didn't murder her, sir, I just sent her on."

"Excuse me." Mica could see beads of sweat pop out across the thick upper lip. "But isn't that the same thing?"

This time Mica laughed—and saw every uniformed head twist toward him.

"*No*, sir. You can only *murder* somebody who's alive. Mrs. B was already dead when I—"

"Sent her to glory," Jerome said, snapping the notebook shut. "Yeah, you already said that. Would you mind accompanying me into the house, Mica? There're just a few more things I'd like to ask you about."

"I'd be pleased to, Jerome."

Mica fell into step next to the big detective and pretended not to see the man twirl a finger next to his temple. But that was all right . . . they'd understand soon enough.

Stopping just short of the back steps, Mica turned around and lifted his cuffed hands to those assembled— the uniformed police and paramedics, the white-jacketed ambulance attendants, the overalled evidence technicians . . . the neighbors and street people hanging over the back and side fences—lifted his hands the way Howard Beale had lifted his hands to the television cameras.

"And I say onto you all that the Lord God Most Mighty is looking down on us right now and Smiling . . . Smiling because we have come together this day to bear witness to the great *miracle* He has wrought. Right now He's probably singing along with the Heavenly Choir, rejoicing about the evil that has been put asunder."

Mica felt the Spirit flow into him from above and shook off the sweaty hand trying to pull him into the house.

"YES, Lord . . . we're with You. *Praise* Him, brothers and sisters . . . lift your voices and let Him know!"

The scream of a fire engine roaring down Highland seemed unnaturally loud in the otherwise silent back yard. Mica lowered his hands slowly. They were all just standing there. Looking at him like he'd just squatted down and taken a crap on the bottom stair.

Jerome was the first to shake the look off. Taking Mica's arm, the detective turned him around and led him up the back steps.

"I think you just cinched the insanity defense, son," he said as he opened the squeaking screen door. "You can calm down now."

For a split second Mica forgot Mrs. B wouldn't be shuffling up to meet him, a cup of coffee or plate of kolatchky in her hand—and when he did remember, it almost knocked him to the floor.

"You okay, Mica?" The detective said. "Want to sit down?"

Mica shook his head and pressed his lips together. He couldn't show sorrow for having done a righteous thing. He just *couldn't*.

Say Hallelujah.

The house smelled worse than usual. Mica hadn't noticed it when he carried Mrs. B into her bedroom to lay her out "proper" before calling the police. But he noticed it now.

There was a stench that went deeper than the boiled cabbage-mildew-dust-spoiled bananas-aged mothball-old lady smell of the house. It was a darker smell . . . rank, like a toilet had backed up somewhere and kept going.

Mica got as far as the kitchen table and sat down.

"You're not okay, are you, Milo?"

Mica looked up and shook his head. No, he wasn't okay. He should be shouting praise to the Heavens for letting him free the old woman's soul . . . instead of wanting to bury his head in his hands and sob his lungs out.

"Want to talk about it, kid?" Jerome said, pulling up Mrs. B's chair and waving the other cops/detectives/attendants/etc. away.

Mica felt his mouth open and had to force it shut.

"Okay, Milo," Jerome said, "suit yourself. Feel up to identifying the body?"

Aw, shit, Lord. Is this really necessary? Didn't I do enough?

The detective stood up without waiting for an answer and physically hauled Mica to his less than steady feet.

Okay, Lord, I get the message. Praise Your name.

Mica followed the detective past Mrs. B's mismatched orange and olive green bathroom *(". . . that was back when we opened the shop, all peace and love and psychedelic colors—what a year THAT was . . .")* where a female tech was carefully dusting along the edge of the mirror with an oversized brush.

He wanted to stop and tell the woman she didn't have to bother—that, being a vampire, Mrs. B wouldn't have touched the mirror—but Jerome seemed to be in a hurry, practically dragging him into the bedroom.

The stench was almost suffocating in the tiny room. The breeze coming in through the open window didn't seem to be doing any good.

It still smelled like *Hell*.

Mrs. B was still on the bed, just where Mica had left her—eyes closed, mouth tipped upward, feet and legs

253

covered discreetly with the bedspread . . . her hands folded just below the Holy Mother's gore-crusted feet.

Mica felt better.

"She looks real peaceful," he said. "Doesn't she?"

"Yeah," Jerome answered, "*real* peaceful. Can you identify this woman as Anna Berkovich?"

Anna . . . Mica had never called her anything but Mrs. B. Anna suited her.

"Yes sir. That's Anna."

Jerome nodded and checked something off in the notebook. Still nodding, he walked to the head of the bed and pointed to the Holy Mother sticking out of Mrs. B's chest.

"And *you* did that?"

"Yes, sir," Mica said as proudly as he could without sounding boastful. "I helped her back from the abyss and set her feet onto the Path of Glory."

"So you *did* kill her?"

"No sir."

Both of the detective's eyebrows met in the middle of his forehead. Mica felt his own forehead mold itself around the scar-cross. *Didn't we already go over this ground, Lord?*

"So now you're telling me you *didn't* kill her." Jerome looked about three shades lighter than when they started the conversation. "Is that right, Milo?"

Mica lifted his cuffed hands and clasped them to his chest. *Okay, so we go through it AGAIN.*

"Like I already told you and a half-dozen of your peo-

ple, Detective, I *didn't* kill Mrs. B because she was AL-
READY dead." Mica took as deep a breath as the stench
would allow and rolled his eyes. "Look at her, man . . . I
mean *really* look at her. Can't you see the Glorified
smile on her face?"

The detective looked down at Mrs. B.

"That's the heat," he said. "They all smile like that
when they're left out too long."

"Lord," Mica said out loud because he wanted
Jerome to know *exactly* Who he was dealing with, "remove the scales from this man's eyes and let him *SEE!*"

Nothing.

"Shit, man," Mica yelled, "she was a fucking *vampire!*"

Jerome's notebook snapped shut and he reached
down toward Mrs. B's puckered mouth.

"No . . . wait!"

But it was too late. Mica's shout had been too loud.
And the detective's reflex actions just a little too good.

Jerome's hand accidentally knocked into the side of
Mrs. B's face . . . and all Mica could do was watch her
head roll backward off the stained pillow and hit the
floor.

It bounced twice and came to rest on its left ear—the
freshly washed and blow-dried hair Mica had worked so
hard on collecting dust bunnies like a magnet.

"Damn."

When he looked up, Jerome's ebony face had
drained to the color of old fireplace ash.

"That's part of the ritual," Mica explained slowly . . .

in case Jerome wanted to make more notes. "People think that a stake destroys them outright, but that's wrong. A stake through the heart only pins the soul back to its body. You have to cut off the head so that soul can never animate that body again."

Mica looked down at Mrs. B's head and sighed.

"After the head's been cut off you're supposed to stuff the mouth with fresh garlic, but she didn't have any." Mica looked up at the detective. "You think garlic salt will be okay?"

"You . . . you . . ." Jerome cleared his throat with so much force it made Mica drop his chin. "You cut off her head? But she doesn't have any teeth. Aren't vampires supposed to have teeth?"

"Well, of course she doesn't have them *now*," Mica said. It was like trying to explain something to a wall. Didn't the man ever read a comic book? "Once I released her soul from the Evil, all the embodiments of that Evil disappeared as if they never existed."

"How convenient," Jerome muttered as he turned away from the bed—turned back toward Mica, his fingers clenched tight around the golden pen.

"There is something else I have to tell you," Mica made it sound like he was going to confess to some wrong so the detective would listen.

It worked. Jerome stopped in his tracks and cocked his head to one side. "Yeah?"

"There are others," Mica whispered—aware that the policeman with the mirrored sunglasses could be listening, "the ones that *did* this to Mrs. B. I know where they are and even though this burden was laid at my feet I'm willing to accept your help in destroying the remaining vampires."

Jerome's head began going back and forth in time to the Felix clock.

"You gotta be shitting me."

"No, *sir!* I'd never do that. There are four of them . . . one of them used to be my best friend and there's this new one with red hair—"

Allison . . . forgive me

"—Anyway, they work at the same place I do . . . Luci's Fur Pit over on Sunset. Now if you could just equip your men with stakes, I have enough Bibles to—"

All the air was driven out of Mica's lungs by the force of Jerome's fingers grabbing a handful of shirt and skin.

"That'll be enough information. *Sir.* Thank you for being so cooperative. Now, turn around and start walking back to the patrol car. Keep your hands low and in sight at all times." Jerome's face was blank as he released his grip on Mica and pulled a laminated Miranda Card out of his coat pocket.

"I'm sure that one of the other officers has already told you this, but let's just make *doubly* sure, shall we? You have the right to remain silent . . . should you give up this right, anything you say can and *WILL* be used against you in—"

Mica stopped listening as he turned around. Instead

he focused on the reflection of Mrs. B's headless body in the full-length cheval mirror. And smiled.

A dusty beam of sunlight was tickling the Holy Mother's feet as it illuminated the dead body.

Just a dead body. No fangs, no blood lust, no longer invisible to the power of mirrors. Just the dead body of a good woman.

"Praise His name," Mica whispered.

And accidentally *fell* into the bedroom door.

TWENTY-FIVE

Shit!

Allison tucked her knees under her and snuggled deeper into the rattan chair—trying to find the *least* uncomfortable position.

It didn't help.

Nor did the constant massaging.

The skin between her breasts still ached.

One of the makeup chairs flew across the room and scattered against the far wall. Allison ignored it. It was the third chair Gina had destroyed in the last hour.

"Gina, boobala, sit," Miriam said. Again. "There's nothing you can do right now, so why wear out your legs."

Gina growled and Miriam shrugged.

"You see . . . you try to be nice and what does it get you?"

Miriam was scrunched into one corner of the daybed, another moth-eaten cat—even uglier than the one Allison had seen her with the day before, if that was possible—purring wheezingly in the folds of her Mexican peasant dress.

Allison watched the old vampire pick a flea off the cat's mangled left ear and pop it into her mouth. Just the thought of eating . . . of hot blood pouring down her throat made the pain in her chest worse.

"*Jeeze* . . ." she moaned, "Miriam."

"Ah, poor li'l baby got an upset tum?" Gina snarled as she picked up an unopened jar of cold cream and tossed it almost casually over her shoulder. It made a creamy white puddle in the middle of the broken chairs. "Well, if you can't take the heat Fledgy, best'a get outta the kitchen . . .'fore you burn yourself!"

"Gina!" Miriam's hiss made the cat lay back its ears. "We're all in this together . . . you either be nice or go somewhere else."

Another jar, this one shattering into a goopy yellow splotch, joined the debris on the floor. Allison was about to look away when she saw Gina claw at her chest.

"Yeah, bitch," she said when she noticed Allison looking, "hurts like hell, don't it?"

"You mean you feel it, too?"

Gina rolled her eyes toward Miriam and curled down into one of the last remaining makeup chairs.

"'Course I *feel* it, Fledgy, what'd you 'spect—that *you'd* be the onliest one? Shit . . . I was greener'n grass when I got turned an' *I* still knew 'nuff not to go stickin' my nose in where it weren't wanted!"

Gina's nails left four gouges in the table's formica top. "We never had us no trouble 'till you showed," she growled. "Why don't you leave 'fore another one of us gets staked."

Allison swung her legs slowly off the chair. Not once, while she was still a *Breather,* did she even *think* about fighting someone physically . . . although there'd been a few men she would have loved to have shot outright . . . but something deep inside her told her that the time had finally come. Gina would continue to ride her ass like a boil until Allison did something to stop it.

"You gotta be shittin' me," Gina said, smiling for the first time that Allison could remember. "You think you can take *me* on, Fledgy? Sheee-IT, I took out mean'r white folk'n you 'fore your granddaddy learned how to pee standin' up. But, if you want t'try . . ."

Gina turned toward her, drumming three-inch, ebony talons against the table top.

". . . don't let *me* stop you. I ain't killed one o'my own in a long time."

"Stop it, you two!" The cat high-tailed it off Miriam's lap when she clapped her hands together like a kindergarten teacher trying to restore order. "You think like you're the only ones suffering here? Hah . . . you don't know from suffering. My first year in this country and I went through such hell it could only happen to a dead person—so let me tell you, feeling the echo from a staking ain't such a much."

P. D. Cacek

Gina huffed and clawed more furrows into the table.

"What do you mean by *echo*, Miriam?" Allison asked, even though she was sure she wasn't going to like the answer.

"Aw, such a baby we got here, Gina." Miriam tsk-tsked and tried to persuade the cat back onto her lap—without much luck at sounding sincere in either instance. "It's the blood line . . . it connects all of us no matter who our Makers were. When one of our kind is destroyed we all *feel* it—how *much* we feel it depends on how close the one who got staked was. I remember one time on the lower East Side . . ."

"The one got staked last night was *real* close, Fledgy. *Too* close," Gina barked. "And it was that damned boyfriend o'yours that done it."

Boyfriend? "Seth?"

"Fuck me, bitch, weren't you listenin' . . . I said *BOYfriend*, not Maker!"

Allison caught the inference in Gina's snarl and felt her skin crawl over itself along her backbone. *The Preacher-boy?*

Well, congratulations . . . you AIN'T as dumb as you look!

Allison suddenly realized that two were missing from their happy little Band of the Damned. The Watcher and . . .

Luci? Is she the one who got—She couldn't even bring herself to think the possibility. As fragile as *life* was, death didn't seem any sturdier.

"Is Luci the one who got what?" Luci asked, walking

262

into the room with Gypsy close on her heels. "Laid? Hell no." She winked at Allison. "Try though I did."

Another jar went flying through the air—this one smashing *just* above Allison's head.

"Oops," Gina said, "missed."

"Boy," Luci said, "I leave you guys alone for a couple of hours and you start acting like Valley Girls. Miriam . . . *Miriam,* will you stop playing with that damn thing and pay attention!"

Miriam stopped trying to attract the animal back onto the daybed and dutifully folded her hands in her lap.

"So what's up that you told me not to open the club tonight?" she asked. "There's a Garlic Growers Convention in town we should know about, maybe?"

Allison started to smile—until she saw Luci's face. Whatever the reason for the unscheduled holiday it must have been serious. Luci looked frightened. And that scared the shit out of Allison.

"Gypsy found the Preacher-boy," she said. "He's being held at the station on Colfax waiting a psychological evaluation. That's only a couple of blocks away from here . . . which is lucky for us."

"Why?" Allison asked.

When Luci turned, any trace of fear that Allison *thought* she'd seen on the angelic face had disappeared.

"Because, sweet-cheeks, we're going to bust him out."

Ask a silly question, Allison thought.

.

TWENTY-SIX

Become a vampire . . . and see the world.

So far she'd seen one parking lot, two alleys, a cemetery, a deserted courtyard in one of L.A's most *well-
known* tourist spots and the inside of the *world-famous*
Hollywood police station.

And I thought my LIFE was fulfilling!

Allison crossed her legs under the flowing navy skirt
and glanced at the other women sharing the wooden
slat-backed bench with her: Blond, brunette, fake red-
head, one streaked grey—all wearing tight, skimpy
clothes and arch-breaking high heels. If they'd been
prettier and younger . . . and *dead,* they might have
found jobs at the Pit. Instead they were just waiting for
their pimps to come up with bail.

Luci was standing next to Gypsy at the admitting desk

talking to a khaki-uniformed officer. Occasionally—on cue—the Watcher would reach over and pat Luci on the shoulder. Comforting her in whatever fantasy she was concocting. Allison picked a stray piece of lint off her dress—refusing to eavesdrop. Whatever the plan was, she'd find out about it soon enough.

Unfortunately.

Shit-eating son-of-a-bitch! I hope somebody blows him a new asshole!

Luci's mental bombshell made Allison look up. The words filling her mind were completely opposite to the softly sobbing woman walking slowly toward her—face buried in her hands, leaning heavily on Gypsy's sturdy arm. One of the whores sitting next to Allison yawned loudly.

"Luci?"

For Christ's sake, Alley-cat—look stricken! Your fucking brother's in jail for murder.

Allison felt her jaw unhinge. *Who?*

Better, Luci said, finally raising her head to accept a tobacco-stained handkerchief from Gypsy and pressing it to what looked like real tears. She smiled sadly down at Allison. *Your brother . . . our own dear little Preacher-boy. I'll explain, later.*

But Luci—?

Later, I said. "Oh, Allison . . ." Luci said, crushing the handkerchief into a wad and pressing it against the all-too-real sounding sob. "It's *him* . . . it really is our poor Milo!"

Milo?

Luci nodded sadly even while her voice buzzed in Allison's mind. *The Preacher-boy's real name. Now stand up and shake out the terribly sensible dress you're wearing. If you can squeeze me out a tear or two all the better.*

When she still didn't move, Gypsy reached down and half-dragged, half-lifted Allison to her feet.

"There, there, little girl," he said loud enough for anybody who was interested in the drama to get an ear-full. "You're brother's going to be okay. There has to be some kind of mistake. Milo's the *sweetest* kid I ever met."

Allison bowed her head and hid behind her hand. *You going to tell me what this is all about?*

In good time, Alley-cat—but for right now just follow my lead and everything'll be fine. Okay, girlfriend . . . it's Showtime.

Allison let Gypsy help her back toward the admitting desk the same way he'd helped Luci away from it. Her calf-length skirt kept flapping between her legs, but Luci had insisted on it as *well* as the pert, Peter Pan collared blouse that made her look like some suburban PTA president . . . circa 1953.

"Part of the disguise," she said, cocooning herself in a modest, knee-length business suit. "The Preacher-boy won't know what hit him."

Allison didn't ask then just like she didn't ask now.

She really didn't want to know.

Okay, sweet-cakes, Luci's voice murmured at her, *see the nice man sitting behind the desk? He's a real dickhead but we have to play up to him or we won't get to see the Preacher-boy. Okay?*

Allison sniffled—and it wasn't because she was acting. Mica . . . *Milo* was somewhere close by. Dammit.

Good girl, Luci said, *Now try a few tears. Male Breathers are suckers for a beautiful woman in tears . . . it brings out their latent maternal side.*

Great. *Luci?*

Yeah, Alley-cat?

Why don't we just use our supernatural powers to render them helpless and just walk in?

Luci stopped just short of the chest-high counter and turned toward Allison—a sad smile trying to break through the tears.

Will you fucking stop pretending this is a vampire movie? THIS is reality, baby . . . it may suck but so do we. Okay?

"This is Milo's sister," Luci said as she hugged Allison to her breasts. "She's been staying with me . . . because . . . because . . . well, he's always been a little overzealous in his beliefs, and when he found out she was gay, well . . ."

WHAT?

Luci's smile dipped slightly as she planted a quick kiss on Allison's cheek.

"I'm afraid Milo never could accept us being lovers . . . in fact, just the other night he said he'd do something *drastic* if Allison didn't leave me and go home."

Luci's hand flew dramatically to her throat—a move Allison wished she'd thought of first. With a claw hammer.

"Oh, my God, Allison . . . you don't think he did this because of *us?*"

Luci's unexpected sobs even made Allison jump. But

it worked. Even the policeman behind the desk looked convinced. Convinced and revolted by their supposed sexual preference.

"Oh, Allison—if it's true I'll never forgive myself!"

Neither will I.

Luci winked at her. *Just tell the nice dickhead you want to see your dear, crazy brother.*

No.

You're not paying attention, Alley-cat.

Fuck you!

Maybe later, Luci said, *but right now we have to go see the Preacher-boy. Do it.*

Allison was about to go another round when Gypsy pulled her close—just a big, hairy friend showing his support—and poked something hard into her ribs. It hurt. It really, really, *hurt.*

Gypsy moved his hand just enough for Allison to see the pointed three-inch stake he was holding.

Think of it as a loaded gun, Alley-cat, Luci said. *Ask nice.*

Allison stared at the *Fuck the Pigs* graffiti someone had scratched into the front of the desk.

"I . . . I'd like to see my brother." *Nicer.* "Please?"

And me.

"And can my . . . *friend* . . . come with me?"

"I'm afraid that won't be possible," the officer said.

Gypsy ran the point of the stake down her hip.

"Please!" Allison yelped. "Mic—Milo needs to see that . . . we're just like everybody else."

Very good, Alley-cat . . . I couldn't have put it better myself.

TWENTY-SEVEN

"Okay, nutcase," the officer said, directing him to the empty table in the middle of the room, "keep your hands on your side of the barrier and your butt in your chair and we'll both be happy. Try to get cute and I'll be all over you like ugly on your mama. Sit."

Mica sat. Quickly. And didn't even start breathing until the officer had left the room and closed the door behind him. Then he almost hyperventilated.

The guard had taken him out of the holding cell— where he'd already saved three drunks and a crack-head—saying he had visitors.

Mica didn't have to ask who it was. No one should have known where he was . . . *no one alive*.

He began praying the moment he heard the door re-open.

"And Jesus said 'Love your enemy and do good' . . .

271

but these are not just my enemies, Lord, these are the enemies of *all* Your people here on earth!"

Mica felt the temperature of the room drop a dozen degrees—like it always did when they entered a room. He squeezed his fingers tighter together until the pain drove the fear out of his heart.

The cross on his forehead burned with Holy Fire.

"These are foul, soulless creatures of the night who feed upon the blood of the Innocents and corrupt what is pure and natural until what is left stinks and writhes in the depths of its own putrefication."

Mica stood up—safe in the Lord's Hand—and pointed a trembling finger at them

. . . at *her* . . .

. . . at *Allison,* the one who wasn't and never could have been Piper!

"Begone foul Whores of Satan! I revoke your entrance into this place!"

The officer who already gave his lecture about conduct becoming a criminal, suddenly reappeared. Grabbing Mica by the shoulder, he manually helped his butt mold itself to the chair.

"Take it *easy,* pal," the guard ordered. "These are the nineties, remember, we're all supposed be a little more liberal in our thinking. One more outburst and I haul you outta here. Understand?"

"I'm sure that won't be necessary, officer," Luci said.

"Okay, but I'll be right outside." The officer gave Mica's shoulder a hard pinch and let go. "In case you need me."

Mica curled his right hand into a fist and covered it

with his left. They were talking about him like he didn't exist . . . like *he* was the unnatural creature.

Lord . . . You gave me the strength to vanquish ONE of Your enemies . . . now let my voice shout out Your praises to the Evil gathered before Us!

Mica took a deep breath and arched his back, ready to take whatever abuse was about to be heaped upon him in the Name and Glory of the Lord's—

Don't.

Mica's opening jaw snapped shut with a click.

Lord?

Not even, the voice said. *Just sit there and don't go crazy for at least another minute, okay?*

Allison.

Mica jerked his head up. Allison stood against the far wall, tucked into the corner next to the door, hugging herself. She looked ill. Her creamy skin looked like sour milk under the harsh florescent lights, her hair the dull red of leaves touched with frost.

How the hell had he once thought she was the most beautiful woman he'd ever seen? And how the hell had she gotten into his mind? *How?*

Later.

Mica closed his eyes and exhaled slowly. She was as corrupt as the others of her night-flying kind. And the Lord had made him mankind's only line of defense against them.

"Thank you, O Lord," he whispered out loud. "Make me worthy of this honor."

Mica heard Luci's sigh—long and suffering—as well

as the guard's "fucking lunatic" mumble. Mica kept his eyes closed until he was sure the guard was safely out of the room.

Forgive him, Lord, Mica prayed as he opened his eyes to Luci's radiant smile, *and open his eyes to the Evil surrounding him.*

"Goddamned, blood-sucking, whores of Satan," he said softly. "Fucking vampire cunts!"

"And it's so nice to see *you* again, Preacher-boy," Luci said as she walked past the visitor's table to the tiny, unobtrusive intercom just above the door leading back to the cells. Glancing through the tiny wire-mesh reinforced window, Luci waved at the guard at the same time she reached up and yanked the wires out of the box.

"There," she said, dusting off her hands as she walked back to the table and sat down opposite Mica, "that should give us a little more privacy."

Mica inched his chair back from the table. "Why didn't you just destroy it with your supernatural powers?"

Luci laughed and Allison suddenly flinched as if physically struck.

"You two should *really* get together and compare notes," she said, tossing her moon-bright hair. "You were practically *made* for each other."

Mica's stomach rolled over on itself at the very thought of Allison's body pressing against his while she sank her fangs into his throat and he pushed his engorged cock up into her icy cavern. Oh God—What

would it feel like? To Come and go at the same time?—
Sweet Jesus—Her body so cold and hard and

Mica. Stop it!

His eyes flew open as the air pounded against his
lungs in short, shallow gasps.

It's Luci, Mica. She's doing it. Fight her.

Mica blinked Luci's smug face back into focus.

"Problem, Preacher-boy?" she asked.

"No. No problem." Mica looked over at Allison, still huddled against the wall, still looking like death warmed over.
"Then what are *you* doing to me?"

Luci hooked one arm over the back of the chair and
glared at Allison.

"Nothing's going on, Luci," Allison said out loud. "He's
crazy . . . you told me that yourself. Huh? No. You know
I wouldn't lie to you."

Mica raised his fingers to the scar and slowly traced
the cross—tried to control the trembling in his hand. It
was more than just a little disconcerting to listen in on
only one half of a conversation.

"I hope you're telling the truth, Alley-cat," Luci said,
turning back to face the table. "I'd really hate to see
what was left after Gina had her way with you. And as
for *you*, Preacher-boy . . ."

"Get out of here," Mica said softly, lowering his hand
so the cross was visible, "I gave you no leave to be here.
A—a *vampire* can't enter a place unless it's invited and
I didn't give you the right!"

Luci's smile parted over the tips of her fangs.

"You're an alleged psychotic murderer, dear," she said, "the state took away your rights when they finger-printed you. Now, cut the late-night movie shit and I'll give you our proposition."

Mica looked over Luci's head to Allison. *What proposition?*

She didn't answer. Just looked away.

Good-cop/bad-cop . . . vampire style.

Mica straightened his back—*Whenever You're ready, Lord*—and heard Allison groan.

"What proposition," he said out loud. To Luci, this time.

"See there, Alley-cat," Luci said, beaming, "didn't I say the Preacher-boy would listen? *She* thought you'd run a stake through us the moment we showed up."

Give it time and I will.

He saw Allison flinch. And was glad.

"We're here to help you . . . *Milo*." Luci giggled. "Unless you *want* to spend the rest of your life rotting away in some state-run Home for the Criminally Nutzoid. Because that's where they're going to put you.

"You may have brutally killed a little old lady with malice and forethought, but—given the brilliant minds and bleeding hearts that are currently running our judicial system—if you keep telling everyone she was a vampire and you were only doing what comes *naturally* to self-appointed Holy Crusaders, you'll be wearing tie-in-the-back pajamas for the rest of your life."

She smiled and winked at Allison.

"But *we* can save your worthless ass, Preacher-boy."

"I've already *been* saved," Mica said, struggling to

keep his hands flat on the table—as per instructions—and away from her throat. "And there's fucking *nothing* you can do to me that's going to change that!"

Luci's fangs dropped another quarter of an inch. "I wouldn't be so sure of that, Milo. There are more things between Heaven and Earth, remember? More than just black and white."

She stood up and held out her hand. Allison came to it slowly, like a dog who'd been beaten once too many times but still felt blind loyalty to its master. Mica's heart almost went out to her.

His cock tried, as well.

Stop it!

Allison looked at him, puzzled, but kept quiet. Praise the Lord.

"We'll talk again, Preacher-boy," Luci said, walking Allison back to the visitor's door and tapping on the glass. Her nails made a dull, metallic sound. "You can count on it. Alley-cat, wave bye-bye to your crazy brother."

Allison didn't move. Didn't speak. Mica wished he'd had more time—he could break the chair apart and use a leg to end her eternal damnation.

"And the Lord said, 'Suffer not a witch to live'." Closing his eyes, Mica clasped his hands together and listened to the sound of his own words as the vampires left. "Whatever happens to this body I now wear is nothing to compare with the rewards that shall be mine in Heaven.

"I am Mica, the Lord's Own Stone, and I shall crack the bones of those who go against His Word and Will. I shall tear away the black cloak of darkness and let in the cleansing rays of God's Own Divine Light! The Lord will guide my hand so that I may drive them back into the void of endless pain from where they came!"

Mica opened his eyes and glared at the closed door. He was alone.

"And the Lord will cover me with Everlasting Glory."

You sanctimonious asshole.

Allison's voice floated back to him through the layers of wallboard, brick and steel bars that separated them. She sounded so close his cock twitched.

Stop boasting. Remember what happens to pride . . .

Mica stood up when the guard returned and followed him back to the holding cell without unclasping his hands.

Pride goeth before a fall. A warning? From a vampire? Impossible.

"Please let it be impossible, Lord," Mica whispered. "I *need* things to be in black and white. I need Your narrow line to follow."

"Amen to *that,* brother," a thick voice slurred as the cell door clanged shut. "We all gotta toe the line."

Mica pressed his back against the bars and closed his eyes. It wasn't much of a Sign . . . but he took it as one anyway.

Allison.

TWENTY-EIGHT

"Gee, that was fun," Allison said as the three of them crossed the Police Station's sodium-drenched parking lot. "What'd you want to do now? Drown a couple of newborn puppies?"

She kicked out at a car tire and was startled at the sudden *whoosh* of air as it deflated.

SHIT! I want to go home!

Luci stopped between a shiny black Porche and a fifteen-year-old station wagon, and turned around.

"Home's a million miles away, *Dorothy*. And unless you didn't figure it out already, we haven't been in Kansas for a *long* time." Luci brushed the hair out of her eyes and nodded Gypsy to her side. "And if you're finished having a hissie fit, why don't you just shut the fuck up and listen . . . maybe you'll finally *learn* something.

"Okay, Watcher, what's the procedure with the Preacher-boy?"

The Watcher glanced back at the station house and hawked a glop of spit toward it.

"He's Murder One, that's hot property and the boys in blue are going to play it real close to the bone with him. God help them if word slips out they have a vampire killer in there." Gypsy smiled—his teeth a pale pee-green under the crime light. "But I know the Public Defenders in this town. If he doesn't already have a half-dozen lean and hungry young lawyers fighting over him I'll shave my legs and join you up in the spotlight."

Luci chuckled but Allison could tell it was just for show. Hell, she'd laughed at enough men's idea of wit to know when someone was being polite.

"So he's got a lawyer? Then what?" Luci looked over at Allison and winked. "I don't stay in nights watching all those cops-n-robber shows."

Hah hah.

"Well, with a headline hungry lawyer and the way he did the old broad, my guess would be the psycho ward over at Queen of the Angels." The Watcher pulled a fat cigar out of his vest pocket and stuck it between his back molars. "I know back from my wilder days that the individual precinct stations usually run the preliminary evaluation right on the premises, but it'll be a real quick 'shit 'n git' kind a' check out."

A wide grin spread around the stogie. ". . . Hollywood's always been a different kind of place. If they tried to really evaluate crazies here, they'd never get anything else done."

Allison watched Luci nod, taking it all in, then frown.

"We're going to have to get him out before that happens." Luci suddenly spun and clawed the Porche—cutting the paint job right down to the bare metal. "Goddamned old *bitch!* I sucked her so dry she should have attacked him the minute he walked in."

That was the *second* time Allison could remember Luci sounding . . . "worried."

"I don't see what the big deal is," Allison said. "I mean, you just said yourself that the police think he's crazy—right? So why are we still here?"

Luci's head turned slowly beneath the shimmering curtain of pale hair. It had to be the piss yellow lights playing optical tricks—*had* to be . . . because the creature staring at her was no more Luci than the Watcher was.

Behind the smooth, tight skin and flowing hair was *another* Luci—one whose loose flesh hung down from the yellowed, almost bald head. Only the eyes . . . *Luci's green emerald eyes* glaring out from the bruised, sunken sockets . . . remained the same.

"We're still here because the Preacher-boy's still here," Luci said and the image of the crone disappeared. "We're safe at the moment *because* they think he's crazy. Vampires? They'll laugh themselves sick and tighten his straight jacket up another notch."

"Then I don't understand why—"

"That's just *it*, Alley-cat," Luci snarled, "*you* don't understand. I've been on this side long enough to know that eventually . . . though maybe not today or even next month . . . it'll happen. Somebody'll stop laughing and start listening. And then things, like unsolved murder cases and disappearances—even if we weren't responsible—might suddenly begin to make sense.

"Try to remember what it was like to be a Breather, Alley-cat. The real world is so big and indifferent you'll grab at *anything* that will make it less frightening. Even something straight out of the movies."

"Three little bites, baby . . . and you won't ever have to worry about gettin' old anymore."

Seth's words. Right out of the movies.

"It's like an epidemic when that happens," Luci said. "One infects another until we're up to our asses in Hunters. I lost a real good Watcher the last time. They hung him from a tree and set him on fire while he was still alive. And once it starts there's no stopping until we're gone. One way or the other."

Allison had begun to shake her head long before Luci finished her little tale of terror.

"You can stop the bullshit, Luci. I may not be as . . . *experienced* at this as you are, but I think I would have heard something about roaming bands of vampire hunters. On the ten o'clock news, if nowhere else."

Luci walked over to Gypsy and pressed up into his arms—a little girl wanting her daddy to comfort her. And *that* frightened Allison more than the verbal tripe Luci was trying to force-feed her at the moment.

"You were a Breather back then," Luci said—as if that explained everything. "If stakings are reported at all it's always as something else . . . suicide, hit-and-runs . . . *accidents*. Gina was right about one thing, Alley-cat, it is more dangerous for us to be in groups."

Then she smiled and patted the Watcher's belly.

"But I've always *lived* for danger, haven't I, Gypsy?"

"Far as I know."

Allison walked past them and looked back at the squat stucco building. Even the back of the station had flood-lit palm trees.

"So what do we do?" she asked.

"We break the Preacher-boy out," Luci said, coming up and throwing an arm over her shoulder.

"Then what?"

"Then it's up to him," she said. "He's always talking so much about choices, well we're going to give him a beaut. The best of both worlds . . . Death or Life Everlasting. We're going to see just how strong his fucking faith really is."

Allison heard the anger in Luci's voice echoed by a drunk that three policemen were hustling up the back stairs into the station. The man didn't want to go but he didn't have any choice.

Just like her.

Just like Mica.

Allison rubbed her hands over her arms and watched the man disappear behind the frosted glass doors.

Why bother? she asked.

Luci slipped her hand off Allison's shoulder and onto her right breast.

"Same reason, Alley-cat," she said. *Because I still WANT to.* "Why do we ever do anything?"

Yeah, Allison thought. Why?

TWENTY-NINE

Gypsy touched the tip of his tongue to the blood splattered crescent wrench and grimaced.

"I don't know about this," he said. "I think I still prefer beer."

Chuckling, he bent down and wiped the tool off on the front of the dead officer's uniform. The second officer was lying on his back a couple of yards farther up the alley—his legs and arms thrashing as Luci fed.

Mica swallowed the bile racing up his throat and watched Gypsy stand up and head for the squad car.

Lord, why didn't I see it coming?

Because it all seemed so believable, Mica thought he heard, *that's* why. Stop blaming yourself.

Like that was possible.

Even in Hollywood—where rape and murder and other acts of violence occurred with enough regularity to be classified as a hobby—he should have realized something was up when the half-naked woman darted out of the alley *just as the squad car was slowing for a red light* only to be pulled back into the darkness by a bare-chested man.

He *should* have known.

It wasn't until the first officer failed to answer the second's shout that Mica realized who the man in the alley was. His own shout went unheard as the policeman pulled his gun and got three steps away from the car before meeting up with Gypsy's wrench.

"Forgive me, Lord," Mica said as the back door swung open. "I didn't see it coming."

"Neither did he, pard," Gypsy said. "Now, let's haul ass before more uniforms show up to find out what happened to their little lost lambs."

Mica stared at Gypsy's hand as it snaked into the backseat and latched onto the sleeve of his shirt. He once wished he had hands like the big biker—strong, big-knuckled, 'I don't take shit from nobody' hands.

Now all Mica wanted was for those same hands to go away and leave him alone.

They did neither.

"There, now," Gypsy said as he got Mica to his feet and dusted him off, "doesn't that feel better? I know *I* always felt like second-class scum riding in the back of those things."

Mica took a quick step to the side—trying to avoid contact with Gypsy's hands—and tripped over the leg shackles he forgot he was wearing.

"Easy, there, Preacher-boy, you'll make yourself fall."

"But not as far as *you* fell!" Mica twisted out of Gypsy's hands and fell backwards against the car. "You threw away Life Everlasting as a child throws away a candy wrapper. Shit, man . . . is this life so wonderful that you'd forfeit your soul to *stay?*"

Gypsy leaned against the door frame and absently dug a toothpick out of his vest pocket.

"Hey, pard," he said, sticking the pick into his mouth and shrugging, "when it's the only thing you got . . ."

"But it's *not*, Gyp!"

Swallowing hard, Mica reached out and grabbed the front of the man's vest—and tried just as hard not to think about the corrupt flesh he felt against his fingers.

"Shit, man, haven't you been *listening?* This isn't the only thing we've got . . . this isn't even part of it. All you have to do is ask the Lord's Forgiveness, Gyp. That's all. Just *ask* and He'll wipe away your sins. C'mon, man. They can't have that tight a hold on you yet. Kneel with me and we'll pray your soul back fr—"

Gypsy's thumb pressed in on Mica's Adam's apple and brought the discussion to an abrupt end.

"Now, *you* listen, Preacher-boy. I've put up with your Holy-Roller crap this long because it was funny. You reminded me of one of those little floor mop dogs . . . y'-know a Pekingese—all the time yapping and growling and making a fool of yourself."

Gypsy moved his thumb just enough for Mica to pull in one wheezing gasp.

"But I'll tell you something, Preacher . . . you *stopped*

being funny a while back." Working the toothpick around to the other side of his jaw, Gypsy dragged Mica away from the curb and nodded toward the deep shadow made by a giant trash Dumpster. "He's all yours, Alley-cat."

Mica's spine tried to push its way out through his skin when she stepped out of the shadow and started toward him.

Allison.

From what he could tell, she was still wearing the deceptively modest dress she'd had on earlier that night—but now it clung to her . . . molding itself to her breasts and thighs.

Mica took a deep breath and looked away.

Having trouble with the old libido, Mica? Her voice whispered inside his head as she took the interconnecting links of the handcuffs and snapped them apart as easily as a child would break a twig. *Good. Keep it up . . . and I'm not trying to be funny. If they think you still have a yen for me they won't interfere.*

Mica stared down at her . . . at the eyes that seemed to glow in the darkness . . . at the face that still looked like Piper no matter how much he tried to deny it.

Don't worry, her voice whispered, *they can't hear us. In fact, I'm the only one who can hear you.*

Why?

Mica thought he saw a tiny shrug raise her shoulders as she bent down and broke the straps binding his legs.

Maybe God really does have a sense of humor.

"Really something, isn't she, compadre?" Gypsy said, smiling down at her. "But you be careful down there, Alley-cat . . . don't go spoiling your appetite with a quick snack."

Mica's balls jerked up into his shorts just thinking about it.

"Oh, stop fretting, Preacher-boy," Luci said, finally finished with the policeman and wiping her mouth off on the uniform sleeve she carried. Mica wouldn't have minded so much if the arm wasn't still inside it. "Our little Alley-cat isn't much into cock-sucking. Can't say that I blame her . . . I've always thought pussy was much tastier."

"Please, Gyp . . . there's still time. It's not too late, man. Fight them, Gypsy. Fight for your immortal soul."

Gypsy's laughter echoed down the innercity canyon.

Too late, Mica. Allison said deep inside him. But he'd already known that . . . known it deeper than even her voice reached.

Known it and mourned it as he shot a quick glance at Allison. She was watching Luci spin the policeman's severed arm as if it was a baton and they were in some kind of nightmarish marching band.

Marching them to the car and whatever lay beyond.

Mica swallowed and crossed his fingers. A child's game. If you crossed your fingers it meant you weren't responsible for whatever you did next.

What are you going to do with me? he asked.

Allison's head turned just enough to let him know she'd heard him.

But she didn't answer. She sneezed.

And Mica didn't feel up to blessing her for it.

Miriam had closed the club with the excuse that it was booked for a private "party."

Except the guest of honor didn't seem to be enjoying himself all that much.

Allison could see Mica—gagged and hogtied to a chair in the first row—staring up at Luci as she danced, *sans fur and all flesh,* to the revoltingly sentimental strains of Neil Diamond's "Listen."

Once upon a time . . . she had loved that particular song. Once. A long time ago . . . in a galaxy far, far away.

Swinging the stool back toward the bar, Allison lifted the blood-filled crystal goblet to the mirror and saluted—nothing.

The goblet looked like it was floating in mid-air.

"Well," she said to the nothingness where her reflection should have been, "if *this* gig doesn't work out you can always get a job doing special effects.

"Here's looking at *you,* kid."

The clotting blood went down like warm jello.

Because it was to be a "special" night, Luci sent Gina out on the prowl. The panther-woman returned less than ten minutes later, smiling and laughing, her arm protectively around a Hispanic teenage girl with purple and green hair and a pierced nostril.

A brave little girl of the streets—hardened by life and able to handle any and all situations.

Except the one with fangs that ripped out her throat.

Luci had done the pouring herself, tossing the girl's limp body over one shoulder like she was a jug of cheap wine.

Five glasses. Four for them and one extra.

For Mica.

Once he was turned.

Allison licked the girl's short life off her lips and swallowed. The memories were as grainy as her life had been.

"Rest in peace, kid," she said, crushing the goblet between her fingers.

You still with me, Mica?

She watched his reflection in the glass. He was ignoring her—staring into the empty ice-blue spotlight. Except Allison knew it wasn't empty. And judging by Gypsy's reaction, she knew Luci must really be going to town. The Watcher was shouting and hooting and making more noise than an entire room of Furverts.

Allison flipped the broken stem around in her fingers and stabbed it into the bar.

Alley-cat! Stop being an old stick in the mud and get over here. You're missing all the fun!

Ah, hell, let her stay over there. Gina. *We don't need her.*

We need who I say we need. NOW, Alley-cat. And smile pretty, your boyfriend's waiting for you.

Allison spun the stool and stepped down. Luci and Gina were "69-ing" each other like starving minks.

Miriam was eating another kind of *pussy*—this one a moth-eaten tabby—and Gypsy was giving the performance a standing ovation.

Mica had his eyes squeezed shut. Allison could hear his hushed prayers racing through her mind.

'What you don't see can't hurt you' only works for kids, she said as she crossed the empty room. *Believe me, I know.*

Help me.

Allison's hip collided with a chair as she jerked to a stop. *Who are you talking to?*

Allison . . . help me.

He turned his head and stared at her. The cross-shaped scar seemed to glow in the reflected blue light. Radiant.

Allison. Please.

"Well, what are you waiting for, Miss-Knocks-Into-Furniture, a written invitation, maybe?"

Allison sniffled and walked to the chair directly behind Mica. She didn't want to have to look at that scar anymore than she had to.

Allison.

Allison!

Do what you do best, Preacher-boy, she whispered back. *Pray.*

He turned to look at her and Allison's own quick glance told her the suggestion only helped so much. It had always been her experience that True Believers—of *anything*—wilted slightly in the harsh light of reality.

Allison . . .

She sat down and reshaped the flowing dress into something more appropriate for the occasion: A blood red bustier with matching garter-belt and stockings. Making sure he had a good view of all her most endearing charms . . . including the wounds on her throat.

Just the thing for a whore of Satan, don't you think, Preacher-boy?

A single tear followed the curve of his cheek down. She watched it until it soaked into the gag.

"All *right*, Alley-cat!" Gypsy said, clapping his hands—momentarily distracted from the cardinal sin being performed on stage. "Damn, you're one hot little chili pepper!"

"And I used to *love* chili peppers," Luci said as she sat back on her haunches and wiped Gina's juices off her chin. "*Ate* them all the time if I remember correctly."

Allison giggled and blew a kiss . . . much to Luci's delight and Gina's snarling anger.

Allison, don't! Mica's voice was so loud she almost jumped. *Gina's dangerous. Don't get her mad at you.*

Worried? About one of the undead? I'm honored, Mica. He looked so hurt she almost stopped. Knock it off, Allison, she told herself, this ain't no school picnic. *Divide and conquer, Preacher-boy . . . nothing personal.*

His eyes softened.

You are still praying, aren't you?

Always.

Good. Allison stood up and wiggled her way toward him. *This is still nothing personal.*

Understood.

Yeah, she thought looking down at the bulge between his legs, your mind may be saying that but your body definitely has other ideas.

Running one hand slowly through Mica's hair (and willing herself not to sneeze), Allison cocked her head and smiled.

At the Watcher.

"See anything you like, Gypsy?" she asked, aiming her .38's at him.

"Everything."

Ignoring his other charges, Gypsy unbuckled the wrist band and held his arm out to her. The swollen flesh made her mouth water.

"How 'bout a quickie?" he whispered.

Taking Gypsy's outstretched hand in hers, she leaned over Mica's suddenly tense body and ran her tongue over the tender meat.

Allison . . . don't do this! You're NOT like the others. I know it . . . I can FEEL it! You're different.

She let a drop of blood bubble from the corner of her mouth as she drove her fangs into Gypsy's flesh.

Still think I'm different, Preacher-boy?

Allison closed her eyes as she swallowed . . . and tried not to listen to the sound of Mica's sobs deep inside her mind.

Nothing was different, she reminded herself.

Again.

THIRTY

Mica was sobbing so hard he could hardly breathe. Another drop of Gypsy's blood hit the side of his face and oozed slowly down toward the gag. *Oh God, please don't let it reach my mouth . . . PLEASE Lord!*

Allison shifted suddenly, dropping Gypsy's hand so that it brushed against his cheek—smeared the blood across his skin.

You did that on purpose.

She didn't answer, just reached over the top of his head and lovingly pinched Gypsy's cheek.

"Thanks, Gyp," she said, "you're sweet."

Mica looked up as she moved away and saw Gypsy's normally lopsided grin go arrow straight.

"Oh, man," he said, slumping back into the chair next to Mica. "You don't know what you're missing. Yet. Hey, now . . . cut the waterworks, Preacher-boy. Don't you know these ladies have this thing about *holy* water?"

Gypsy laughed as he slapped Mica across the shoulders and untied the gag.

"You gonna be good and keep your homilies to yourself?"

Taking a ragged breath, Mica nodded and cranked his jaw from side to side.

"Good," Gypsy said, using the gag to wipe the tears and crying snot off Mica's face, "because I don't think you'd like to spend the rest of eternity without a tongue."

"I don't plan to spend—"

Don't say it!

Mica watched Allison walk over to another table and pick up the broom the assistant bartender had left behind. Standing it on end, she sniffled and wiped her nose off on the dusty straw. Ignoring him.

"—eternity like that," he finished.

I'm proud of you.

"Well, I'm proud of you, Preacher-boy," Luci said, verbally mimicking Allison's silent thought. "Maybe you won't be as hard assed about this thing as I thought you'd be. Kind of a pity in a way. I was hoping for a real knock-down drag-out with you."

Mica bit down on his tongue to remind himself of just how quickly he might lose it. A yard away, Allison suddenly jumped and jerked her head toward Luci. In the cold blue light her hair again looked like autumn leaves covered with early frost.

Hoarfrost.

Whorefrost.

Mica pressed back against the chair and tried for the hundredth time to work his hands free of the rhinestone collars tying his wrists together. They were even stronger than the plastic zip-lock cuffs the cops had him in earlier.

"No," Allison said. "You know I can't."

Luci shifted her weight, folding her arms across her naked breast.

"Shit, Luci," Allison said again, "because I'm fucking *allergic* to him, that's why. I get within a yard of him and my nose starts running. I don't even want to find out what would happen if I . . ."

Allison's voice trailed off and Mica blessed her for it. *That* only got him a pained looked.

Sorry.

Just keep those damn blessings to yourself, her voice whispered to him. *Understand.*

Mica nodded—realizing at the last moment that he probably shouldn't have done something so obvious. Luci cocked her head and walked to the edge of the stage, the blue light dancing across her naked body like waves breaking on a marble shore.

"Something going on between you two?" she asked.

"What the fuck would be going on between us?" Allison said quickly, twirling the broom like a baton and smiling. "I already *told* you I can't stand being near him."

Mica watched Gina move in quickly—a coal black shadow against Luci's shimmering white one.

"I don't buy that shit for nothin'," she snarled, glaring down at Allison. "She be talkin' to him sure as I'm standin' here."

"That true, Alley-cat?"

"'Course it true. Just look at 'em . . . they be talkin' behind your back, Luci." Smoke-gray talons suddenly curved out from Gina's fingertips. "I said she wasn't t'be trusted, didn't I? Didn't I say that, Luci?"

Luci reached around behind her and patted Gina's thigh. "I asked you if what Gina said was true, Allison."

Allison set the broom aside and raised her right hand while drawing an *X* over her still heart with her left index finger.

"I *swear* there's nothing going on between us, Luci." She looked over her shoulder at Mica and sneered. "So help me, God."

Allison!

Mica watched her pull out a chair and sit down. *I'm already damned . . . what more could HE do?*

"Yeah, like you 'spect Luci t'believe that?"

"Don't fret, Gina," Luci said as she squatted down—spreading her legs just enough for Mica to see straight up into her open vulva—and slid off the stage. "I don't think Alley-cat would lie . . . not to me."

Then Luci came straight at him. On tippy-toes.

"Oooo! This floor's so *cold!*" she said as she straddled his lap—squirming up against him . . . molding her coldness to the heat rising out of the front of his pants. "But you'll warm me up, won't you, Preacher-boy?"

LORD! I am MICA! Make me impervious to the temp-

tations of this creature's dead flesh! Make me as unfeel-
ing and cold as the rock for which I am nam—

"HOLY JESUS!"

Luci scooted back to his knees and began running a
long red nail up and down the front of his zipper.

"Got nailed to a cross for shooting off his mouth about
the glories of life after death." She dropped her hand between his legs and squeezed his sack hard enough to
make his eyes water. "Well, why just pray to a man you
never met when *I* can tell you all about it . . . in person."

Mica saw her fangs descend through his tears.

"Be . . . gone . . . unclean . . . spirit!"

Even Miriam applauded.

"I'm *impressed,* Preacher-boy! I didn't think you had
it in you." Luci dug her claws in through the fabric of his
jeans. "But I can yank it out if you like. See?"

Allison . . .

Every dark fantasy Mica had ever had since puberty
became an even darker reality when Luci ripped away
the crotch of his jeans. His penis—stiff and bloated as it
came free—dwindled to a limp mass in Luci's icy hand.

"Aw . . ." Luci said, jiggling him, "I think I broke it."

"NO! Dear Lord—why have you forsaken me?"

Luci tightened her grip on his weakened flesh—
bringing his attentions back to earth.

"Hey, if Big G didn't bother saving His own Son . . .
why the fuck would He save a worthless, egotistical,
psalms humping—"

Luci twisted on his lap without letting go. It was all
Mica could do to swallow back the moan.

"What was that word you called him, Alley-cat?"

Mica eased one eyelid up.

"Sanctimonious," she said softly . . . not looking at him.

"Yeah," Luci said turning—*Thank you, Lord*—back to him, "sanctimonious . . . great word. You got one, Miriam?"

"A schlemiel," the tiny voice piped up, "with delusions of grandeur, yet."

"Alley-cat?"

Mica looked over at her—still silent, still looking away.

"Aw, come on, Alley-cat . . . think of a name."

Blue light poured down Allison's hair as she shook her head.

"No."

Holy man.

Only Mica heard the name. And only Mica understood its meaning.

"Okay, next? Gina . . . do *you* have a name for the Preacher-boy?"

"Yeah," the black shadow said leaping off the stage, "how 'bout *dinner*."

Luci's fangs were dripping with saliva as she smiled.

"Good choice . . . but first a little fun . . . just to heat up the blood a little."

Mica felt his body arch back as Luci pumped his cock rigid and slipped him into her. *NO! God NO! Please, Lord . . . You can't!* It felt like he was sticking his rod into a vat of ice cold oatmeal.

Smiling, she leaned forward and kissed the scar on his forehead.

"No," Mica gasped, "you can't . . . it's my—my sign!"

Luci traced the outline of the cross with her tongue.

"First rule, Preacher-boy, if you don't believe in something it doesn't exist. Just like vampires, huh?

"So just sit there and enjoy the show, Preacher-boy," Luci said, tipping his head forward so he could watch himself appear and disappear below her dead white curls. "*Then* we'll see to that all-precious soul you're always talking about."

my god my god my god my god my god my god my

"Just let it go, Preacher-boy," Luci said, quickening her pace—the stench of her filling his lungs and making him wish he still had the gag in his mouth. "You know you always wanted me. Every time you saw me you *know* all you wanted to do was get me down and hump me raw. Isn't that right, *Milo?*"

"Sure as hell did," Gypsy chuckled. "Most nights I thought I'd have to hose him down."

"See," Luci purred into his ear, "everyone *knows* how much you wanted to fuck me. So come on, Preacher-boy . . . let it go.

no

"Give it to me, Preacher-boy . . . enlighten me . . .

No

"Fuck me, you sanctimonious bastard!"

"NO!"

Too late . . . always. Too late.

Mica's body jerked against the chair as he shot his load—straight out into the middle of the room . . . following Luci's sudden—*backwards*—withdrawal.

"Wh-what . . . ?"

believe

Luci was dancing in circles a yard in front of him—struggling with a broken length of broom handle protruding from her mouth.

"YOU FUCKING CUNT!" Gina scream—claws and fangs extended. "I'LL RIP YOUR HEAD OFF!"

Mica ducked as Gina sprang, even though he wasn't anywhere near the line of fire. There was just something about a woman instantly changing into a black panther that made a man want to duck and cover and—

Believe, Mica!

Allison's voice. Again. Telling him . . . *commanding* him.

"I do believe!"

"Then fucking say it!"

Mica took a deep breath and began the *Lord's Prayer*—the first thing that sprang to mind—as Gina took the straw end of the broom straight through the heart.

Three groans, all female, almost drowned him out.

believe

The pain in her chest was worse than the first time . . . *much* worse. It felt like a rat was trying to chew its way out, but Allison couldn't stop to think or even acknowledge it.

Gripping the edge of the table to steady herself, she saw that she wasn't the only one suffering. Miriam was curled into a tight little ball on the floor next to her overturned chair—trembling—the mutilated cat pressed to her belly like a favorite toy.

This? We take you in and treat you like family and this is what you do? I should have let Gina tear you a new asshole that first night.

Luci wasn't in much better shape. Worse maybe. The punk-girl's fresh red blood still bubbled around the broom stick, covering Luci's pale flesh from chin to crotch . . . but she was still trying to get up . . . still glaring at Allison.

Still dangerous.

Mica . . . Allison called. *Get ready.*

His face was stark white—eyes bulging, jaw slack—but he nodded.

"Okay," she said out loud. "Two down, one dog to go."

Because that's what Gypsy looked like: A big, scruffy dog caught between two masters . . . whimpering and rocking back and forth as his eyes went from Allison to Luci and back again.

Pushing away from the table, Allison took a step forward and jerked her head.

Time to show the dog which master's in control.

"Back off," she commanded, side-stepping toward Mica. "I'm taking the Preacher-boy. *Move and I'll kill you.*"

End of discussion.

Gypsy whimpered again and looked at Gina's moldering corpse. It took a minute before he moved . . . but in the wrong direction.

He was coming toward her.

"Gypsy! I told you to back *off!*"

He won't listen to you, Alley-cat. He was never supposed to.

Luci suddenly stood right behind Mica—the bloodied, jagged piece of broken handle pressed to his throat.

It'd be a real waste, Luci said as blood trickled from her unmoving lips, *but you'd be surprised how well these work on Breathers.*

She jabbed one of the points just under his skin and gurgled.

It would be sort of poetic justice, wouldn't it? An eye for an eye?

"Let him go, Luci."

Mica's blood oozed around the sliver of wood. The inside of Allison's nose burned.

You gonna make me, bitch?

"If I have to."

The gurgling got louder. Luci was laughing.

You're already down to EIGHT lives, Alley-cat . . . and I promise I won't go down as easy as Gina did.

Luci pressed the wood in deeper . . . drawing more blood. Allison's mouth began to water.

Look at you! Bloody foam gushed from Luci's mouth, as if she was trying to say the words out loud. *You're one of US, dammit. Why are you doing this?*

Why?

She had no idea.

Squinting so she wouldn't look directly at the cross on his forehead, Allison met Mica's eyes and nodded.

Are you ready?

Just tell me what to do.

Panic swept through her as the words froze in her mind. She couldn't say the words . . . couldn't make herself think them. A moment later she didn't have to.

Allison sneezed—long and loud and hard.

"Bless you," Mica shouted.

And so it began.

THIRTY-ONE

Allison's body hit the floor at the same time Luci's did—writhing and shuddering as if they'd been struck by lightning.

"What . . . ?"

Again. Allison's voice shouted. *You have to do it again!*

"What? What did I do?"

Allison rolled over to face him, clutching her stomach.

"B—bless us."

Mica was suddenly glad they could speak without moving their lips, because his jaw felt like it had become permanently detached. *Excuse me?*

She looked up at him and smiled. *Believe, Preacher-boy.*

Mica closed his eyes and took a deep breath. *Okay, Lord, I know You move in mysterious ways and I won't argue with You about Your methods . . . but a VAMPIRE?*

Mica!

"Lord, this may be the strangest thing I've ever asked of You, but *Bless* them, Lord! Bless these vile creatures of Hell and let them feel the strength of Your Mercy."

He could hear their screams—both inside and *outside* his head. Allison's was so weak . . . so *hurtful*.

I'm sorry.

"Forgive them their evil ways, Lord, and Bless them like You never Blessed anything before! They made a bad choice and fell into corruption! They were led astray . . ."

Mica opened one eye and looked at Allison. She was shivering—the flesh on her arms and legs literally crawling over her bones. He squeezed his eyes shut and dug his fingernails into the palms of his hands. *I'm sorry I'm sorry I'm sorry.*

"They were tempted by the dark pools of sin and fell away from the bright light of Truth and Love. Show them You Love them, Lord—Love Thy Enemies and Bless them, Lord! BLESS THEM!

"In the name of the Father . . ."

Mica felt their agony like a living thing—spinning around him like a cleansing Oklahoma tornado.

". . . and of the Son . . ."

Luci. Miriam. Allison. Luci.Miriam.Allison. LuciMiriamAllison.

". . . and of the HOLY SPIRIT, Bless them!"

Silence.

"Thank you, Lord," his voice sounded so loud it echoed off the inside of his skull. "Amen."

Panting, sweat dripping down the sides of his face, Mica took a deep breath and steeled himself for what would probably be the most gruesome sight he'd ever have to witness.

"Shit."

In every vampire comic he'd ever read, the final panel always had the creature either bursting into flames or melting into a pool of decaying goo. Nothing *that* dramatic had happened.

Except for Gina, who was nothing more than a greasy smear on the carpet, the results of his blessings were disappointing to say the least.

They were just laying there. Silent.

Dead?

Allison?

She was curled into a ball not five feet in front of him—shredded carpet under her nails, her hair a dull red fan covering her face. *Oh, God . . .*

"Allison!"

"She's *dead!*" A voice shouted at him. "Just like the others, you mother-fucking son-of-a-whore!"

Mica turned his head just as something the overall size and shape of a runaway Peterbuilt body slammed him and the chair to the floor. The frame held less than a second before the chair shattered beneath their combined weights.

Gypsy.

"Nobody does that to *my* people and gets away with it!"

Lord? You still listening? HELP!

"G—Gyp! You're free of them, man . . . you're fre—"

Gypsy's hands wrapped themselves around his throat and squeezed.

"You fucked up my job, you Bible-humping, tight-assed turd! These were my *ladies,* man, and you fucking *killed* them! You fucking—"

A loud buzzing drowned out the rest of Gypsy's tirade and Mica smiled as an Angel stepped into the pale blue light. It was a bright Angel with red hair . . . holding a raised sword . . .

. . . no, not a sword . . . a chair . . .

The Angel was holding a raised chair above Gypsy's head. And, lo, the chair descended and air filled his lungs. And it was Good.

A miracle.

"I don't think this would qualify even in a *New Age* Bible."

Dropping the remains of the broken chair, Allison reached under him and snapped the collars tying his wrists as easily as she had the handcuffs. Rhinestones flew through the air like frozen drops of rain.

"But please . . . keep the religious talk to a minimum for a while. I feel like I just ran the L.A. Marathon carrying an elephant."

Mica reached out to touch her when the blood returned to his finger—just a friendly touch—but she jerked away as if he'd been carrying a switchblade.

"No! Don't touch me, okay? Shit, I don't even know why I did any of this." Allison kept her back to him. "Put a hat on or something."

"Allison."

"No. Look, whatever just happened here doesn't change anything, Mica, and it never will. I'm still a *vampire* and you're a . . . a . . . Preacher-boy with your own personalized *cross!*"

She laughed softly and Mica watched her hair ripple down her back.

"Talk about strange bedfellows, huh?"

The statement immediately brought Mica's hands together over the gaping hole in the front of his jeans. Allison hadn't seen, but she laughed again.

"That's *not* what I meant."

"Oh, yeah, I know . . ." *It was only a little lie, Lord.* "It's okay. Wait a minute."

Keeping one hand tucked firmly in place, Mica leaned over and pulled the cap off Gypsy's crushed skull. The leather was sticky with blood and brain fluid . . . but Mica could feel his friend's forgiveness as he put the cap on and pulled it down low over his forehead.

Over the cross.

"There." He just finished pulling his T-shirt out of his pants and over himself as Allison turned around. "All decent."

She looked from the cap to the hem of his shirt. And pretended she didn't notice the sudden slight *lump* that momentarily appeared.

"I can tell." When her eyes finally got back to his face the laughter had died. "Are you ready to finish it?"

It?

Allison looked back over her shoulder—drawing Mica's attention to the naked, gasping *thing* laying on the floor. The comic books finally got something right. Bombarded by his impassioned sermon, Luci had transformed into her "unnatural" state.

At least Mica *thought* it was Luci.

All he was sure of was that it was female.

Sort of.

The sagging, wrinkled breasts quivered each time the creature moved. And it *was* moving. Very slowly, very painfully it was trying to pull itself across the floor to the storage room.

Getting to his feet, Mica took one step then another . . . and another until he was standing directly over it. Even in the blue spotlight, the vampire's flesh looked as yellowed and lined as old newspaper.

Patches of ash-white hair caught in the carpeting as it moved, tearing loose from the scab-crusted scalp like a dog with the mange. Mica watched one clump flutter away in the club's air-conditioned draft.

The sweet-rotten stench of carrion rose off her body as she turned and hissed up at him. Although sunken deep within the moldering skull, Luci's emerald green eyes were filled with hate.

"Gloating, Preacher-boy?" Luci's voice was thin and raspy . . . as dry as an Oklahoma summer. "Isn't *pride* one of the Seven Deadly Sins?"

The forced laughter that followed made Mica's skin crawl.

"You have to finish her, Mica," Allison said, tossing him the same piece of broom handle Luci had threatened him with . . . a brief *lifetime* ago. "If you don't she'll come after us."

That thought was enough to make his body act on its own behalf. Kneeling, Mica grabbed the makeshift stake with both hands and placed it against the narrow chest.

"It doesn't have to be like this," Luci wheezed. She sounded so pitiful . . . so weak . . . so *helpless*. "Get rid of that bitch and I'll turn you so easy you won't feel a thing."

Cold, skeletal fingers encircled his wrists as Luci's fangs pressed against her cracked bottom lip.

"Just think of it, *Mica*—preaching the Big G's name for all eternity? Saving souls? Creating a whole band of psalm-singing—"

"VAMPIRES!"

Mica's scream was joined by Luci's howling wail as he fell forward onto the stake and pinned her to the floor like a bug—a very old and very *lethal* bug.

The echoes seemed to take forever to fade away.

Lord, humble the pride of Our enemies and let the might of Your right hand crush their arrogance.

"Amen."

Sitting back, Mica looked over at Allison and smiled. Then frowned.

Allison was holding onto her knees, rocking slowly back and forth on her rump.

"You *felt* that?" he asked.

She nodded and brushed the blood red tears off her face. They smeared into a perfect blush.

"Just another thing they don't put in the recruiting

posters. I really should talk to my congressman about it." She looked up at him and smiled. "But don't get too comfortable, *Preacher-boy,* you're not finished yet."

He looked down at Luci's shriveling remains and shrugged.

"Not *her,*" Allison said, lowering her knees into an Indian position, "me."

"Now wait a minute . . ."

"Just do it quickly, okay?" She lifted her chin and closed her eyes—a brave little girl about to get a shot, with nothing but the tiniest quiver along her lips to show how scared she really was. "And no prayers . . . at least not until *after.*"

Mica looked down at the stake protruding from the rotting corpse at his knees and—

Jesus destroyed Your own temple because He found it to be Evil, Lord . . . and You destroyed the whole of the world with the Great Flood because Evil had taken over. Evil must be rooted out and destroyed where ever we find it and these are Evil creatures, Lord. EVIL! Whores of Satan who prey on the souls and desires of men and feed on them. FEED ON THEM as if we were merely cattle. They are evil . . . EVIL . . .

"I can't kill you," Mica shouted as he stood up. "You saved my life, dammit. I can't just . . ." He looked at the stake again and felt the room twist under his feet.

"I *won't,* Allison."

"But won't that get you into trouble with . . ." She pointed one finger straight up.

Mica smiled and tugged on the front of his shirt.

"He'll forgive me."

Allison was shaking her head as she pushed herself to her feet. Mica fought both the urge to rush over to help . . . and to gasp out loud when the red lingerie became jeans and a tank top. He was going to have to get used to that.

"Now what?" she asked.

"Now we get out of here—you and me."

Allison dipped her head and gazed up at him through her lashes.

"You really are as crazy as Luci said you were. I'm one of the bad guys," she said, sprouting fangs. "Wemembur?"

"Huh? No, wait, listen to me . . ." He took a step toward her and watched her back up. Quickly—her nose twitching a mile a minute. "Sorry. You're *not* like these others . . . if you were I'd be dead right now. Drained.

"Okay, so you're a vampire . . . you fucking saved my life tonight. More importantly, you saved my soul, Allison. I think . . ." Mica took another step forward and smiled when she stood still. "I think we were brought together to give each other a second chance."

"I'm dead, Mica," Allison said. "All my chances are gone."

"Not if you *believe*."

Another look flickered across her face.

You're going to pray for my soul. Aren't you?

Mica touched the brim of the cap with three fingers.

Religiously.

Then kill me now.

It was a joke—and Mica laughed at it.

"So where does a poor single vampire and an escaped homicidal maniac go to start a new life." Allison looked him up and down and shook her head. "Or *afterlife*, in my case?"

Mica was about to say something stupid like "Anywhere they want" when Allison suddenly bit her bottom lip and pointed.

Miriam—butt high on her hands and knees—turned around and hissed at them.

Mica bent down and pulled the stake out of the moldering lumps of flesh that had once been Luci. He'd think about taking off the head later . . . if there was still a head to worry about once she finished rotting.

"I forgot about her," he said.

"Me, too." Mica watched Allison pull out another chair and sit down, already rubbing a spot between her breasts. "Don't worry . . . it's just like a bad case of heartburn."

Right.

Taking a deep breath, Mica wiped the stake off on the leg of his jeans and walked toward the minuscule vampire. He always knew working for the Lord was a twenty-four hour job . . . but he never thought it would involve quite so much manual labor.

EPILOGUE

The bus station was still packed even though it was heading hard onto four in the morning.

Fresh meat coming in . . . losers going out.

Honeymooners starting out on a shoestring, senior citizens sticking close to their bleary-eyed tour leader, kids thinking the bright lights meant easy pickings, high rollers who lost it all on that "one last toss."

Hookers moving slowly up and down the walkways—vultures in black spandex and heels.

Mica *loved* it.

". . . and Jesus destroyed the temple because it had fallen into corruption and evil. Pleasures of the flesh and gambling abounded and it was wrong. *Wrong!*

"Those of you who are slinking back home with your tails between your legs *know* how wrong it is. Those of you who are coming in thinking this is an easy way to the good life had better just turn around and head back to where you came from. Because this *isn't* easy. You're all standing at the rim of the Abyss about to take that first long step down!"

A sleepy child looked up at Mica from the safety of her father's shoulder and yawned. *Bringing a little thing like that to a place like this . . . Lord, humble that man and make him see what treasures he already has!*

"But it's still not too late," Mica said to the crowd in general—and to the child's father in particular. "You made a bad choice but it's still not too late to turn that mistake around. Read *this* before you let those bright lights draw you into the flames of HELL!"

Mica shook the latest edition of his pamphlet, *GOD's Slot-Machine—The only one that really PAYS OFF,* at the crowd and was ignored.

Again.

Just like every night.

But no one said this job was going to be easy, did they Lord?

Stuffing the pamphlets back into his nylon brief-case, Mica ignored their ignorance and blessed them just the same.

Most of them were going to need it before night fell again.

Mica felt her watching even before she spoke.

Ready to head out?

He turned and saw her standing near the terminal entrance—just another showgirl in shorts and top wait-ing for her man.

Allison . . . now called Raven. Just like he was *John*. The MTV Generation's voice calling in the wilderness.

She'd added a little padding to her curves ("This is Vegas, Mica . . . and they want tits and ass more than Luci ever did") and wore her *natural* blue-black hair in a short fluffy cut (". . . easier to get those damned head-dresses on . . ."). Although, sometimes when they were alone, she would literally let her hair down—long and loose and the color of autumn leaves in the sunset.

Yeah, Mica said, zipping the case closed, *no one's paying any attention anyway.*

Now there's a surprise!

Throwing the shoulder strap over his arm, Mica tugged the *I went to Las Vegas and this is all I WON base-ball cap* lower over his forehead and pushed his way through the crowd.

Toward her.

"Hello, beautiful stranger," he said when he got to her.

"Hello right back at'cha."

They kissed—an old married couple kind of kiss—and threw their arms lightly around each other as they headed out. It had only taken Allison a couple of months to develop a kind of immunity to him. Now she only sneezed if—and *when*—he was able to sneak up on her from behind.

"Rough night?" he asked as they jay-walked with the rest of the crowd through the heavy pre-dawn traffic. It seemed that in the six months they'd been here, Mica had never seen the roads leading to and from the famous Strip empty . . . or at least passable. But, of course, he couldn't say anything about what the streets might look like from dawn to dusk. He slept during the days now.

"Not too bad," Allison said. "After the show this one guy offered me a thousand bucks for a quickie up in his room."

"And?"

Allison patted the thick belly pack she wore low on the hip—then patted her belly.

"Which reminds me," she said, "did *you* eat?"

Mica nodded and belched. "I grabbed a burger and fries."

He could hear her sigh deep inside his head. *Do you know what that garbage is doing to you?*

Yeah, he said, *making me unappetizing.*

She swatted him hard enough across the seat of the pants to raise him up an inch.

"Cretin."

Mica hugged her close as they passed a dark plate glass window. The reflection showed a thin man with shoulder length blonde hair (courtesy of Miss Clarol's *Living Color*) and full beard walking down the street with his arm floating in mid-air.

Going solo.

"Anyone tell you lately how pretty you are?" he asked, turning back to the more substantial illusion in his arms.

"Just dinner," Allison said, patting her tummy again.

Mica shook his head—she loved doing that to him— and hurried her across a less traveled intersection at Scotland Lane.

The glitz and glamour of Las Vegas was behind them and they were heading into *their* section of town— older, run-down . . . heavy industry mixed with "working men" bars. A part of Vegas the travel agents and Chamber of Commerce didn't talk about.

A part of town that actually looked *better* in the piss-colored glow of the sodium street lights.

Home.

The hot night wind caught them as they took the first right. Mica took a deep breath and filled his lungs with her scent—musk and rust with just the faintest tang of raw meat left out too long. He'd gotten used to that, too . . . like not being able to see her refection in glass.

It wasn't that bad. All things considered.

You sure you had enough? he asked. *We could pick up someone on the way home.*

Allison slipped her hand into the back pocket of his jeans and began kneading his ass.

"I'm fine."

You're better than fine . . . You're great!

Mica hadn't planned it, but he stopped and pulled her into his arms, kissing her passionately. Her tongue tasted like his socks smelled. He'd gotten used to that, too.

Allison punched his arm gently when he let her go. And sneezed.

"B-word to you," he said.

"Thanks," she sniffled. "Mind warning me the next time your hormones decide to kick in?"

"What? And loose all that spontaneity?"

She tugged him back into a walk and ran a hand through her shortened locks.

"The Lord's gonna get you for that, *Preacher-boy*."

"Nope . . . the Lord will Forgive me my trespasses as He'll Forgive you yours."

Allison pressed her hand to her chest and groaned. *Shit.* "Sorry! I'm sorry . . . I keep forgetting. I'm sorry!"

Allison looked up at him, the pain leaving her face, and shook her head.

"That's okay," she said, "I'm getting used to it."

Mica kept silent for another hundred feet before the tattered remains of police cordon tape and a faded chalk outline on the sidewalk in front of them gave him something else to think about.

"You know, maybe we should think about moving to a better area. With the money you get at the casino . . . and *other* places, we could even buy us a condo over in that new Yuppie part of town."

"Why? So we can have bar-b-ques and hang out at the jaccuzi like all the other up and comers?"

It was an old argument—six months old, in fact—and Mica didn't have any illusions about winning it. It bothered him that Allison had to live in such a rundown section of town.

She deserved better.

"Well . . . I'm serious, Allison. This neighborhood's pretty dangerous—"

A low snarling shape suddenly darted out of the narrow alley just ahead of them. The dog's jaws were open and dripping, its black lips curled back over massive fangs.

Allison spun to meet it head on—her own fangs more than a match for the pit-bull mix.

The animal back-peddled frantically, claws digging into the broken concrete and leaving behind a trail of dog shit as it took off in the opposite direction. What was left of its cropped tail tucked protectively over its balls.

"You were saying?" Allison asked as she stood up and took his arm. Protectively.

"Nothing at all."

Hugging her tight, Mica ruffled his beard against the top of her head and sighed contentedly.

"What would I ever do without you?" he asked.

Allison looked up at him and sniffled.

"God only knows," she said.

THE WIND
CALLER
P. D. CACEK

Listen to the leaves rustling. Hear the wind building. These could be the first signs that Gideon Berlander has found you. They could be the last sounds you hear. Gideon hasn't been the same since that terrifying night in the cave, the night he changed forever—the night he became a Wind Caller. But the power to call upon and control the unimaginable force of the wind in all its fury has warped him, twisted his mind, and unleashed a virtually unstoppable monster. Those who oppose Gideon are destroyed . . . horribly. No one can escape the wind. And no one—not even Gideon—knows what nightmarish secrets wait in its swirling grasp.

JACK KETCHUM
THE GIRL NEXT DOOR

Suburbia. Shady, tree-lined streets, well-tended lawns and cozy homes. A nice, quiet place to grow up. Unless you are teenage Meg or her crippled sister, Susan. On a dead-end street, in the dark, damp basement of the Chandler house, Meg and Susan are left captive to the savage whims and rages of a distant aunt who is rapidly descending into madness. It is a madness that infects all three of her sons— and finally the entire neighborhood. Only one troubled boy stands hesitantly between Meg and Susan and their cruel, torturous deaths. A boy with a very adult decision to make...